T0036464

HATE MACHINE

STEPHEN BLACKMOORE

DAW BOOKS
New York

First Printing, October 2022
1st Printing

Raves for Stephen Blackmoore's Eric Carter novels

"For a book all about dead things, this novel is alive with great characters and a twisty, scary-funny story that teaches you not to tango with too much necromancy. My favorite book this year, bar none." —Chuck Wendig, author of the Miriam Black series

"Breathtaking . . . Carter's wry voice is amusing as ever, but the grief he carries is palpable, adding depth and a sense of desperation to this action-packed adventure. Readers will be eager for more after this thrilling, emotionally fraught installment."
—*Publishers Weekly* (starred)

"Not only met, but exceeded, my expectations. . . . Plenty of action and magic-slinging rounds out this excellent second novel from one of my favorite authors." —My Bookish Ways

"In *Dead Things*, Stephen Blackmoore expands upon the Los Angeles supernatural world he first conjured in *City of the Lost*. Blackmoore is going places in urban fantasy, and readers fond of dark tales should keep their eyes on him. Highly recommended."
—SFRevu

"Blackmoore can't write these books fast enough to suit me. *Broken Souls* is hyper-caffeinated, turbo-bloody, face-stomping fun. This is the L.A.-noir urban fantasy you've been looking for."
—Kevin Hearne, author of The Iron Druid Chronicles

"Eric Carter's adventures are bleak, witty, and as twisty as a fire-blasted madrone, told in prose as sharp as a razor. Blackmoore is the rising star of pitch-black paranormal noir. A must-read series."
—Kat Richardson, author of the Greywalker series

"Fans will find plenty to enjoy in the long-awaited third outing of necromancer Eric Carter. Blackmoore infuses his increasingly detailed and dangerous urban fantasy landscape with grim yet fascinating characters, and ensures that every step of Carter's epic journey is a perilously fascinating one." —*RT Reviews*

Novels by Stephen Blackmoore
available from DAW Books:

CITY OF THE LOST
DEAD THINGS
BROKEN SOULS
HUNGRY GHOSTS
FIRE SEASON
GHOST MONEY
BOTTLE DEMON
SUICIDE KINGS
HATE MACHINE
CULT CLASSIC*

*Coming soon from DAW Books

ACKNOWLEDGMENTS

About a week or so ago, somebody walked into a school and shot up a bunch of students and teachers. The obvious tragedy aside, you know what's fucked up about that? You have no idea which one I'm talking about.

Apocalypse shouldn't have a plural.

The last few years have been an absolute horror show. A pandemic, a government that can't get its head out of its ass, Russian invasions, Chinese saber rattling. A mass school shooting on top of all of that just feels like a kick in the nuts.

We have lost too many, too quickly. And as is so often the case, we've lost a lot of the wrong ones.

So, a shoutout to all of you. You who have had to face this dumpster fire of a decade in ways you never expected and never wanted. You who have given so much of yourselves as nurses, caretakers, morticians, grief counselors. You who are just trying to get by in a world that feels like it's against you more and more.

To all of you who haven't given up, who've kept putting one foot in front of the other. You have been an inspiration to me. A reminder that no matter how bad it gets, it doesn't mean I have to give up.

Thank you. This book of violent, profanity-laden bad decisions is for you.

Chapter 1

Everyone dies alone.

Doesn't matter if you crack your head on the shower floor or go up in a fireball surrounded by a hundred-fifty people in a cratered Boeing. It's unique no matter how it happens. It's your death and yours alone. Your experience of it—and believe me, no matter how unconscious you might be, you're experiencing it—is shaped by context.

Who you are, what you believe, the things you've done. They're what make your dying an experience that no one else will ever have.

Let's take Las Vegas. There are places on the planet that shouldn't exist. Vegas is near the top of that list. An artificial oasis in the middle of a desert wasteland fed by the waters of Lake Mead, it's about as fake a place as you can find. But there's one authentic thing about it you won't find anywhere else in the U.S.

See, Vegas is the suicide capital of America. You don't get much more real than that.

You'd think it's people who blew all their savings at the blackjack tables or the locals who just can't handle living in Sin City, anymore, right? Not even.

The ones holing up in their hotel rooms with a fifth of Jack and a bottle of Ambien come to Vegas with a plan. They come to party, gamble, maybe hire a hooker or two, and then make their exit. A final blowout before their final blowout, so to speak.

This is where being a necromancer and seeing the dead gets to be a problem. We can't shut it off. I get to watch the Echoes, Haunts, and Wanderers of the desperate and lost as I drive by the hotels on the Strip. Even the ones I can't see directly, I can feel. I know they're there.

You got those who went with guns; always a popular choice, particularly with the largest demographic, middle-aged white men. Hanging, of course. That's number two on the list. Drugs and alcohol are a distant third. And that's as true in Vegas as anywhere else.

There used to be a lot more jumpers, though. Last time I was here it was like watching a fucking waterfall. But hotels started sealing their windows a long time back and a lot of those ghosts have faded over time.

Sure, it's only a couple hundred visitors a year offing themselves, but that stacks up fast. I was last here almost twenty-five, maybe thirty years ago. That's something like six thousand new dead just on suicides and about a third of them leave ghosts behind.

And for however much all those deaths seem similar, every single one is unique. Every one. Viva Las Vegas.

Vegas isn't all corpses and slot machines. Take Candyland, for instance. It's not a strip club, though there's a lot of that going on, and it's not a sex club, though it's got a lot of that going on, too.

To call Candyland high-end would be an understatement. Saudi princes, movie moguls, the wealthiest people you've never heard of. They're here for the exclusivity, the mystique. Not just anybody gets in. Sometimes not even the Saudi princes.

The club sits in an old, squat office building, gutted and rebuilt with pure hedonism in mind. When most people find out about it, they're surprised more people don't know it. That's just its magic at work. If you know about it, you're supposed to know about it. If you don't, you don't.

The line for Candyland is half a block long. Men and women in sharp black suits open doors to help the uber-rich out of their limos while taxis disgorge the hoi polloi at the curb.

Everybody standing out here is a Las Vegas high roller or wants to be. The only thing they have in common is that most of them aren't getting through those doors. But they'll stand out here waiting and hoping. Why? Because it's fucking Candyland.

I walk past the line to a group of well-dressed bouncers, stupidly wealthy clubbers glaring daggers at me. The bouncers are what you'd expect for a place like this, big, beefy, immaculately dressed. They're well-schooled in the rules of *Roadhouse*: be nice until it's time to not be nice.

One man stands at a podium checking names off of those allowed to get in tonight. I can tell he's a mage. He's got a subtle—for this town, at least—spell going. At a guess I'd say he's turned up his senses and is sniffing around for any magic. I don't have any spells going and I'm not drawing any power from the local pool, so as far as he's concerned I'm just some random asshole trying to cut in.

Those are really the only ways you can identify a mage. Like we're all walking around with concealed guns but nobody else knows about it until we either pull it out to load or start shooting. Mage fights are kind of annoying that way.

"End of the line's down there, sir," he says.

"Here to see the Twins," I say. "I'm expected." I better fucking be expected.

"Name?" The bouncer pulls a clipboard from behind the stool he's been sitting on.

"Eric Carter." The bouncer freezes. I can feel a tension in the other bouncers behind him.

"You're, uh . . ." He swallows hard. "You're not on the list."

"Look harder." He flips a page and the relief washing over him is like watching a cresting wave.

"Yeah, you're good. Go on in. They're in room one."

"Thanks." The men covering the door step aside as if they might catch something contagious from me. I stop right before stepping through. "Am I really that scary?"

"I saw your fight last week."

"Ah."

"Yeah," he says.

I helped a friend out by fighting her cousin in a death-match. Complicated family politics. A group of people who make the Borgias look like amateurs. I thought I'd throw him off by having the ring owner make the fight public. I just hadn't realized how public.

Thousands of people saw me in person, and thousands more streaming live or later online. Anything resembling anonymity among the mage community has gone straight to hell. Doesn't help that I paraded the other guy's severed head around the ring. They say any press is good press. I can tell you from experience that that's not the case.

I don't say anything else, just push my way inside and let them think whatever they're going to think. There's power in anonymity, but there's power in being recognized, too. No matter what, I'm going to be different things to different people. The constant seems to be that they fear me or hate me. That's okay. I do, too.

The inside is the classiest not-actually-a-strip-club you'll ever see. Multiple stages with beautiful dancers, men and women, lots of dark booths, VIP rooms, bars. And loud, though you're only going to hear what's in your immediate vicinity once you get to a table. They use magic to bend the sound away. Gives it an air of intimacy and also lets you actually hear a conversation.

Another bouncer in a black suit and tie with a maroon shirt and a conspicuous bulge that isn't happy to see me stands watching a staircase to the private rooms upstairs. That's where I'm headed.

"Mister Carter," the bouncer says, stepping aside to let me pass. "You'll want room one. Great fight, by the way. Hope you do another one soon."

Fuck, I don't. If I hadn't had an ace up my sleeve, I'd be a smear on the floor right now. I just nod and head up. The music fades a bit as I go up the stairs, leaving a persistent squeal in my ears.

I stop at the top of the stairs. Do I really want to do this? The place has changed drastically, which is probably just as well. I have, too.

I was murdered on a school blacktop in Los Angeles about five years ago. Because of a deal I'd made with an Aztec goddess, my soul went to Mictlan, the Aztec land of the dead. The deal was to act as a stand-in for the god Mictlantecuhtli. To sort of grow him, in a way, with my humanity as the core. It's complicated.

About a month ago the human part of Mictlantecuhtli was pulled out of Mictlan and dumped into a new body. That would be me. Or us. I'm still not clear on what pronouns to use.

I'm also still having trouble adjusting to being human again. Breathing, eating, sleeping. It all still feels a little alien. The worst part is that, though I'm not Mictlantecuhtli anymore, I still have all his memories up to the point we separated.

Mictlantecuhtli's been around in one incarnation or another for thousands of years. That's a lot of memories to shove into somebody's head. Sometimes I forget myself and start speaking Nahuatl or go on a rant about Spanish colonialism and how they should all burn. Most of the time it's both.

So yeah, though Candyland's changed, I suspect I've changed more.

If you're looking for information in Las Vegas, the Twins are who you talk to. They're tied into the mage community like nobody else. Some of that's because they've been around so long, but mostly it's because everyone really wants to get into Candyland and the best way to do that is to be their friend.

The Twins. Whenever anyone says it, you can hear the capital letter. Ken and Kendra. Not their real names. I hear they change them up every so often. Bob and Bobbi, Del and Delilah, you get the idea. When I was here last, they went by Vic and Vicky.

The Twins look identical so long as they have their clothes on, and even when they don't it can be tough to tell them apart. They're beautiful. Be careful or you'll find yourself staring at them for hours—which they're just fine with, by the way. Not too tall, not too short. Slight build, close-cut black hair, otherworldly purple eyes. I'd say they were contacts, but my eyes turn into pitch-black orbs when I'm pissed off, so I'm not really in a position to judge.

They have the same androgynous features, dress the same, sound the same, move the same. Neither looks any more or less like a man or a woman. They trade off who's who. You think you're talking to Ken and suddenly it's Kendra, but it doesn't actually make a difference because they're finishing each other's sentences anyway.

I hear they've been in Vegas since before Vegas was Vegas. Story is that they ran brothels when the place was just a watering hole in the desert for the railroad. Before then, they were in New Orleans, Paris, who knows where else.

Are they human? Who cares? Personally, I think they're one person with two bodies. I couldn't prove it if I wanted to, and they're not saying.

But the most interesting thing about them is that they are two of the most powerful erotimancers in North America.

Yes, erotimancers. It's a stupid word, but "Sex Wizard" sounds like something airbrushed onto the side of a van with a waterbed and a disco ball in the back.

Every mage has a knack, one thing they're stupidly good at. Some people get sex magic. I got necromancy. We all have our crosses to bear.

Room one is, of course, the first along a dimly lit, carpeted corridor. The music from downstairs fades into a low whisper of bass and melody. I knock on the door, and when I hear a muffled "Come in" I open it, and stop.

What exactly is the etiquette for walking in on somebody with their head buried in someone else's lap? I skipped that day in charm school.

"Bad time?"

"Oh no, it's fine," says a voice to my right. "My sister's merely indulging. Kendra, dear? We have a guest. So terribly sorry, Stacy. We'll call you up later tonight."

The woman on the giving end of the evening's festivities gets up, dabs a napkin on her chin, kisses both twins, and walks out the door, closing it quietly behind her. Her flushed and lucky recipient hikes up her pants.

"Eric, it is so good to see you," Kendra says. "Forgive me?"

"For getting your rocks off? What's there to forgive?"

This is their thing. Some people think sex magic is all tantric blowjobs, raw-dogging it in the middle of a pentagram, or some bullshit like that. Sometimes it is. Mostly it isn't.

Most people think that an erotimancer's most powerful trick is to make other people want them, like it's mind control, which it totally isn't. Not that some of them can't do it on purpose. It's more they have an instinctive empathy and understanding of what a person wants or needs, and like my seeing the dead, they can't shut it off.

Like anything else there are good and bad aspects. Maybe you want to make the world a better place one handjob at a time. Or maybe you want to seduce secrets out of your enemies' trusted companions.

Magic isn't the Force. There's no light side, no dark side. There are no sides. It's just energy. It doesn't care what you do with it. Feed a starving city? Murder a hundred thousand people? Magic's got you covered.

The thing with erotimancers isn't just their powers of desire. Unlike most mages, who can only get power from their own reserves or by tapping into the well of magic that's everywhere around us, erotimancers get it from the raw energy of sex and desire itself.

They're not unique. There's a whole school of emotion-based mages out there. The scary ones are the ones who draw power from suffering. Ran into one of those once. He had a basement filled with dead boys and girls and a few live ones chained to the wall.

He kept them just barely alive and when they were spent, he'd just toss them onto the pile. When I got to them the three survivors were so broken that they each picked up the first sharp thing they could find and slashed their own throats.

This ability of erotimancers to pull magic from desire and sex makes Candyland like the Hoover Dam for sex mages. What do they do with all that energy? Fuck if I know. I've never been to a ritual. Nobody wants to invite a guy who can summon dead eyeball-eating rats to the orgy. Go figure.

Las Vegas is a popular city for them. The place is soaking in sex. You can't go five feet along the Strip without having it shoved in your face.

They have a ridiculous amount of power, though they can't do a whole lot with it on their own. Good for rituals, not as good for slinging spells. But the ones they do pack a wallop.

The biggest problem for them seems to be all the normals, the people without magic who see Satan in everything from porn to videogames and decide to take matters into their own hands. You might not hear about it but trust me, burning witches is still a thing.

See, a lot of erotimancers are sex workers, though by no means all of them. Makes them easy targets. The witch-hunter types are a nuisance at best and deadly at worst. Sex is a sin, you see. Killing the sinner is perfectly justified.

I don't get the "sex is evil but violence and death is A-OK" crowd. They should get a load of me sometime. I can correct that thinking in about thirty seconds. And I have.

"A hug," Ken says, standing and wrapping his arms around me. I wince and of course he notices.

"Oh dear. From the fight?" Of course they know about the fight. Probably bet against me. Anybody with a bit of sense would have.

"The fight," I say. "The day before the fight. The day after the fight. The day after that."

"Dear god, that was just four days ago."

"What can I say? I'm a busy little beaver."

"Let me get a look at you," Kendra says, turning me around and looking at my face. The bruises are already fading, but I don't think that's what's got her attention.

"You're different," she says. "No. That's not it. You're the same. You haven't aged a day since we saw you last." She tugs at my shirt collar to reveal the mass of brightly colored sigils and spells I have tattooed all across my body. "The tattoos are new."

"Throat to wrists to ankles," I say.

Ken cocks an eyebrow at me. "Oh, we must see this for ourselves, sometime." Kendra's still examining my face with the attention of a dermatologist going over a freckled redhead.

"Uh, I think we all need to sit down," I say. It takes her a second to get what I'm talking about and when she does her eyes pop.

"Oh, I am dreadfully sorry," she says, letting go of me and stepping back. I sit in a chair across from them and adjust my pants. The thing with the Twins being as powerful as they are is that the effect they have on people is intense whether they want it to be or not. Being around them is like walking through Chernobyl. Do it too long and you're not coming back.

"No, you're not," I say. She knows exactly the sort of effect she has.

"Oh, I have missed you," Ken says. "You are adorable."

"You're sweet," I say, "but let's be honest, nobody's missed me."

"I was trying to be polite," he says.

"You know I don't do polite."

"Fine, have it your way," Kendra says. "What can we do for you?"

"Looking for somebody. You're two of the least likely people to try to kill me in this town. I figured I'd start with you."

"Ah, business," Kendra says. "We don't do business without alcohol. It's uncouth. You still drinking old fashioneds?"

"I'll drink whatever's cheap," I say.

"My dear boy, you must raise your bar on alcohol consumption," Kendra says.

"You know he only does that because he likes to punish himself. Don't take that away from him."

"How dare. I absolutely will not serve swill in this club," Kendra says.

"As you wish, ma sœur." Ken taps a button on the table between us. "Clarice, can you send up, oh, let's say five old fashioneds, please? Top shelf, of course. You're a dear."

"Now, while we wait," Kendra says, "How are you? Are you staying in that stinking jail cell with your deceased friend?"

"I am not," I say. "I'm in a grown-up hotel room and everything."

"And your ageless, battered beauty?" Ken says. "I know how we do it, how do you?"

"I died," I say. "Also, I moisturize." I'm not crazy about being interrogated, so I throw it back on them. "The club's changed."

"A moment," Kendra says. "Did you say you died?"

"Yep. Gutted on a playground in L.A." They look at me, willing me to go on, but I don't elaborate.

"You are always such a surprise," Ken says after a moment. "Like a piñata filled with snakes. As to your question, everything's changed. Oh, the glamour, the glitz, the illusions we spin to take well-earned dollars and stuff them into our G-strings are still the same. But there's a certain je ne sais quoi about the place that's been lacking since they started blowing up the old hotels and building new ones."

"It's absolutely criminal what they've done to the Strip," Kendra says. "Mandalay Bay is simply hideous."

"They should have kept the Hacienda," Ken says.

"It felt honest, somehow," from Kendra. "People knew why they came to the city. Now, I'm not entirely sure. Now it's so . . . so . . ."

"So Disney-fied," Ken says. As they talk their voices merge together in my head and it's like listening to one person talking.

Took me a while to get used to that. I met the Twins a few months after I got to town. Mages don't really need to work to get money. Magic a few ATMs and you're flush for a good long while. But I was bored.

Heard the Twins were having trouble getting some information out of a guy on account of him being dead. Well, dead's right in my wheelhouse.

I'm asked to retrieve a safe combination out of a fresh corpse. I get the combination, give it to the Twins. Suddenly I'm on speed-dial.

Pretty soon me and a few of the Twins' protégés are working together knocking over mansions, museums, a couple banks. It was fun for a while.

We believed we were friends for no other reason than we spent a lot of time around each other. It was a seductive lie.

There's a knock on the door and a shirtless waiter in leather pants sporting a six-pack carved out of marble comes in with a tray of drinks, sets them down, and leaves.

"Randal is such a dear," Kendra says. "He knows exactly when not to speak." Ken hands me a drink and they each take one themselves. "Now that we're well liquored, what is it you're here for?"

"The Oracle," I say.

"I beg your pardon?"

"You know, the Las Vegas Oracle. Don't tell me you think he doesn't exist."

"Oh, we know it exists," Kendra says. "The question is

how do you know? Not a lot of people are aware of that fact."

I'm more aware of that fact than probably anyone else, seeing as I'm one of the people who made him.

The Oracle is a severed-but-still-living head with two souls stuffed inside: the person the head belonged to and a demon that can predict the future. Something about the combination turns it into a sort of uber-Magic 8 Ball.

"Ran into someone who worked with him," I say.

"I see. And you, what, want revenge?"

"Oh, Christ no. Need some information. I've exhausted all my other sources. I just need to ask him some questions."

"The Oracle doesn't answer questions, Eric," Ken says.

"The Oracle makes things happen," Kendra says. "It's dangerous. I hope whoever made the damn thing burns in Hell."

"I get it," I say. "I know he . . . twists reality. Sees different futures and what needs to be arranged to make the one he wants to happen happen. That kind of shit is terrifying."

"You're surprisingly well informed."

"I prefer to do my homework before jumping headlong into a situation," I say. Apparently, that's the funniest thing they've heard in ages. I sip my drink and wait for the laughter to die down.

"Oh, my boy," Ken says, wiping a tear from his eye. "I needed that. You are a poster child for poor impulse control."

"People grow," I say.

"Not that much."

"Fair enough. Look, I need to find the Oracle. You know everyone in this town. I just need a lead. I mean, I could go around busting heads until somebody tells me something, but I don't know which heads to bust so I'd just bust everybody's. Might not make a guy popular."

"You have changed," Kendra says. "I'm impressed at this newfound restraint."

"Like I said, people grow. Plus, it takes too long."

"Well, I am so very sorry to disappoint," Ken says. "But we don't know." He takes a sip of his drink.

"It was a long shot," I say. I know they're lying. They know I know they're lying. They're wary about these sorts of questions. I just don't know why. Maybe I need to tackle it from a slightly more oblique angle.

"I'm also looking for a couple of mages," I say. "Would have been here around the time I was, and they might still be."

"My memory's not that good, Eric," they say together, their voices creating weird harmonics in the room. Kendra sips at her old fashioned while Ken keeps talking. It feels weirdly like watching a ventriloquist dummy act.

"I'm sure there are others in town who would remember better than we would," Ken says. "Why not go to one of them?"

"Because nobody here likes me."

"I like you," Kendra says.

"No, you just dislike me less than anybody else does."

"I'd like to argue that point, but I don't think I can. All right, who are you looking for?"

"Sebastian McCord," I say. The glass is halfway to her lips and she freezes. "You know him."

"Know of him," she says, smoothing over her surprise with practiced ease. Ken's face is impassive, his eyes boring into me. "He died around the time you left. They found him shot to death in a half-built house in a suburban development. Grisly scene. Plastic tarps covered in blood, a headless body strapped to a table." So, Sebastian's dead. I can't say I didn't expect that.

"How about Nicole Hawthorne?" A flicker of surprise, then it's gone.

"Never heard of her," Ken says. Bullshit.

"Well, like I said, it was a longshot," I say.

Sebastian was a two-bit casino owner. His girlfriend Nicole was the smart one. They're the ones who came to me about making the Oracle. They tried to double-cross each other, each wanting me to use the other's head to make it. I could see what was at the end of that road, a quick knife in my back.

So, I stabbed first. I drugged both of them with a paralytic, propped them up in a corner and duct taped a gun to each of their hands, fingers on the triggers, before leaving the Oracle with them. Whoever came out of their stupor first would have the better negotiating position. Sounds like Sebastian lost that round.

The rest of the evening was me and a saw and a guy whose screams cut short as soon I got through his windpipe. It was messy, loud, and by the end of it I had a talking head with a tarred over neck stump that could tell the future, and enough nightmares to last me a couple of years.

The Twins exchange an uneasy glance. "Rachel may know," Kendra says.

"She does keep her ear to the ground," Ken says.

"McManus? Last I recall she didn't much like me."

"It's been almost thirty years, Eric," Ken says.

"She shot at me," I say.

"From what I recall, several times," Kendra says. "And if she truly didn't like you, she wouldn't have missed. Some people don't carry grudges their entire lives."

"Hasn't been my experience, but you do you."

"If you hold people by who they were in their youth," Ken says, "you'll always be disappointed."

"I'm offering possibilities," Kendra says. "I know you have bad blood with your old crew—"

"They were never my 'crew,'" I say. "They were clients with jobs that needed particular expertise. And when that ended, we went our separate ways."

"Eric, we funded those jobs," Kendra says. "We know why you left and what David did. You did the right thing. And if the rest of them knew about it they would have agreed. But you disappeared. Hard for a man to clear his name when he's not around. While you were here you were as tight knit as a bunch of childish reprobates could possibly be."

"In other words," Ken says, "they were your crew." Goddammit. This was why I didn't want to come back to Vegas.

"Fine, they were my 'crew,' whatever the fuck that means. So, why Rachel?"

"She's connected to parts of Las Vegas mage society that we aren't," Ken says.

"We move among a particular class of people," says Kendra. "Rachel's circles are a little more . . . rough around the edges."

"You're saying she hangs around people like me."

"No," Kendra says. "Maybe? All right, yes. Though you are better dressed than most of them."

"And that does make all the difference," Ken says.

"What's she doing these days?"

"Runs a, what does she call it?"

"A prepper school," Kendra says.

"Right. A prepper school. Out in the desert. Survival training, weapons, how to drink your own urine, that sort of thing."

"Expecting the Apocalypse?" I say.

"Aren't we all?"

"Know how I get there?"

"It's the twenty-first century, Eric. God made Google for a reason. I'm sure you can figure it out."

I finish my drink and stand. I've learned all I'm going to here. Any longer and we'll start talking about other things that happened years ago, and that's a conversation I don't need right now.

"Thank you," I say. "This helps."

"Eric," they both say with that weird harmony that I never got used to. "You said we don't like you. Just that we dislike you the least. That's not true. We do like you. Because we know you tried to do the right thing." I open the door and shove down the memories.

"Thanks for the drink," I say, and take my leave.

Chapter 2

Death is a lot of things. Simple isn't one of them.

With death, it's easy to fall into the trap of thinking in binaries. This or that. On or off. Dead or alive. I'm still struggling with it and I was dead for five years myself.

A lot of magic is an answer to a question. Need a fire? Want to fly? Kick the shit out of that guy who looked stink-eyed at you at the baseball game? Magic'll do that easy. Pyromancy, aeromancy . . . I don't know if there's a kick-the-shit-out-of-somebody-mancy, but there really should be. You have a problem, magic gives you a solution.

But necromancy? It asks way more questions than it answers. How dead is dead? How alive is alive? At what point does a corpse become meat? What exactly is a ghost? A soul? Where does it go? Necromancy blurs lines and reveals more questions the more it answers.

I had a roommate my last few months in Vegas. Guy named Jimmy Freeburg. Not too bright. Had a little magic but didn't know it. Not until I told him about it. It was all subconscious. Guy was like a black hole. Divination, tracking spells, that sort of thing just slid right off him. If you're trying to keep a low profile, he was a great guy to hang around. Spend enough time with him and nobody could see you either.

Around this time these two mages get their hands on a spell book that shows how to make this thing called an oracle. Funny thing, it's mostly a necromancy spell. They don't understand it.

Thing reads like a recipe that's missing every third word. Unless you know enough about cooking to fill in the blanks, you'll never figure it out. They needed a necromancer.

Lots of things are called oracles, but this one looks like it might be the real deal. Less Delphi, more Genuinely Magic 8-Ball. At least that was the goal. I should have read the fine print.

The idea was that you take a person, slam their soul against a demon's like a high-speed car crash until they're pretty much one thing, then cut their head off and seal both of them inside.

Boom. Talking, demon-filled, fortune-telling head.

That was the easy part. The hard part was when Jimmy volunteered. He was dying. Cancer. Scared shitless about where his soul was going.

I had no answers. I'm, like, twenty years old. I know ghosts. I know fuck-all about souls. I mean, I've got some ideas, but it's not like I've got firsthand experience with dying. That bit came later.

Anyway, he's convinced he's going to Hell, which, yeah, probably, and he's convinced that being a talking head is better than getting buttfucked by demons.

Jimmy asks me if it's gonna hurt. Of course it's gonna fucking hurt, I'm sawing your head off, not giving you a blowjob. I tell him I won't do it. Over and over again. No, nada, nein.

I honestly don't want to cut anybody's head off. In fact, I'm planning to bail with the spellbook before I have to do the ritual, so nobody loses their head.

Up to that point I had killed exactly one person and I was damned if I was going to kill another. I'd beat the crap out of somebody if I had to, sure, but kill? Fuck no. See enough ghosts, you don't want to murder anybody.

But like I was saying to the Twins. People grow.

Except. I kinda screwed things up when I was doing a dry run and summoned the demon early without an appropriate sacrifice. So basically I've got twenty-four hours to cut somebody's head off or the demon's coming after me and there's no way I'm gonna win that fight. And here's Jimmy asking me to cut his head off. Him kinda dead or me very dead? Not a tough choice.

That, I thought, was that. But like I said, I should have read the fine print.

———

The Twins weren't a total bust. I know more than I did when I walked in there, that they know something about Nicole, maybe where Jimmy is. And they're pointing me toward Rachel, which I'm not crazy about.

This whole situation is fucking with my head. How much coincidence is at work here? How much of it is Jimmy's doing? Did he not want me to find him? Or find Nicole? Or did he want me to learn something else and I just can't see it?

I'm overthinking it, I know, but when you're dealing with something that can shape today from events set in motion ten years ago you start to wonder what else it's done, and then free will gets into the mix, and thinking about that shit just gives me a headache.

Then there's my very existence. I died. I took over for Mictlantecuhtli, the Aztec god of the dead, for five years, and then got a piece of me pulled out and shoved into my grandfather's corpse. Voila, instant necromancer. With some reshaping and plumping out and puking out lots of embalming fluid.

Mictlantecuhtli's several thousand years old. Grand-dad died in his, I dunno, eighties? I don't remember meeting him. All I know is that he tried to murder me when I was a baby, so it's probably just as well.

Then there's me. If I'm doing the math right, I'm pushing fifty, but I look like I'm in my late twenties, maybe early thirties. But technically, I've only been alive for about a month.

And I seem to have their memories. All of Mictlantecuhtli's stuck in my noggin, though I can't always remember them. And grand-dad's kind of sneak up on me.

Keeping my memories and Mictlantecuhtli's separate is easier than I expected. He's just so different from me that I know right away if something's from his experience. Robert Carter could be a problem. So far I've only had a couple of flashes of his memories. If that's as far as it goes, I'm fine with it.

But I'm told he and I were alike in more than just our looks. The memories I've had of him have taken a bit of effort to separate out. If I can't tell where he ends and I begin, that's going to be a problem. The last thing I need is more people in my head.

Not for the first time I find myself wondering why I'm even doing this. I don't mean being in Vegas, I mean any of this. I was dead, for fuck sake. I liked being dead.

But now that afterlife is closed off to me. If I kick now, where does my soul go? Back to Mictlan? Or will one of the various gods I've pissed off grab me to use as a celestial punching bag for eternity? I don't know where I belong.

Outside in the parking lot I get some distance from the crowd and call Amanda. Amanda's the scion, I guess head now, of the Werther family, one of the most powerful groups of mages in the world. She's nice. Family's horrible. Like lock them all in a room and set them on fire horrible. Fortunately, I managed to kill the worst of them. Amanda inherited everything when her uncle murdered her father and things pretty much went to hell from there.

The fight where I killed her cousin that has everybody either scared or pissed off at me was to help her. Actually, it was more because I ran into some of her asshole family members and they pissed me off, but it worked out the same way.

Those people. Jesus. By the end of this last weekend we had a load of corpses who totally deserved it, and her father in a weird half-dead state where his body had stopped but his soul was still tethered to it.

All courtesy of Jimmy Freeburg. Ten years ago Amanda's uncle had an audience with the Oracle. It told him how to take over the family. Actually, it told him how to safely bump off his family. Once that happened, the dominos started tipping.

Which is where it gets weird. The payment for all this was to tell me that Jimmy Freeburg gives his regards, or wants to talk. Something like that. I don't exactly remember. I was too rage-filled at that point.

And why was I burning with so much anger? The spell that hit old man Werther also hit Gabriela Cortez, a mage who went by the street name La Bruja. Gabriela is Amanda's girlfriend and my . . . I'm really not sure what we are. Friends, though that's been iffy a time or two, and more recently something more, though I couldn't tell you exactly what that is. She was the one who brought me back from the dead, if that's any indication.

Needless to say, Amanda and I have a shared interest in the situation. Hence why I'm looking for Jimmy.

"Hey," Amanda says, yelling into her phone. I can hear the staccato thud of EDM in the background. Amanda likes clubbing. It also helps that a lot of mages in her particular circles like it, too. Now that she's the head of her family she needs to show the flag. For her, dancing is business the way golf is for old white men.

"I can hear you just fine, you know," I say. I hear a door open and close and the music fades away.

"Sorry about that. How's Vegas?"

"Oh, you know. Bat Country. I just had a talk that at least gave me a name, though I honestly don't expect anything to come of it. How about you?"

"I'm spending too much time getting across to the stupid that I'm the new sheriff in town," she says.

The Werthers have been well known in L.A. for decades. Scratch that. Old Man Werther has been well known in L.A., Amanda, not so much. She's twenty-three years old. Her father Attila was over two hundred. A lot of people probably don't even realize he had a daughter. With him gone, people see a power vacuum. Amanda's making sure they know it's been plugged up.

"You kill anybody?"

"Not yet," she says. "A couple of them will be walking funny for the rest of their lives, but they're still breathing."

"I'm sure you'll be very popular," I say.

"If the three guys coming up to me are any indication," Amanda says. "Looks like they followed me from the last place I twisted somebody's nuts into a knot. We parted on less than cordial terms."

"Go figure."

"Bringing some friends looking for a rematch."

"Have fun," I say. "Stay safe."

"You too," she says.

"When have I ever done that?"

"Fine. At least don't die. Again. I gotta go," she says. "Looks like they want to do this here in the parking lot."

"If you can, take a selfie with the bodies. I could use a laugh."

"I'll text it to you," she says and hangs up.

Las Vegas. Never thought I'd see this place again. Learned a lot out here. Can't deny it. Hardcore necromancy, good ways to steal shit. Just how thoroughly I can piss people off.

The night I made the Oracle, the night I killed Jimmy, was the last night I spent here. I was in Salt Lake City by the time the sun came up. Never looked back.

God fucking dammit, Jimmy. I thought I was quit of this place. Now that I've talked to the Twins, it's just a matter of time before news gets out I'm back and looking for the Oracle, if it hasn't already.

I wasn't lying when I told the Twins they were the ones who disliked me the least.

Speaking of. Footsteps behind me. My razor appears in my hand. Maybe I don't know if there'll be trouble, but the razor sure as hell thinks so.

"You're actually here." I know that voice. I turn around to see a man with a crooked smile, shoulder-length blond hair with too much product in it. He's wearing the same black leather jacket he did thirty years ago and his jeans are still too tight. It's like I never left.

Except that his face is too gaunt, his eyes too sunken, too haunted. Sallow skin, lines around his eyes, his mouth. Thirty years of hard living. He doesn't look great. Hell, he doesn't even look good.

"David," I say. I don't move other than to shift the razor in my hand so light glances off it. His eyes flicker to it and the smile falters.

"Heard you were in town," he says. "I didn't believe it. Because the Eric Carter I knew wasn't stupid and wouldn't have come back here."

"Oh, I think we both know Eric Carter is plenty stupid."

Now he looks full on at the razor. He knows I use it for ghosts. And he knows I use it for people.

"Hey man, water under the bridge. If you still got a beef with me, fine. But I ditched my grudge with you a long time ago. How about we call a truce? Go somewhere quiet. I'll even buy you a drink. Think of it as a frenemy thing."

I fold the razor closed and slide it into my coat pocket. Water under the bridge, my ass. Last time we saw each other we exchanged words, then fists, then magic. We beat the crap out of each other. I knocked his teeth out with a crowbar then summoned a bunch of dead cockroaches to run up his body and into his bleeding mouth. Pretty much ended the fight when he ran away choking and screaming.

"Sure. Thought I saw a Denny's down the road. Let's go there." Brightly lit, good sight lines, no cover.

"I was kinda thinking my casino. There's at least one quiet bar in it. We could—"

"You know that's not gonna happen."

"Jesus. Fine. Denny's. Want a ride?"

"I'll see you there."

"Dude, come on. I got a new car. I don't get to show this thing off to anybody." He walks to a slick black Tesla at the curb.

"Looks great," I say. "Very you."

He shakes his head and gets into the car. He tries to rev it and, well, it's a Tesla. I can almost feel him seething as he drives off.

David Jewel. Looks like he hit the big time. Always had big dreams. A casino, huh? Wonder who he killed for it.

I steal a Porsche and head down the half mile or so to Denny's. These places are fucking everywhere. Open twenty-four hours for all your greasy-burger, overdone-pancake needs. Almost as good as Waffle House. Almost.

I'm not crazy about this development, but I'm not

surprised. David's on my list of people not to talk to. It's a long list, but he's at the top of it. Pretty much guaranteed I'd run into him eventually. Just wish eventually had taken a little longer.

The list used to be bigger, but I've crossed most of the names off as I've learned they've left town, died, or otherwise disappeared. Tragically, David wasn't in any of those categories.

He was the de facto head of what the Twins so irritatingly called "my crew." Not because he was particularly good at planning jobs, he just liked believing he was in charge. The real work was all done by the rest of us, Lucas in particular. We didn't do anything too elaborate. Get too complicated and things have a tendency to fall apart.

The part of Vegas near the casinos and strip bars is a twenty-four-hour town like no other. You go into a casino and you could be there for hours and not realize it. They've got no windows, they've got no clocks. They pump in oxygen to keep you awake. You lose all sense of time or place and everything is flashing lights and ringing bells and the waterfall coin crash of the occasional jackpot.

Out here it's a little tamer. People know when the sun sets, know when it comes up. They've got jobs to get to, children to raise. Even so, any part of Vegas has its nighthawks. The Denny's isn't full, but it's full enough. David isn't stupid enough to start any shit here. Not in a diner full of normals.

I park the Porsche next to David's Tesla and resist the urge to key his car. For one thing I don't have any keys, and the straight razor would go through the door like warm cheese.

David is sitting in a closed off section near the back at a table in a sea of empties. Three sides of the room are glass, so no matter where I sit, I'm going to have my back to a window. I join him and sit down.

"You're still a dick, I see," I say. He shows me that crooked smile that makes me want to punch him.

"I thought by now you'd have gotten over your whole sitting-with-your-back-to-a-window paranoia."

"Just cautious. I get shot at through windows a lot. But don't worry, I've got a charm that'll make the bullet pass through and hit whatever's in front of me."

I don't, but David doesn't know that. He thinks about this for a second and then it occurs to him that he's sitting in front of me. His smile falters for a tick then comes back a little more crooked than before.

The waitress comes over, totally comfortable with the fact that we're sitting in a closed-off part of the diner. I get a good look at her and see that her eyes are a little glazed over. I take a look over at the occupied section. Everyone is eating their food, but weirdly in sync. They might as well be robots.

"I'll have coffee," he says. "Cream and sugar. Eric?"

"Coffee," I say. "Black." She doesn't move until David dismisses her.

"You've gotten better at that," I say. Mages like David call it "charming." The rest of us just call it mind control. It's creepy and fucked up, which is pretty much David in a nutshell. When I knew him, he could do it to one, maybe two people if he pushed it.

"Time goes on," he says. "We learn a trick or two. So, what's with you? I heard some shit about people thinking you were dead. What, you were like in a coma or something?"

The waitress brings us our coffee. David starts to doctor his with cream and sugar. I don't touch mine. I wonder if I punched him right now really, really hard, would he lose control over his new puppets? I'm tempted to find out.

"No, I was dead," I say. "Dead's kinda my thing. Necromancy, remember? Or did you forget about the cockroaches?"

Anger flashes on his face and disappears behind that smile with the perfect teeth that are all fake because I shattered the real ones with a crowbar.

"Okay. Dead. Right." He clearly doesn't believe me and I don't care whether he does or not.

"Looks like the heist business has been good to you."

"Stopped doing that crap years ago," he says. "Robbing houses and museum vaults barely paid the bills. Plus, after that job where you bailed on us, it all fell apart. Bridget's in prison because of you."

"Sorry to hear it," I say. I'm not, actually, but I am surprised. Bridget was an asshole. She and David were an item briefly until he realized that she was more of a sociopath than he was, which is saying something. Being blamed for whatever happened to her is par for the course, but keeping a mage in prison is what has me surprised. Somebody ward a supermax?

"She got off easy," David says. The surprise must show on my face because he says, "No, really. It was that bank job. Could've gotten killed."

"You had a mouthful of busted teeth and you went through with it?" I say. I watch his hands tense.

"Magic can do a lot of things, Eric. You know that."

"Yeah, it can," I say. "That's why I'm a little surprised to hear she's in prison."

Bridget was a pyromancer. Really good one. Specialized in cutting vaults, which takes a lot of power and a lot of skill.

"She burnt herself out," David says. "Pushed herself

too hard." If a mage channels much more energy than they can handle they can burn out. That point on, they're lucky if they can ever do magic again.

I'm having trouble buying that. I've seen Bridget do everything from melting engine blocks to burning precision holes a quarter of an inch in diameter through half-inch steel. The fuck could she have done that would have burned her out?

"And you left her there?"

"We were getting shot at. I had a bullet in my arm. I had one teleportation charm for all of us. Got everybody else out, but when I went back for her, she was already surrounded by a dozen cops. There's no way I could have taken them all. I mean, not like you."

I can see what he's trying to do here. It's a thing with David. He tries to manipulate, but he's not very good at it. Backhanded compliment with a heavy implication that it was my fault since I wasn't there, at the same time exonerating himself of all blame. It would be clever if it ever worked. But I don't rise to the bait. Ironic, really. The mind control mage who can't convince anybody of anything.

"How come you didn't get her out after?" I say.

"Why the hell would we do that?" he says. "She's a normal now. What good would she be?"

Of course. She's a normal, someone without magic, a regular person. A peasant. Why bother helping her out? She's lost her magic, lost her worth.

Oddly enough, I appreciate David's honesty. It's the mages who pretend they give a fuck that really piss me off. Do some of us actually care? Sure. Most of us just don't do anything to change it. There are few things more hypocritical than a mage with a conscience. David's still an asshole, though.

"So, Bridget's in jail, you own a casino. What are Rachel and Lucas doing?"

"Rachel's running some prepper shit out in the desert. And fuck Lucas. I haven't seen that fucker in years, and if I do I'll kill him."

"He made you look like an idiot, didn't he?"

"Blow me," he says. I'd call that a big yes.

Lucas is one of the best ward-crackers I've ever met. Getting to a mage's vault and knowing how to open it means nothing if you can't get past the wards. You're likely to end up dead or worse. Wards, alarms, traps, Lucas could do it all. And he always made it look easy.

Same with the plans he came up with and let David believe were his ideas. They weren't foolproof, but they were good. He was able to work around the fact that we were all a bunch of amateur Willie Suttons going after safes and vaults because, as the man says, that's where the money is.

"So, it's just you and a big ol' casino all on your lonesome?"

"Me, a big ol' casino, and a whole lotta money," he says. "Why? You lookin' for a sugar daddy?"

"You're not really my type. Say, are those dentures?" His face goes flat and it takes him a tic longer to get his expression under control.

"You were always funny," he says. "Always crackin' jokes."

"I'm a regular Shecky Greene," I say. "What do you want, David? You didn't come out to the Twins' club for shits and giggles. How long you been following me?"

"Aren't we full of ourselves?" he says. "I actually had some business in the area. Total coincidence that I ran into you. I'd heard you might be in town, but I honestly didn't expect to see you."

"Come on. We twist reality around like meth-head

clowns making balloon animals. People like us get involved, coincidences aren't usually all that coincidental."

"I didn't expect to see you, and I sure as hell didn't
want to see you," he says. "Why are you in Las Vegas?"

"I came for the waters," I say. "I was misinformed."

"What?" David never was a film fan.

"What do you care?" I say. "Afraid I'm gonna fuck up
some big score? What's the job? Casino robbery? Go after some ancient artifact with immense powers sitting in
some rich guy's safe in Summerlin? Or are you just gonna
burn an apartment building down with a bunch of families inside? Again."

He's trying to control his rage and not doing a great
job of it. His face is getting warm and his hands are
clenching.

"That was an accident and you fucking know it," he
says.

"No. An accident is bad wiring in the kitchen, not a
Molotov cocktail in the carport. Figure, what, four people per apartment, call it an even dozen families. That's
forty-eight people you could have murdered."

"And didn't."

"No, you only killed thirteen of them. I got the rest
out." Thirteen people died when David's fire reached an
empty apartment where they'd accidentally left the gas
on over the weekend. Ten people next door went up in
one big blast. The other three kicked when a second-
floor bedroom collapsed onto the first.

I don't know what the official report says. Cool thing
about being a necromancer? We can feel when somebody
dies. It's like getting your nuts hit with a golf ball, a real
hoot. So, I know exactly how many people went up in
that fire and when they did.

"You're still a fucking bleeding heart," he says. "A
necromancer who's afraid to kill anybody."

"Oh, that life ended a long time ago," I say. "I saw the error of my ways. I've lost count of the people I've killed. I burned over a hundred thousand to death five years ago. A month back I flat out murdered a couple thousand who were being used as human shields because somebody didn't think I had the balls to do it. This past weekend was a little light. I only killed four or five. One of them twice."

I decide not to tell him about the nightmares I still have about both those events. The deaths of hundreds in a matter of seconds slamming into me like a cannonball.

"The fuck is wrong with you?" he says.

"If we go that route we'll be here all night. I have to wonder what's wrong with you. I've clearly struck a nerve."

David leaps to his feet, all fury, kicking his chair across the room to hit a booth. He throws his coffee cup at the table and it shatters into a hundred shards, coffee splashing. I stop it all with a spell, let the shards hang for a moment in a porcelain-and-coffee cloud, then I pull them all back together and tell their molecules to play nice with each other. I refill the cup with the coffee floating in the air and then gently lower the cup down to rest in front of him without so much as a ripple. I take a sip of my coffee.

"I've gotten better, too," I say, doing my best to hide the fact that that spell kicked my ass. Power I can do. Control, especially that level of control? I'm honestly surprised I didn't make the table explode.

"I don't know why you're here, but whatever it is, you stay the fuck away from me. Or I will fucking gut you."

"You want to go another round with the cockroaches?"

"Fuck you, Carter." David storms out of the diner as the waitress is walking up to the table. His control spell drops and she blinks, confused. I throw a wad of bills on the table, twenties, hundreds, I don't know how much.

Maybe it'll make her feel better when she wakes up screaming in the middle of the night, remembering in dreams what happened to her, but I doubt it.

Chapter 3

I hit the road in the morning taking the 160 out to the other side of the Spring Mountains. Freedom Preppers, Rachel's desert survivalist school, is a group of buildings at the end of a dirt track. Glad I took the time to steal a Jeep this morning.

Rachel MacManus was our muscle. Scottish, scraggly red hair, freckled face. She always looked like she was either about to start a bar fight or had just finished one. Sometimes both were true.

Her dad had been a mercenary. Did a lot of work in West Africa in the nineties. She followed him into the family business, but something happened in Sierra Leone that got him killed. She never told me what and I didn't ask.

Knacks aren't always a particular type of magic, like necromancy or pyromancy. Sometimes they manifest as just being insanely good at something. I know a woman whose magic expresses as her being able to run fast. Like, really fast. Up the side of a building fast. She's not great at any other sort of magic, but if you need to get from point A to point B as quickly as possible, she's your gal.

Rachel's knack is like that. Couldn't cast spells worth a damn, but you give her a weapon and she's a fucking maestro. Knives, guns, clubs, hammers, machetes, swords. If it can fuck you up, she was all over it.

I can tell something's wrong before I pull into the small

dirt lot outside a double-wide trailer with the Freedom Preppers sign over the door.

The lot isn't packed, but it's not empty. A handful of different cars, mostly trucks. It's the five identical black Suburbans parked in a neat row right outside the trailer that grab my attention. Five vehicles, eight people a pop. I'd like to think that this is just some group of doomsday preppers out here on some package vacation deal, but my gut tells me it's not.

There's gunfire nearby, though I'd expect to hear that in a place like this. But it's uncontrolled. Like the range master just handed a bunch of monkeys .45s and let them go to town.

I park the Jeep behind a nearby dumpster. Dumpsters are shitty cover, most bullets will just go through them like they're cardboard, but you work with what you got. Somebody's yelling but I can't make out what it is.

I get out of the car, stay low, and head toward the gunfire, my SIG Sauer at the ready. After being dead for five years and acting as a stand-in for a death god, it's still a little disorienting being human again. Not everything works perfectly. Like my situational awareness.

"Turn around. Drop the gun."

"In that order?"

"Smartass, huh? Drop the fucking gun."

I do what he says, tossing the SIG into the dirt. I turn around slowly. I don't really like the idea of being shot. It hurts, and at the very least it's a pain in the ass to deal with afterward.

The guy's decked out in black BDUs, Kevlar vest, a full-face gasmask, and an HK MP5 submachine gun tricked out with a silencer and Picatinny rails holding a reflex sight, flashlight, and an assault grip, because I guess he had a lot of money to piss away.

His gear screams military but his posture, the way he's holding his gun, and the more-than-slight pudge hanging over his belt tells me he's really more a weekend-warrior type. Not to mention the HK, which I don't think anybody important uses anymore.

"Aren't you hot in all that?" I say.

"What?"

"Hot. You know. Desert? It's at least ninety out here." I'm wearing a white short-sleeve shirt and khakis which is so not my style, but wearing black out here is an invitation to heat stroke.

"Who the hell are you?"

"Why haven't you shot me yet?" I say.

"I'm asking you the fucking questions."

"I mean, it doesn't make sense. Whatever you and your friends are doing out here, I can't imagine it's good. You're here to kill somebody and I can guess who. But if you do that, you're going to have witnesses unless you kill them, too. So why haven't you shot me yet?"

"I—" I can only make out his eyes through the gasmask but it's clear he's not sure what to do. I can see what's happening. He didn't know what he was signing up for. Probably why he's out here guarding the trucks and not out there murdering people.

"You've never killed anybody before, have you?" I say.

"Answer my goddamn question."

"Shit, sorry. What was it?"

"Who the fuck are you?"

"Oh. Name's Eric. You?"

"Why are you here?"

"I hear the sushi is to die for. First time jitters? I know a breathing exercise that'll help." The thing about gasmasks is that visibility is for shit. His breath is fogging up the lenses, and they collect dirt and dust like you wouldn't believe.

I've been slowly inching my way closer to him and he doesn't seem to have noticed. Bummer for him. I figure I'm close enough now.

My straight razor's in my hand before I even think about pulling it out. Not sure I'm ever going to get used to that. It seems to know when I need it. The last weapon I had with a mind of its own was this old Nazi Browning Hi-Power that was a real asshole. Made hella big holes, though.

The razor doesn't seem to have an opinion on what I do with it. It just seems to want to be useful. Like a puppy. A decapitating, throat slitting, insta-death-kill puppy.

I take a swing with my left arm, stepping forward and shoving his gun aside. The razor goes through his throat like it's Jell-O. Blood fountains out of the gash as his head tips back like a Pez dispenser. He's dead before he hits the ground.

And now I'm covered in blood. I don't know why I don't just walk around wearing a fucking raincoat. This is why I prefer to wear black. I have a spell for manipulating blood that will pull it out of my clothes, my hair, off my skin. I'm about to use it when I feel magic flare in the distance.

I figure it could be Rachel, but then there's another one, and another. There are at least three mages out there. If I fire off a spell they'll be on me like flies on shit. I'd rather they have to react to me instead of the other way around.

Well, it's not like I've never been covered in blood before. A lot. I grab the guy's MP5 and stuff a couple extra magazines into my pockets. Jesus. He had the gun set to full auto.

The grounds of Rachel's school are a series of half-buried bunkers, Quonset huts, gun ranges scattered across acres of desert gravel and scrub brush. I move out of the parking lot, keeping low and staying in whatever shadows I can find.

I feel the dead before I get anywhere near them. There are a few fresh Haunts and Echoes nearby. They're confused, shocked, angry. At least the ones with enough awareness to be anything at all. Maybe a dozen all told. Not everyone leaves a ghost. On average it's about twenty-five percent, give or take. There could be anywhere from twenty to fifty dead up ahead.

I duck behind a building and listen. The gunfire has died down, though the smart money's on it starting back up with a vengeance any second.

"All we want is the Keeper." A man's voice. "Give her to us, and we'll let you go."

"You just shot everybody out there, you fuckin' bawbag." All this time and I can still pick out Rachel's Scottish accent and her ability to make anything she says sound like "go fuck yourself." "You expect me to believe you why, exactly?"

There's something about this exchange that seems very familiar, and then I realize she's stalling for time pretty much the same way I do, by swearing violently. I usually end up more beaten-up, though.

"Fuck this," the man says. "We're gonna burn you and your fucking kid out of there and then we'll—" A single gunshot cuts him off.

I need a better vantage point. I duck between a couple cinder block buildings but pull back because one of these assholes is standing in the way. He's wearing desert camo, a pair of Oakleys, and a pretty stripped down M4 hanging at his side from a sling. These are definitely not pros. There's no uniformity.

I press myself against the wall and pull the razor. I don't want to shoot him. Silencers are not silent. I hear his feet crunching on gravel as he walks in my direction.

The sun is behind him, giving me his position without giving him mine. I only have one shot at using that.

He steps out between the two buildings and though I only barely shift my weight, the noise is enough. He spins, blocking my arm as I slash with the razor.

He jabs at my throat with a finger strike, but I tilt my head just enough that he misses. There's a loud crack as his hand slams into the wall. That's what you get for trying to be fancy.

He steps back and comes at me with a kick. This time it's my turn to block. With the razor. It takes his leg off just above the knee, mostly because of his own momentum.

There's always this split-second pause when a person suffers a catastrophic injury before their brain catches up to what's just happened. When it does, he's going to start screaming, and that's going to be a problem.

I slash up and across with the razor, slicing through his throat before he can make a sound. He falls to the ground clutching at the gash. He tries to get his gun up, but it's tangled in the sling, and even if he did manage it his trigger finger is a bent and twisted mess.

It won't take him long to bleed out, but I don't know how much time I have. A quick stab at his chest goes through the ribs and tears into his heart. He's dead in less than thirty seconds.

I drag him back between the two buildings and prop him next to some bags of cement covered by a blue tarp. I drape enough of the tarp over him that it might buy me a few seconds if somebody comes back here.

A metal ladder is bolted to the side of the building. I climb it up to the roof as slowly and quietly as I can. One time I tried this exact same thing, only to pop my head up looking straight into the barrel of a gun. I'd rather not repeat the experience.

I get lucky and there's no sniper up here, and from

what I can see of the nearby rooftops there aren't any at all. From a tactical standpoint even the dumbest weekend warrior is going to want someone up top covering them. It's almost as though they're trying to get themselves killed.

I crawl to the edge and look over to see an open area of dirt and gravel with about fifteen men and women in a bizarre assortment of tactical gear. Black, blue, desert, woodland. One guy's wearing fishing waders.

They're each taking cover behind anything that looks like it might stop a bullet and firing on one building, a bunker half buried in the dirt. There's a hatch in the front like on a submarine and lateral slits that look like they can be opened and closed from the inside all along the doorway. I can't tell for certain from where I am, but I think there might be more on the sides.

I'm wondering what those are for when I get my answer. A rifle barrel pokes out of one and fires. Fishing waders goes down with half his head blown off.

I'd say Rachel's done pretty well for herself so far. There are about a dozen corpses in black BDUs outside her door. But they're just bait. The mages in charge, because it's always the mages who are in charge, want to see what she can do and how she does it. They're probably the only professionals in this crowd.

They'll hang back and try to figure out a way to blow through that door. Eventually, they will. I hope she has a lot more ammunition.

The real challenge is going to come from those mages. I can feel three of them casting spells looking for weak spots in the bunker, unwarded spots they can exploit.

I'm pretty sure I'll have to kill all of them. I need to talk to Rachel, and I'd rather do it while she's still breathing. They're making that less likely.

And then I look at the corpses they've littered the

grounds with and see a kid who can't be more than five or six lying in his own blood that's seeped into the dirt, his dead eyes staring at me.

"Pretty sure" goes to "Absolutely will in the most painful fucking way possible."

Death is a thing. Like rocks or air. There's no consciousness to it. It doesn't choose who dies. It's indiscriminate. It doesn't care. It happens to all of us.

But suffering is something that's done to us by other people. None of us have to suffer. We can all make it stop. Except that humans are fucking trash who'll murder a five year old because they're standing in the way.

Most of the dead look like civilians, tourist types. Men, women, girls, boys. There are at least two dozen corpses down there who aren't armed in tactical gear.

The shooters have gunned down everyone they've run across and I will murder every fucking one of them for it. Yes, I recognize the irony.

The wannabe soldiers are all carrying assault rifles. Between that and the mages, even with the element of surprise there's no way I can take them all on.

All the carnage below gives me an idea. Maybe I don't have to take them on at all. I duck behind an air conditioning unit and think about it. I should—might?—have enough power for the spell I'm thinking of without tapping the pool, but I'll need to tap in pretty much right after. As soon as I do any magic I'm gonna light up like a wildfire up here, and with what I have in mind I might not have much left over.

But I've been itching to do this since I got back. As someone pointed out to me recently, knowing how to do a thing is the hardest part to doing the thing. And thanks to Mictlantecuhtli's memories, I know how to do a lot of things I didn't before.

There's a lot of crap up here on the roof. Debris blown

in on desert winds, flyers, rocks. Paper charms are spells written on a piece of paper, or anything really, then crumpled up and thrown to the ground, where they detonate like a grenade. The more power you put into them, the more powerful the spell when it goes off.

Got hit with one in L.A. that triggered an earthquake once. It didn't last long or go far, but it took down the building I was in.

I find a hefty rock, pull out a Sharpie, and start marking it up with runes. They're not strictly necessary, you don't need to write down $v=u+at$ to make your car move, after all, but this is how I learned it and old habits die hard. These aren't the spell. They're more like glue to make the spell stick.

Once I have that done I concentrate on the spell, pulling strands together in my mind before I actually commit. I lose threads a few times and need to start over, but eventually I have something that I think is going to work. If it doesn't, well, it'll suck.

I cast the spell on the rock, not even sure if it's going to stick. I do have the mages' attention, though. Gunfire erupts around me, bullets ricocheting off the edge of the air conditioner. I wait for the fire to die down then throw the rock over the side.

"Grenade," someone yells, and everyone hits the dirt. The rock bounces a couple of times before landing near the corpses Rachel has taken out.

It goes off with a brilliant flash of blue light, a ring of energy that blows outward like waves from a meteor crashing in the ocean.

It doesn't take long before the wannabe soldiers down there realize they're not dead. There's a new burst of gunfire until one of their number yells at them to stop.

"I don't know who the hell you are," he yells, "or what

that was supposed to be, but it didn't work." I poke my head out from cover to see him. I kind of expect somebody to take a shot at me, but no one does. Just as well, they're gonna need the ammunition.

"You sure about that?"

"Seeing as we're all still here, yeah, I'd say so."

"Nobody ever taught you how to count, did they?" His expression goes through amused, confused, and slowly into terrified as he realizes what I just did.

Nobody really likes necromancers. I get it. We freak people out. But all the rumors are not doing anybody any favors either. Did you know I eat babies and drink blood? I've heard that from a couple dozen people over the years.

My favorite is that I've got an undead army at my command. How exactly is that supposed to work? Where am I going to put it? Do you have any idea how much it costs to run an industrial freezer? Or how long it takes to thaw out a corpse?

Besides, why would I keep an army on ice when I can just make one on the fly?

Everybody down there, living and dead, is on their feet. The first few soldier-wannabes who realize this are too slow to do anything about it before the shooting begins.

Animating the dead hasn't always worked out for me. Bugs, rats, those I could always manage. But it wasn't until everything happened with Santa Muerte and Mictlan that I unlocked enough power to animate a human corpse without a fuck-ton of assistance.

And even then all I could do was puppet them around like marionettes or issue very simple commands. They were just dancing meat, and I had to maintain focus.

Honestly, I wasn't sure this would work. But having

Mictlantecuhtli's knowledge and understanding of the dead, when I can remember it, seems to let me do a hell of a lot more now than just make puppets.

A wave of exhaustion and nausea hits me. I pushed myself too hard for this one. I hear screams and more gunfire. Flares of magic go off down below as the mages join in on the fun.

And then there's a flare right in front of me. Well, fuck. I hate teleporters. I was hoping I'd have a couple more seconds before someone came up here to kick my ass. At least I don't have to pay attention to my little battalion of the dead down there. They'll handle their own shit.

This guy looks more put together than the rest. I don't mean that as a compliment. He's wearing black BDUs and brand-new polished boots. He doesn't have a gun. Typical. Depending on his magic to do all his work. Mages can be really stupid, sometimes.

I fire the MP5 and then realize that no, maybe I'm the idiot here, because he manifests a flaming sword and brings it down on me blocking the gunfire. I have to say I am impressed. It slows him down for a second and I roll out of the way before he can cleave my skull in two.

I bring the MP5 back up and empty a clip at him. He doesn't need the sword to block now. He's got a shield up. My mistake. I brought a gun to a magic fight. I drop the gun and keep moving, the straight razor taking its place.

The mage lunges at me with the sword as I bring up the razor. I don't know what the hell I think I'm going to accomplish. Sword versus razor is kind of like rock versus scissors.

Except it doesn't work out that way. The razor holds. More miraculous is that as a result, I hold, too. That much force impacting that small a thing should have knocked it spinning and sent the sword straight through my hand.

But it's not all unicorns and handjobs. The guy's sword is on fire, after all. I can feel my skin blister under the intense heat.

That's when I notice he's left himself open just enough for me to try something. Never say I'm too proud to take a shot at somebody's nuts when the opportunity presents itself. I kick upward and connect, putting as much force into it as I can. It's a very solid hit. His eyes cross a little and I've clearly thrown him off.

I don't need to hide myself anymore, so I tap the pool, pulling in as much power as I can. He notices and at first it's no big deal. But then I keep drawing more. And more.

He's not a stupid man. He does the logical thing; try to kill me before I let loose whatever spell it is I'm about to cast.

Only I'm not planning on doing anything like that. I just needed to buy a little time. By the time he's steady on his feet, reshaping the sword into a massive fireball to throw at me, I've got everything where I need it.

The trick to staying alive in situations like this is to make sure you have options. For example, just because they didn't put any snipers on the rooftops doesn't mean I can't.

A single bullet fired from the top of the next building by a reanimated body that's missing most of its chest catches the mage just under the right ear, bursting his head like an overfed tick. One of these days I'll learn not to be so close to blood-fountaining headshots.

I would have had my sniper up sooner but it turns out there are some things these corpses can't do on their own. Getting a corpse to understand the concept of climbing a ladder to line up a shot is surprisingly difficult.

The last couple of minutes I've been feeling a string of deaths, but when I look over the edge of the roof I see a cluster of these clowns holding their own and taking down my corpses by shooting them in the head. Who says zombie movies aren't educational?

Before I can do anything about it there's an explosion below me. Screams cut short, shrapnel rips through the air like angry hail. Deaths burst in my consciousness like popcorn.

The corpses are somewhat autonomous but getting hold of a grenade and thinking to use it might be a stretch. I can only think of one other source for the blast.

"All right, ya fuckstick. Show yourself or I'll blow up the fucking building you're standing on." Ah, Rachel. Don't ever change.

I slowly walk toward the edge of the roof with my hands up. I don't have a shield spell going right now. That'd just be a provocation I don't need. The question is, if she tries to shoot me, can I activate it in time to stop a bullet?

"Eric Fucking Carter," Rachel says. Her face cycles between surprise, confusion, disgust, and anger, finally settling on an impressive combination of all four.

"Aw, Rach," I say. "You remembered my middle name."

"What the actual fuck?"

"Been a long time. You look good."

She's got the same frizz of red hair. Same pale, freckled complexion burnt red in the desert sun. But there's experience etched into her face that suits her.

"I see your bullshit excuse for charm hasn't changed."

"What? You're alive, aren't ya? Looks pretty goddamn charming to me."

Chapter 4

"Polis are on their way," Rachel says, hanging up her phone. Rachel's Scottish accent might not be very strong but she never bothered to change how she pronounces anything. A little rebellious "fuck you" to Standard American English.

We're in the double-wide out front. Office, reception desk, and living space all in one. Long, wood-paneled front office that smells of stale cigarettes with old flyers stapled to the wall behind the counter. An old air conditioner strains beneath the Nevada heat with a rattle that would give a ninety-year-old emphysema patient a run for his money.

Some of those flyers on the wall are years old. Gun shows, truck shows, tough mudders, gunsmithing. Rachel's been doing this a long time. Not really surprising. It all feels very her. What stands out is the short stack of books on the counter.

"The Book of the Law?" I say. "Practice of Enochian Magick? You're reading Crowley. And . . . Jack Parsons' Book of Babalon? Seriously? You know both these guys were cranks, right?" I pick up another one. "The Royal Arms of the Great Eleven. Why does this sound familiar?"

"Haven't read any of them," she says. The mess of Post-It Notes sticking out from between the pages says otherwise, but whatever. She grabs the book out of my hands and sweeps the entire mess under the counter.

The books are unusual, but the real surprise is Kyle. He's very clearly Rachel's kid. Early twenties, maybe. Same scraggly red hair, same too-pale, freckled complexion.

But his other features, the high cheekbones, the gawky frame are pure David. The last time I saw them together Rachel and David were a hair away from killing each other. Or Rachel killing David, actually. Between the two of them he wouldn't stand a chance.

I'm not exactly in a position to judge romantic partners. You do you. But David? Seriously?

Kyle sits opposite me at a circular table in the corner. He's got the same sullen look of all teenagers with a new coat of holy-shit-what-the-fuck-just-happened on top of it.

Rachel sinks heavily into a plastic chair next to him, sets a massive first aid kit onto the table. "Let me see your hand," she says.

"My hand is fine," I say. "See? It's at the end of my arm where it belongs and it even has all the fingers." She grabs my hand, her fingers brushing against the burn on the back of it. My eyes cross from the pain.

"Fine, huh? So, you don't mind if I start poking at it?"

"Okay. It's not fine. One of those assholes had a burning sword. I got too close."

"Wow, yeah. I can see that. Second degree burn, blisters, got some weeping here. I can help with that, but if you really want to tough it out like a real man and get infected and then have to cut off your arm, who am I to tell you no?"

"When did doctors get so pissy?"

"I'm not a doctor," she says. "I'm Scottish."

"That explains it."

"This is gonna hurt." She pulls out an aerosol can and shakes it a couple of times before spraying it on the burn.

"It already hurts," I say. "I'm sure it— Jesus H. Pig-fucker Christ. What the hell, Rachel?" My hand feels more on fire than it did when it was actually on fire.

"It'll be fine in a minute. Drama queen." The pain calms down and she covers it with gauze and tape. "That should speed the healing up. Should be fine by tomorrow morning."

"No shit? What is this stuff? Could have used some the last few days." I can still feel the bruises, healing burns, and assorted stab wounds from my ordeal at the Werther estate. I kinda want to grab that can and bathe in the stuff.

"No idea. Get it from a guy in Flagstaff. I'll give you his name." She puts the first aid kit away. For a moment she's got nothing to do. The façade falls and she slumps deeper in her chair, exhausted.

"What did you do out there?" she says. "Seeing as you're the only one who was standing afterward I assume it was you."

"You probably don't want to know." Most people get weird around death. Some folks don't care one way or another. You should watch out for them. Some of them are worse than I am.

Other people get physically ill, creeped out, run away. All normal reactions. But it's the desecration crowd, the holy roller types who see anything with the dead as a capital-A Abomination that I could do without. We're talking torches and pitchforks. You throw zombies into the mix, well, it's a whole new ballgame.

"I have seen more than my share of shite," she says. "Spill." I glance over at Kyle. He doesn't seem to be paying much attention to us.

"He's fine," she says. "He knows what's what."

"All right. I raised the corpses and had them kill every-one who was still standing. Thanks for the grenade, by the way. Zombies are great at pulling triggers but seems they can't reload for shit. Once they were out of bullets it was all hand to hand. Or bite to hand as it were."

She doesn't say anything for a second and I can tell from her widening eyes what she's thinking. "Jesus. Everyone?"

No point in denying it. "Yes, everyone. Even the children who came with their families. They didn't have guns, though. Mostly they bit their legs."

"Fuck me," she says. "I do not know what to do with that information."

"I told you you probably didn't want to know."

"You made zombies?" Kyle says. He's still stunned but that's got his attention.

"At that point they weren't people, anymore," I say. "Just bodies. The people they had been already went off to wherever it is they needed to go."

"People have souls? Like for certain?" he says. I can tell this is wading into some deep waters. I get a question like that, it's one of two things. Either they just lost somebody, or they're about to lose themselves.

"Kyle," Rachel says. There's a warning in her voice.

"I just want to know." Rachel looks at me with a plea in her eyes. I have no idea what she wants me to say, so I opt for the truth.

"Yes," I say. "They go off to wherever they're supposed to go. When I died I went to a place called Mictlan. Part of my job was helping those souls get settled."

Silence. Then Rachel saying, "What?"

"It's a long story," I say. "My point is, yes, there are souls and yes, they go somewhere. Not always to the same places."

"I told you," Kyle says.

"Goddammit, Eric."

"Hey, he asked. What do you want me to do, lie to him? The kid just saw a bunch of people get murdered out back, more than half of them by me. I think he deserves to know a little bit about what just happened."

"This is such a shitshow."

"Yeah. But from what I saw it's a surprisingly straight-forward one."

"What are you talking about?"

"You were clearly the victim of some mysterious para-military force."

Her face goes sour. "Paramilitary force my ass," she says. "Fuckin' amateurs."

"Then say it was a bunch of psychotic Proud Boys or Murder Clowns or some shit. Say they were shouting rac-ist slogans, or 'Woodstock Uber Alles.' I dunno."

"And then they all shot each other?" she says.

"That's exactly what they did. Except for the ones who died from zombie bites or the ones I cut apart. It's what the forensic guys are gonna say, anyway. Probably say it's a suicide cult. Say they were all yelling about the Great Flying Jesus Saucer coming to take them all away and then let loose."

"What about the kids who were biting them?"

"Last ditch self-defense. Besides most of them were taken out by the grenade. They'll be picking up pieces of them for days. This thing is so goddamn weird the cops are going to want a rational explanation as soon as fuck-ing possible. Believe me, no matter how out there it sounds, it's more believable than the truth."

Rachel looks a little green. I remember Rachel being a badass. I don't remember her being squeamish. But peo-ple change. Maybe having a kid has soured her stomach for these sorts of things.

"Might be a harder sell than you think," she says.

"Why?" Kyle says. At first I think he's asking why that story wouldn't work, but no. This one's much more difficult to answer.

"Did I do something bad?" he says. "Is that why they came back?" His movements are slow, like he's swimming through mud. The kid's in shock. Rachel is on him in a flash, kneeling in front of him, taking his hands in hers.

"It's okay," she says, voice pitched low, talking to a spooked pet. "You didn't do anything bad or wrong. There's nothing wrong with you, sweetie. These men weren't after you. The ones who took you, they can't hurt you anymore. They can't hurt anyone anymore."

"Because you killed them," he says.

"That's right, baby. I killed them."

Kyle's face crumples, the shock turning into the heart-breaking cries of a kid who just can't hold it in anymore. He's a sudden mess of tears and snot and hitching breath, his whole body shaking.

Rachel pulls a bottle out of her pocket and shakes out a pill. She slips it between his lips and lifts a Coke can for him to sip. At first I think, Christ, let the kid take his own medication and then feel like an asshole because he clearly can't. I doubt he could hold the Coke can, much less get the pill in his mouth. Rachel pulls Kyle into her arms and rocks him back and forth.

This isn't something I should be in the room for. As quietly as I can, I get up and go outside onto the porch. The heat was bad before, but now the sun is higher in the sky and it's turned into a blast furnace.

Doesn't smell all that nice at the moment. Bunch of zombie bits, exploded corpses baking in the sun fifty feet away will do that. Pretty country, though. Bet the sunsets are beautiful.

A few minutes later, Rachel joins me on the porch with

a couple of cans of Coke. Hands me one. "How's he doing?" I say.

"Better," she says. She takes a swig of her drink. "I promised him he'd be safe. That he'd never have to deal with— Fuck."

"You know who those guys were?"

She shakes her head. "We get the occasional roided-out nutjob who wants to play ninja warrior, but this? There were, what, thirty? Forty? Who the fuck even were these people?"

"Yeah, I got a couple ideas about that. This whole thing left a bunch of ghosts. Soon as I can I'm gonna ask them some questions."

"I always thought that 'talking to ghosts' thing was all bullshit."

"Even with the shit you've seen?"

"That was different," she says. "That was seeing. Not having a conversation."

"We should all be so lucky," I say. "My life would be infinitely easier."

"The fuck are you doing here, Eric?" she says.

"Needed to talk to you," I say.

"About?"

"That's a long story," I say.

"Are you really Eric? Because, and don't get me wrong I appreciate you doing . . . shit I'd really rather not think about, but you look a little young to be Eric Carter."

"That's a much more complicated question than you probably think," I say. "But yes, I'm really me. If you're really worried, let me put it to you this way. If someone wanted to get close enough to you to cause you a problem, you think they'd choose to look like me? Me from almost thirty years ago? Come on. We haven't seen each other in decades."

"Yeah, that's kind of the problem, isn't it? You and I are about the same age. How come you don't look it?"

"Like I said inside, I died. Then I came back."

"I—"

"Whatever you're going to say, table it. For the moment just accept it and let's move on. How many people did you lose?" Place like this doesn't run on two people. She had to have had staff. I just hope most of them were off today.

"Six of my own people," she says. "More than a dozen customers. Fuck. I'll have to contact their families." Rachel looks angry. Given a chance she'll beat the shit out of anybody who happens to get in her way. But I've seen this sort of thing. Hell, I've experienced this sort of thing. It's pain and grief. Rage is its only outlet.

"I'm sorry."

Kyle comes out of the trailer. He's looking better, though maybe not entirely there. Rachel puts her arm around his shoulders.

Sirens in the distance closing fast. "Time to greet the party guests."

"One second." I pull a HELLO MY NAME IS sticker and a Sharpie. I write DON'T MIND ME and slap the sticker on my chest, putting enough juice to make even Rachel wince.

"Christ, that shit again," Rachel says. "If you're going to do that at least stay out of the way. Don't need a repeat of the last time."

"Hey, that security guard walked into me," I say.

"My point."

"Fair enough."

I've taken care of all the blood in my clothes and hair, though I'm still feeling slightly sticky. Even without looking like I took a swim in slaughterhouse runoff, my presence here is complicating. I'd rather not even be a factor.

Three SWAT trucks, six patrol cars, two unmarked, a firetruck, two paramedics, a coroner's van, and a helicopter. I pick a spot on the porch over to the side. The reporters won't be far behind.

Cops are usually a bigger pain in the ass than they're worth. I'm not really up for three hours of interviews in a little shoebox of a room with bad air conditioning. Doesn't mean I can't listen in to some of it.

Rachel waves at the cars as they pull in. One detective comes up to greet her. Big guy with a Tom Selleck mustache. Looks mean, at least until he gets close to Rachel. Then the worry settles onto his face.

"You're all right?" he says.

"We're all right. I don't know who the fuck those guys were. Some suicide cult, maybe? They came in, shot everybody. We got into one of the bunkers just in time."

"And then they killed each other?"

"I got a couple of them from the bunker. But they took out each other after that. The last ones blew themselves up with a grenade. Did a sweep after. Far as I can tell, we're the only ones alive."

"Fuck, Rachel. I wish you would—"

"Enough, Jeff," she says. "Not the time or place."

"All right," he says. "But we're talking about this." He turns to Kyle. His eyes narrow. He glances at Rachel who gives him a short nod.

"How ya feelin', slugger?"

"I'm okay, Dad," he says. His voice is thick, like he's talking through cotton balls.

Detective Jeff's eyes slide right off me as he turns to talk to his people and gets them out to do their jobs. SWAT teams start to comb the area, coroner sets up a tent. Rachel was right, this is gonna be a real shitshow.

And then the family drama kicks in. A woman officer, about the same height as Rachel, similar build to Rachel, same frizzy red hair as Rachel comes up to the trailer. The two Rachels glare at each other.

"You want to help?" Detective Jeff says to Kyle in a futile attempt to redirect the situation. Kyle recoils at the suggestion. "Whoa, it's okay. I meant up here in the car. Monitor the radio. Not gonna take you out back."

Kyle visibly relaxes. "Can I?"

"Of course. Come on." Kyle goes off with Detective Jeff and Rachel's clone. It's just me and Rachel now.

"Okay, what the fuck was that?" I say.

"Diane," Rachel says. "Jeff's new girlfriend."

"I'm thinkin' Jeff's got a type."

"No shit," she says. Clearly she doesn't want to talk about it and honestly I don't really care.

"I'm really sorry about Kyle," I say.

"He'll be okay," she says. "He has good days and bad days. Jeff and I argue about him being here, but I've got every weapon here warded. Not a single one of them will fire without my say so. And it's where Kyle wants to be. Today might change that. Fuck it." She materializes a cigarette in her hand and lights it with a spell. "Been trying to quit."

"I think you're allowed a cheat day when a few dozen people get gunned down by wannabe army men on your property."

"And what about if some asshole necromancer you haven't seen in thirty years shows up just as that's happening?"

"Oh, then you get two cheat days."

"Eric, why are you here? And don't say you want to talk to me. Talk to me about what?"

"Looking for someone. The Twins told me you might know her."

Rachel gets a sudden tension around her eyes, and

though she's doing it slowly I can still feel her drawing magic from the pool.

"Whatever you're thinking of doing, don't," I say. "I'm not here to hurt anybody. I'm trying to save someone."

"Take off those sunglasses," she says. "Look me in the eye and say that."

"Remember last time I said you didn't want me to do something? This is the same sort of thing."

"Humor me," she says. What the hell. I take off my sunglasses. She startles and steps back. She was not expecting pitch-black eyeballs.

"Told ya."

"What the fuck?"

"Present from my ex-wife," I say.

"I don't remember black marbles for eyes on the list of anniversary gifts."

"It's right after leather," I say. "Or maybe paper? I don't remember. They'll go back to normal soon. I am really just looking to help someone, Rachel. Believe me, I don't want to be here."

"Jesus. You know, I pretty much forgot you existed," she says. "That took a while. I was pissed off at you for a long time, you know. Thought you'd just hung us out to dry. Heard the truth a few years later. What David did . . . How many people died?"

"Thirteen," I say. "I managed to get the rest out. Would have been fourteen, but he chickened out and took himself and his busted teeth out of there before I could finish the job."

"How did you even know what was happening? He said you were supposed to wait in the car for him."

"I did. Fun fact: Necromancers feel it when people die. Ten of them went up all at once. Open gas line or something. Blew out the entire apartment. The other three were in a unit that collapsed just before I got there. Found David standing there watching that blaze get out of control. You know what he was doing? Laughing."

"Fuck. I wish I'd known."

"Would have saved you some heartache, huh?"

"What do you mean?"

I nod toward Kyle and Jeff, the boy glued to the officer's hip. "Does Jeff know? About Kyle?"

"I don't know what you're talking about," she says. The lie is so practiced I almost believe her, but her body goes just a little too still.

"Oh, come on. Kyle looks exactly like David. It's pretty fucking obvious."

"Shit. Shit shit shit."

"Whoa. What's wrong? What did I do?"

"You can see that he looks like David. I paid, fuck, so much to get that glamour bound to him. If it's failing—"

"Hang on. Doesn't mean it is," I say. I look at Kyle more closely and let him go a little out of focus. Sure enough, his face snaps into something looks a hell of a lot like Detective Jeff. This feels like when I first came back from Mictlan and saw more into Gabriela's soul than I knew was even there. This one's a little more disturbing because I didn't even realize it was happening. Another holdover from Mictlantecuhtli.

When I finally accepted that I was human again, and not a part of Mictlantecuhtli, I figured all this stuff would go away. As in so many things, I was wrong.

I can't feel his power anymore. It's hard to explain but his magic is nothing like I was taught. It's more . . . pure? No. Feral. Definitely not human. But some things seem to have stuck. My eyes going black, his memories, this thing with my vision.

I finally accepted I was a living, breathing chunk of walking meat a few days ago at the Werther house.

Mictlan was having an identity crisis because as far as it was concerned there were two Mictlantecuhtlis. I renounced it, let myself be human again.

I'm still trying to sort this all out but it feels like I've had an organ cut out and everything around it has to resettle into the space. Renouncing him left a hole inside me that's filling back up. Hopefully filling back up with me. I'm honestly not sure.

And it's a big goddamn hole.

"It's still in place," I say. "I, uh, see things I really shouldn't, sometimes. Does Kyle know?"

"Oh, fuck no. I don't want him getting ideas of contacting David. And Jeff, the timing almost but not quite works out. It was a while before he really believed Kyle was his. Didn't stop him from loving him, though."

"Sounds like a good guy," I say.

"He is. But we had our differences. Magic and non-magic people just, well, you know."

"I do," I say. "Know somebody who managed to hide it from her wife for years. When she finally came out to her it was less than what she'd hoped. He in the know?"

"Yeah, as much as he's willing to be. He had trouble adjusting to it. Does his best for Kyle."

"Kyle got talent?"

"A little," she says. "Intuition from time to time. Nothing big. Enough people around here know not to fuck with me, so I haven't had to worry about anyone trying to use him as leverage against me."

"For what it's worth I won't tell anybody." Just because I'm good at poking my nose in where it doesn't belong doesn't mean I have to be an asshole about it.

She waves it off. "Who are you looking for?"

"I'm looking for a mage I knew when I lived out here. Name's Nicole Hawthorne."

"Jesus suffering fuck, you too?"

"Is that what these assholes were here for? Nicole?" Then it clicks. "She's the Keeper they were talking about."

"I haven't seen her in weeks," Rachel says. "And before you ask, no, I don't know how to contact the Oracle. Why the hell do you want to talk to that thing, anyway?"

"How do you know I don't want to just talk to Nicole?"

"Because I'm not stupid. So?"

"It's yet another long story," I say. "And I think they want you on stage." Jeff and another detective in plain clothes stand at the bottom of the steps.

"Rachel," Jeff says. "We need to get your statement."

"Call me when you're done," I say. "I'll give you the whole sordid tale." I jot my phone number on a HI MY NAME IS sticker and hand it to her.

"Sure," she says. Whether that's for me or Jeff, I don't know, but it works out either way. She waves the two cops into the office.

This is going to take a good long while. I hope these guys get overtime. I'll let them do their investigation. I have my own.

I head behind the office where coroners and forensic specialists are gathering evidence, marking bullet holes, shell casings, bodies.

The spell I'm wearing should hold for a while with normals, but there's no point in tempting fate by doing this all out in the open. I spy a couple large, open-sided tents with tables displaying different survival techniques. A hand-made solar still, traps, deadfalls, a board with different knots on it. It's far enough away from the action and it hasn't been swept by the police yet. They've got their hands full. I should have some time to myself.

I find a spot in the shade, for all the good it does me, and sit cross-legged in the dirt. I pull a small silver cup out of my messenger bag. I cut the one patch on my left forearm with no tattoos. I'm still nervous about using this straight razor, but I'm getting used to it. Hell, I even shaved with it this morning.

I drip some blood into the cup and all of a sudden I have the attention of every ghost in the area. They're too new to understand what's happening, why they're suddenly drawn to me. Some of them never will. They're simply not conscious enough. They're hungry and confused and I've just rung the dinner bell.

"Gather up," I say. Not that I need to. They're already so clustered together in front of me that some of them overlap each other. Some of them are tourists, some of them are members of the kill squad. I make note of the ones who look at me when I talk.

There are about twenty-five ghosts, more than you'd usually get with this many dead. But considering that ghosts are born out of trauma, it makes sense. Not much more traumatic than being knifed to death by your dead buddy.

"Which one of you was the mage I shot?" I say. Nothing. "How about the two other mages who were in on this?" Not a peep. Well, fuck. "You, you, and . . . you. Come here. The rest of you fuck off."

The ghosts I've just dismissed don't move. I don't know why I even bother. They don't listen to anybody most of the time. I push them with a thought and they blow away on the wind. Wish that worked on their side of the veil. Would save me a lot of grief.

"Whoever gives me the best answer gets a prize," I say. I've kept behind three of the wannabe soldiers who look fairly intact. The tourists won't be able to tell me anything I need to know. These guys might.

"What do you want?" one of them says. He crosses his arms and glares at me. He's missing the top right of his skull where a bullet tagged him. Just the fact that he can speak in complete sentences tells me this one's gonna be around a good long while. Probably be a Wanderer. Seems to have the willpower for it.

"Who the fuck are you people?"

"My name's Seth," Head Wound says. "This is Logan and this is . . . I know you, but I don't remember who you are."

Shit. They're already losing themselves. Ghosts are made up of bits and pieces of memories, scraps of soul. Over time they sort of drain away to wherever the rest of them is. Some go faster than others.

It's already happening to these guys. Pretty soon none of this'll matter because I'll be lucky if they remember their own names.

"I'm Peter," the third ghost says.

"Nice to meet you all," I say because it pays to be cordial to ghosts, especially when you're the one who murdered them in the first place. "Who hired you?"

"Nobody," Peter says. "We volunteered. Bryce said he needed volunteers to fuck up a bunch of liberal pedophiles."

"He told me it was vote stealers," Logan says.

"I'm here for JFK Junior," says Seth.

Oh joy. I can see how this went. A couple mages hit up their local chapter of Nazis, Klan, Proud Boys, who the fuck knows, got a bunch of volunteers by telling each of them something different to hook them, then hit them with a compulsion spell to keep them around long enough for the job.

It didn't matter why they were here or what they thought they were doing. These weren't mercenaries, they were pawns. Expendable pieces. I'd be shocked if there were more than two or three with actual military experience.

"Okay, nobody hired you. Got it. Who recruited you?"

"I have rights," Seth says.

"Oh, for—"

"I want to see a lawyer." Ghosts are idiots at the best of times and these guys didn't have much going on to begin with.

"I'm your lawyer," I say. "Now, who recruited you?"

"It was—I don't remember," Seth says. "Where am I?"

"I remember just fine," Logan says. "It was—I just had it."

"Let me guess," I say, turning to Peter. "You don't remember, either."

"I think I'll have the foot-long deli sub with no pickles, please," he says. That's probably the most coherent statement and the best idea these guys have given me. Should've eaten breakfast.

"Right." On top of the compulsion spell, they were probably hit with some kind of memory wipe. They can't tell me anything because they don't know it.

I step back from the silver cup. "All yours, guys. Go to town." And like that, they go completely feral. They descend on the cup with the tiny amount of life in it like dying men fighting over an empty canteen.

And then it's over. They stop scrabbling after the blood and get confused looks on their faces. If they see me, they're not paying attention to me. They shuffle off in a daze like dementia patients who accidentally wandered outside.

I watch them as they head off toward the other new Haunts and Wanderers. I wonder sometimes if it's comforting for them to cluster like that. Be around their own kind in the midst of an empty void they've got no hope of escaping. It's a good thing most aren't aware of much.

Small mercy, I suppose. But then, that's more than most of us get.

Chapter 5

The Bellagio is supposed to evoke a picturesque Italian village. Festive canopies, bright-yet-warm lighting, everything glowing gold.

I don't think there are any picturesque Italian villages filled with slot machines, blackjack tables, drunken fathers, desperate mothers, and broken-down honeymooners, all beneath a haze of cigarette smoke.

The place stinks of sweat, beer, cigarettes and Febreze. Bells, klaxons, the deafening susurrus of a thousand people crammed into too small a space all trying to be heard over each other. Occasionally there's a burst of frenetic energy as someone gets a payout, a dopamine hit for everyone in earshot that drives them on for one more hand, one more pull. This could be the big one. Okay, this one. How about this one?

In a lot of ways it reminds me of the Twins' club. Whether it's a big win at the blackjack table or an hour with that brunette on stage, everyone here is looking for a high.

"Good action at the blackjack tables," someone says. I glance to the side at a man pulling the handle of a slot machine.

"Sorry?"

"What?" he says.

"You said something about blackjack," I say.

"Wasn't me," he says, turning back to the slot machine. "Weirdo."

"There's a space at that table over there." A woman wearing a Mickey Mouse shirt that's a couple sizes too small walks by, seemingly not paying any attention to me.

I wonder if I asked her if she'd be like the guy at the slot machine. Probably. I know magic weirdness when I see it. Doesn't seem to be a spell, though. Which doesn't mean much. Lots out there that doesn't ping our magic radar.

I head over to the blackjack table the oblivious woman pointed out and take a seat. One game is ending, a new one starting. I buy in with ten thousand dollars I stole from an ATM on the way in. The dealer doesn't even blink.

I know I'm at the right table because I'm having trouble seeing the three other players sitting around the table.

"Like to know who I'm playing with," I say. The dealer smiles at me.

"That's up to them," she says.

"Can I at least know who the dealer is?"

"Wendy," she says.

"Wendy?"

"Well, it's Wendy's body."

"I mean—"

"I know what you mean," she says. "And I have very specific reasons for not telling you."

"They're kind of a pain in the ass that way." I turn to the voice on my left. The hazy figure has solidified into a very convincing lookalike of Frank Sinatra.

"It goes with the territory," says a voice to the right. A man in a houndstooth jacket that looks to be from the forties. He looks vaguely familiar but I can't place him.

"Sorry I'm late." A woman in a lapis-and-white sheathe dress with broad shoulder straps. Middle-Eastern? Persian? Egyptian? Hard to say. She's stunning whoever she is.

"Frank Sinatra and . . . Louis Prima? No. Siegel."

Bugsy Siegel and Frank Sinatra. Two people who pretty much created modern-day Las Vegas. Siegel built it, Sinatra and his Rat Pack buddies defined it.

I look at the woman. "You I can't place."

"I'm not like Frank and Bugsy," she says.

"Hey," Bugsy says. "We talked about that."

"I'm sorry," she says. "Benjamin. I'm not even of Las Vegas exactly."

There is something about her that's familiar. Her skin tone, hair, the colors of her dress. "You're part of the Luxor," I say. "I'm not sure how that makes sense, though. These two defined Vegas, more or less."

"We're avatars," Ol' Blue Eyes says. "Manifestations of Las Vegas. We don't really have gods here." The woman conspicuously clears her throat. "Okay, a couple."

"I'm Shait," the woman says. "Egyptian god of—"

"Fate," I say. "I thought you didn't have a gender."

"I don't," she says. "Man, woman, doesn't matter to me. I'm Shait or Shai depending on my mood."

"Just don't ask her about the pig," Siegel says.

"You, what, came over with some of the exhibit pieces in the Luxor?" When it opened the Luxor had a King Tut exhibit on the mezzanine, holding some artifacts from Tut's tomb as well as a lot of reproductions. And then it closed down and they donated everything to the Natural History Museum.

"In a way," she says.

"Shouldn't you be at the museum, then?"

"You would think, but no. This is a city easy for me to manifest in. It didn't take long for me to fit in. I belong to Las Vegas much more than I belong to a dead desert kingdom now. I'm sure you understand, Mictlantecuhtli."

"Yeah, I know how it works." She's a piece of a goddess who grew into herself in a land that didn't realize it was worshipping her. Not much different than my growing into the role of a death god.

"But what I don't know is why I'm here," I say. I give a nod toward the dealer.

"We need to talk to you about the Oracle," Frank says.

"What oracle?"

"Don't be insulting, Eric. We know who you are," the dealer says. She draws a number of cards from the shoe and lays down a king of spades face-up in front of each of us. "We know why you're here." Four queens, all hearts, slide onto the table. "How you got here." The king of hearts, sword shoved far into its head. "And who you're looking for." Alternating jacks, hearts, and spades face-up. Except for mine.

"What's this card?" I say.

"Don't know. Take a look," the dealer says. I flip it over. It's a joker.

"You've got some weird decks in that shoe," I say.

"Okay, no bullshit," Siegel says. "We need you to find Jimmy as much as you need to find Jimmy."

"Why?"

"We're all in a, call it a similar line of work," the dealer says. She sweeps all the cards off the table and deals out a new hand with no card tricks. "Normally none of us would give a shit. He does his thing, we do ours. But things have changed. He's making it hard for us to do our jobs."

"And what jobs are those exactly?"

"This is Las Vegas," Siegel says. "It's built on a dream of making it big. That dream isn't fueled by money, though you'd think it would be. It's fueled by hope, fate, and luck."

"Random chance is why we exist," Frank says. "The people who've made their dreams come true, hit that big jackpot, whether they want to admit it or not, they got lucky."

"You can plan all you want," Shait says. "Become the best at what you do and you still owe all of your success to random chance. But there's a dirty little secret about it."

"What do you know about random chance?" the dealer says.

"That it's random?" I say.

"Funny," Shait says. "That's one of the things it actually isn't. What are the odds that an elephant will come crashing through the ceiling?"

"Dunno. Billion to one?"

"Looked at one way, sure. Unknowable, in fact. There are so many factors, so many unknowns that there's no number that even comes close to accurate."

"I hear a 'but' coming."

"But," Siegel says, "if you look at it another way, after stripping away the context, it's fifty-fifty."

"I suck at math," I say, "but I'm pretty sure you got that wrong."

"It's a binary," Sinatra says. "Everything is. Even the things that aren't. Either an elephant crashes through the ceiling or it doesn't. Which one that's likely to be depends on whether or not there's an elephant above the ceiling in the first place. That's fifty-fifty, too."

"There's either an elephant there or not," I say. "Still having trouble with your math, but sure, let's go with that. What if the elephant walks away?"

"That's fifty-fifty again. Statistically, it could be an infinitesimal number. But ultimately, it, like everything else, either occurs or doesn't. The elephant crashes through the ceiling or it doesn't. The elephant walks away or it doesn't."

"And whether or not an elephant got up there in the first place is fifty-fifty, too?"

"You're catching on."

"I don't know if I'd go that far, but I'll play along," I say. "Whether the elephant comes through the ceiling isn't based on just one, two, half a dozen things. It's hundreds. Billions. Before the elephant can crash through the ceiling it has to be up there. Before it can be up there it has to be in town. Before it can be town it has to be captured in Asia and brought here."

"And before any of that happens the universe needs to be created," Shait says.

"Exactly," the dealer says. "It's a multitude of different events that all have to happen in order for there to be an elephant to drop out of the ceiling."

"And Jimmy kinda fucks with that, doesn't he?"

"Yes and no," Siegel says. "On the one hand, it's exactly how he experiences time. Each moment is a distinct grouping of binaries. What the Oracle does is determine the possible futures to get things to where it wants them and then nudges all of those individual events in that direction. Maybe it changes the choice of a poacher to go out one day, saving the life of an elephant, creating a chain of events that lead it to being captured, sent to Las Vegas and brought to the Bellagio—"

"Where it can crash through the ceiling," I say.

"Exactly," Shait says. "Sometimes it's that simple. When the Oracle has to make more than one change, that's when it gets tricky. It has limitations."

"Like what?"

"It can't change the past," the dealer says. "Only the future."

"It can't change just anything," says Siegel.

"Let's take your situation," the dealer says. "It made a handful of very small changes ten years ago. Not because they were the easiest or best changes for it to make, but because they were the only ones it could."

"Why?" I say.

"First, vicinity," the dealer says. "The Oracle has a very limited range. It can't directly change the future of someone in Barstow from here, for example." Now I get it.

"But he can make changes to the future of a person here in Las Vegas that would cascade out until they affect that person in Barstow?"

"The further away something is," says Siegel, "the less it can influence. Once Liam Werther left Vegas, Jimmy couldn't do much else. Some influencing of the people within the vicinity of him to course correct, as it were, but little else. And there are some people it can't do anything to at all."

"The other is a little trickier," Shait says. "Its starting point is fixed. It can't go back to yesterday and make changes there."

"It has to play the cards it's dealt, as it were," the dealer says. "Every door that's opened means a million others close."

"If all the elephants die," I say, "then there are no elephants for him to bring to Vegas to fall through the ceiling."

"Provided they were all already dead, yes," Sinatra says.

"What does all this have to do with you lot?"

"Like I said, normally nothing," the dealer says. "But there are things happening that are affecting those limitations."

"Meaning he can make changes no matter where he is in relation to what needs to change?" The ramifications of that take a second to sink in. Fuck. "That's a lot of power."

"More than you can possibly imagine," the dealer says. "And I am aware of your recent escapades in Mictlan. I know how much you can imagine."

"It's not quite that bad, yet," Shait says. "Right now, as far as we know he can influence about a city block around him. But it's growing. And it will get worse."

"I still don't see how this affects you."

"The Oracle deals in predestination," the dealer says. "I, and the avatars of Las Vegas, deal in uncertainty. You can't have too much of either or everything falls apart. And I mean everything."

"They're not an avatar of Las Vegas," I say, tilting my head toward Shait.

"No. Nor do I deal in uncertainty," Shait says. "Like the Oracle, I deal with predestination. His efforts are colliding with my own."

"He's changing fates he shouldn't be able to change?"

"Something like that," Shait says. "It's somewhat more complicated."

"It always is. So what happens if he does whatever it is he's doing?"

"Random chance goes to shit and any ideas of fate get trumped by whatever he decides to do."

"Okay, I can see why random chance going away is a problem. But predestination? People have free will."

Shait snorts. "Sorry. They do. And they don't."

I don't think I want to go digging that hole. Not yet, at least. "Do you know where he is?"

"Oh yeah," Siegel says. "But we can't tell you. It's taking everything we have just to have this conversation. We're breaking all sorts of rules."

"They don't speak for me," Shait says. "But I don't know where he is and they won't tell me."

"Pity," I say.

"You have no idea."

"How about a clue?" I say.

"I can't play favorites," the dealer says. "Sorry." Siegel and Sinatra shake their heads.

"I can," Shait says. "Call it less of a clue and more a word of advice. Let Nicole find you."

"Her find me? I'm trying to find her."

"It'll happen," Shait says. "You just being here has thrown everything off. She's been waiting for you. Whether she knows it or not."

"Define everything," I say.

"Here," the dealer says. She flips a chip at me and I catch it. It's not one of the Bellagio's. Unmarked, black. So black it's hard to look at.

"A chip?"

"It only works once. So be absolutely sure it's worth it before you use it. Snap it in half. And be prepared to move. It can be a little unpredictable."

"The hell is it?"

"I'm sorry, sir," the dealer says. "Is there a problem?" I look around the table. I'm the only one there.

"No, I'm good," I say. I slide the black chip into a pocket, scoop up the rest of my chips. I don't know what the hell just gave me this chip, but for the moment at least it sounds like it might be an ally. It definitely knows a lot. Whether it was telling the truth is another matter.

And Sinatra and Siegel. Avatars of Vegas. Are they really what they say they are? Hard to say. But I am sure that Shait's the real deal. She's got a particular vibe that screams deity.

And this chip. It's got power. It doesn't feel like a regular enchantment or a spell, but it feels familiar. Like Mictlantecuhtli's power.

It's identical to that power in the same way that all cars are identical. They have four wheels and an engine, but beyond that you can get away with a lot of variation.

I don't like that. I don't like the whole goddamn thing. Anything that smacks of gods makes me a little jumpy.

No matter what memories I have of Mictlantecuhtli's, I'm human now.

What's more worrisome is the idea that Jimmy is in the same weight class as they are. It makes sense, I suppose. Especially if the range on Jimmy's abilities have increased.

There are a lot of things I've done over the years that I regret. Most of them because they came back to bite me in the ass. This is definitely one of those.

I don't know everything that the spell Nicole and I used to create Jimmy did to him. The sort of demon we merged with his soul is something called a ker. They're Greek. Supposed to be these winged women who feast on the dead at battlefields. Sort of like valkyries, but a lot uglier.

That's because the myths have them completely wrong. They're more like black columns of greasy smoke with nasty eyeballs poking out. They're drawn to death, but will happily make their own if they get a hankering for it.

They are some of the more dangerous demons out there. Partly because they don't just sense death, they sense future death. If you run into a bunch of keres hanging around, shit's about to go down and you really don't want to be there.

The other reason is they can influence it. Not necessarily in a big way. They can nudge someone to fire a bullet at the wrong time, miss some crucial detail that might keep someone alive.

But that's all the influence they have over the future. Something about the spell I used amplified its power. I don't know how exactly, but it's clearly because of the merge with Jimmy's soul.

What I don't get is how the Oracle's powers are being amplified now. I don't know any magic that can do that.

But then, I never expected I could make an oracle, be a god, or be brought back to life, either, so the fuck do I know?

The scariest thing about all this is the possibility of Jimmy having real agency. I knew he had some, but I didn't think it was this much. This has been bugging me since I figured out he was trying to get hold of me through the Werthers and Gabriela. I didn't know an oracle could do that.

When I call him a Magic 8-Ball, I mean it. Everything I've seen says he doesn't work until somebody makes him. Is he acting on his own, or is somebody pulling the puppet strings?

My phone buzzes in my bag. A text from Rachel. I let her know where I am. Maybe now I'll get some answers.

"Swanky," Rachel says, coming up to sit next to me at the bar. "Never struck me as a Bellagio sort of guy."

"I am really more the seedy motel type," I say. "But you take what you can get."

The blood-crusted desert camo BDUs Rachel was wearing have been replaced with jeans and an open button-down denim shirt over a red tank top.

"I think I've only ever seen you wearing BDUs while kicking the shit out of people," I say.

"I can kick the shit out of people wearing this, too," she says. "I'm versatile that way."

"And look good doing it, I imagine."

"I always look good doing it. Let's go sit at a real table."

"Go grab one. What are you drinking?"

"Midori sour," she says. "Extra cherries. Fuck it, make it two. It's been a day."

"You always struck me as a beer sort of person."

"Ugh," she says. "Shit's like sewer water."

"And Midori isn't? I have no idea how you can drink that, but I'm in no position to judge."

"What are you drinking?"

"Jim Beam. Neat."

"You're right. You are in no position to judge."

I get her drinks and another of my own and take it to a table in a corner. The sounds of the casino are muffled, bells, jangling coins, the occasional cheer. Place like this you can talk, but you're going to be reminded of the fun you're missing right outside.

"Why's this place so empty?" Rachel says.

"Did you feel the wards when you walked in?" I say. She closes her eyes for a second in concentration.

"No, but I do now."

"Mages only," I say. "Normals just see it as a regular wall. If they happen to bump into the doorway it pushes them back."

"How did I not know this was here?"

"It's like you said, swanky. Friend of mine owns a suite. Stupid of me not to take her up on it."

"You have friends," she says.

"You sound surprised."

"Was a time I thought we were friends," she says. I don't know what to say to that. For a while I thought we were friends, too.

"Things didn't work out for me here," I say. "I moved on."

"Could have said good-bye."

"Really? You'd have given me a hug and sent me on my way?" I say. "Or would you have shot me for fucking up that last job?"

"Yeah," she says. "You're right. I'm . . . sorry." The words come out like she thinks they're what you're supposed to say, but she's not sure if it's really true. I know the look on her face. I've seen it in the mirror lots of times.

"For what? David fed you a load of horseshit and I wasn't around to say otherwise. You didn't do anything wrong. I could have done a lot more to fix the situation. I could have done a lot more to fix a lot of situations."

"We square?" she says.

"You tell me," I say. "Far as I'm concerned we were always square. Come on, we were kids. Kids do stupid shit."

"Here's to doing stupid shit." She lifts her glass in a toast and downs the whole thing in one long gulp.

"How'd it go after I took off from your place?" I say.

"Pretty much what you said. What I told them was the truth, anyway. I just left out the whole 'corpses rising from the grave' bit. Jeff knows there's more to it, but he also knows when not to ask. I'm worried about Kyle, though."

"You aren't staying out there, are you?"

"No. Kyle's with his dad and I got a hotel room in town for the next few days while the police comb through the crime scene."

"He was having a rough time in there," I say.

"He was twelve when he was kidnapped by some meth-head motorcycle gang who thought Jeff could get their buddy out of prison. Fucking morons. Just amazingly stupid.

"We—I didn't find him for over a week. By that time they'd gone to town on him. The things they did to my boy."

"You killed them," I say.

"Don't fucking judge me, Eric," she says. She's so taut with tension she's almost shaking.

"I'm not," I say. "I can't even if I wanted to. Rachel, I'm swimming in blood. You have no idea. My body count is higher than you can imagine. I'm only sorry I couldn't be there to help kill them."

Something shifts in her expression, like she's just now seeing me. When I was out here last I had one death on my hands. Now I have thousands. I think it's just sinking in that I'm not the man I used to be.

"Thanks," she says. "I wish I could kill them all over again."

"I know the feeling. Not to change the subject, but I'm going to anyway, I talked to a few of those weekend warriors."

"How the hell did you—oh. Right." Necromancy creeped her out years ago and it clearly creeps her out now.

"Compulsion spells and memory wipes. Whoever got them pretty much gouged out the bottom of the barrel and kept digging. These guys were absolute dipshits and they were probably the most solid ghosts out there."

"So nothing, then," Rachel says.

"I wouldn't say nothing. We know they're after Nicole and they'll happily murder a bunch of people to get to her."

"I do not like that idea."

"But it's the truth, isn't it?" I say.

"Yeah," she says. "That's why I don't like it. Fuck." She tosses back her second drink, waves at the bartender for a third. "I can't think about this right now. What about you?"

"I don't particularly want to think about it, either."

"Not what I meant."

"You want to know why I'm looking for the Oracle."

"Yeah. And I'd prefer it if you didn't lie to me."

Fuck it. There's more going on around here than I understand and it seems, if a small army hunting her down is any indication, that we're both on the same side, or at least pointed in a similar direction.

"Okay. No lies," I say.

"Really?"

"Not much point, is there?" I say. "I don't really care about whatever weird bullshit is going on around here. I just need to get some information." She peers at me with an intensity like if she just glares enough the answers will pop out.

"Jesus, you're serious, aren't you?" she says. "All right. What are you doing in Vegas?"

"We might need more alcohol. Let me start with my ex-wife."

Chapter 6

Three scotches, four Midori sours, and two glasses of ginger ale later, Rachel sits back, stares at the ceiling, and says, "Fuck a duck."

"Pretty much, yeah."

"You died? Seriously, really died? No heartbeat, no pulse."

"Cremated my body, even."

"And your girlfriend brought you back? That's true love."

"She's not my girlfriend," I say.

"Sure she's not. Which is why you're out here trying to save her soul? Oh, I'm just giving you shit. Easier than thinking you're some kind of Aztec sun god."

"Death god," I say. "You're thinking Huitzilopochtli."

"I am not even going to try to pronounce that. Almost as bad as Welsh. I'm still a little confused. You said you had a connection to the Oracle, but not what it is."

"No," I say. "Not yet. Your turn. You know Nicole. How?"

"How do *you* know Nicole?" she says.

"I asked you first."

"Fine. About fifteen years back I went looking for the Oracle. She convinced me it was a bad idea."

"That normal? Her steering people away?"

"No. My request . . . got her attention. I owed her after that, though she never brought it up. We got to be friends.

She didn't have anyone she felt she could talk to. Except me. I never wanted anything from her."

"It did a real number on her, huh?"

"That thing is a manipulative sack of shit that fucks with people's lives and doesn't care about the consequences." That sounds familiar.

You can go your entire life not regretting, not even thinking about something really shitty you did years ago. It doesn't hit you until you see the fallout.

"I ever find the fuckstick who made it I'll rip their goddamn eyeballs out and make a pair of truck nuts out of them."

"That was vivid," I say.

"You asked."

"She never told you," I say. "Never mentioned her role in its creation?"

"I know it was thrown at her," she says. "She never had a choice. Why are you laughing?"

"She had choice after choice after choice," I say. "Every step she took she took by her own free will. All the way to the bottom."

"What the hell do you know about it?"

"I was there," I say. "I don't know what she told you, but it was her idea. Well, all but the last bit. That one's pretty much on me."

"You what?"

"Nicole found a spellbook to make the Oracle. Only problem was that it needed a necromancer. And there just happened to be a necromancer in town at the time."

Silence. When she finally speaks every word is clipped, a fragile dam holding a river of rage of behind it.

"Tell me. All of it." I do. When I'm done talking she's staring out at nothing. I know that look.

"Do you really want to get violent over this?" I say.

"You trapped her."

"She got what she wanted, a dead boyfriend and a shot at the Oracle. I got what I wanted, not getting a knife in my back."

"Tell me you at least didn't know what you were doing."

"Of course I didn't fucking know," I say. "Wasn't until years later when I really dug into the magic that I realized what I'd made."

"And you just let it go on?"

"The fuck do you want me to say, Rachel? Did I fuck up? Yes. Did I do the responsible thing and come looking to destroy him because of all the havoc I knew he'd cause? No. I don't even know how I would. By the time I figured it out he'd been in the world for, shit, ten years? More? I had other shit going on at the time."

"You fucked Nicole's life."

"Nicole fucked her own life. She and her boyfriend both tried to use me to kill the other so they could get the Oracle. I set it up so one of them would get the prize they were after. It turned out to be Nicole. You think she wouldn't have tried to kill me, too? She's not innocent in any of this."

"Okay, yes. You're right. But you bear some of the responsibility."

"Never said I didn't. He's as much my fault as he is hers."

"Why do you keep calling it 'him'?" she says.

"Nicole never described him to you, did she?"

"I didn't want to know."

"He was originally a whiny little shit named Jimmy Freeburg. Now he's Jimmy's soul and a demon mashed together and stuck inside Jimmy's severed head. I'm the one who cut it off. Yes, he was alive at the time. And before you completely lose your shit, he asked me to do it."

"I wish I'd never met you," she says.

"You are part of an ever-expanding club."

"It's a severed head. Fine. I've seen weirder shit. Do you have any idea why it would try to contact you?"

"No clue. I also don't know why he went about it in such a complicated way. A phone call would have sufficed."

"Maybe it couldn't?"

"Only thing that makes sense," I say. "Except that he knew ten years ago that this would happen. I was still alive ten years ago."

"Would you have listened?"

"How do you mean?"

"Maybe it knew that if it tried to convince you to help it back then, you would have said no."

"So instead it set something in motion so that ten years later I'd become invested enough to not be able to say no?"

"You're here, aren't you?" she says. "Eric, I don't fucking know. It can't be a coincidence that you showed up at the same time those wannabe warriors did. For me this is just one piece of a bigger nightmare. I'm a little overwhelmed."

Shit. Of course she is. "How many died?" I don't have to say who I'm talking about. She knows what I mean.

"Too many."

"I'm—"

"Children. They shot three children." I'm about to say I saw one of them and then realize that's probably not going to help. For all I know about death, I'm fucking awful at comforting the bereaved. The only consolation I can think of is that none of the children left a ghost. They went quick and probably didn't even know what was happening. Somehow, I don't think she'll see it the same way I do.

"I'm sorry," I say because what else can you say to shit like this?

"Kyle and I were preparing some lessons in the bunker and the gunfire started. And then you showed up." There's a tone in her voice like accusation. I can understand that. I'm the one who walked away. I'm the only one left to blame.

"How's Kyle handling it?"

She shrugs. "Not well. Better than I expected. He was having a good day up until it happened. If he'd been having a bad day— It could have been a lot worse."

"What now?"

"I want to find whoever did this and make them pay," she says. "Could use some help."

"I can't be your first choice," I say.

"Pretty much my only choice. I don't have a lot of friends in the mage community anymore. If I ever really did." I'd like to disagree with her. But mages don't really do friends so much as alliances of convenience.

"Okay," I say. "If you help me find Nicole. I really need to find Jimmy and to do that, I need her."

"I can live with that. Hold on." She presses a finger to her ear and I see an earpiece I hadn't notice before. "You get all that?" she says.

"Yeah," says a voice at the table behind me. "I got all that." Sonofabitch.

Nicole.

———

She's a lot like I remember her. Tall, slender, skin the color of burnt umber. She's wearing a short black dress with a strand of pearls and carrying a clutch that's just big enough to fit a subcompact pistol.

A little older, a little more weary, maybe. But she's still

got the sex kitten thing down. Makes me wonder what would have happened if I'd followed her lead all those years ago. Nothing good, I'm sure. Though it probably would have been fun for a little while.

I don't know if it's an act or if it's just how she is. She slides into a chair between us.

"I hear you've been looking for me," she says.

"Word gets around."

"We all have our own little grapevines."

"Rachel or the Twins?"

"Both," she says. "The Twins weren't sure what the deal was, so they dropped me a line. And then Rachel pinged me this afternoon to let me know what happened. Still playing around with dead things, huh?"

"It's a hobby."

"How've you been, Eric? You look good."

"Make you a deal," I say. "You don't pretend to give a fuck about me and I won't pretend to give a fuck about you."

"Oh, I know you don't care," Nicole says, eyes going dark. "You left me in that house for Sebastian to kill."

"No," I say. "I left you both in that house for you to kill each other."

"You don't deny it?" Rachel says.

"Why would I?" I say. "I'm just getting the pissing contest out of the way. Now, where's Jimmy?"

"And how did I not know it was named Jimmy?" Rachel says. "Or that it was your idea to make it in the first place? Is all that true?"

"It never came up," Nicole says.

"Oh, for fuck sake, Nicki," Rachel says.

"It doesn't change anything that happened later. And it's easier for people to think he's a thing rather than a person."

"Is it a person?" Rachel says. That's a good question.

One I probably should have asked before I cut Jimmy's head off.

"I don't much care," I say. "I just need to know where he is. Where is he, Nicole?" Something in my tone must have come out more forcefully than I'd realized because I can feel them both pulling magic from the pool.

"Slow your roll, cowboy," Nicole says. "That's a complicated question."

"Is it? Seems pretty simple to me." I don't know if I can take them both in a fight and I don't really want to find out.

"It would be," she says. "If I knew."

"You lost the fortune-twisting, talking Magic-8-Ball," I say. "How the fuck did that happen? Did you leave him on the backseat of the car? Somebody wander by and say, 'Oh, hey. Talking severed head. Just what I've always wanted'?"

"Fuck you, Eric," Nicole says, and now she really starts to pull in the power. So I do, too. Rachel notices this and pushes her chair back. Nicole's no slouch, but if she's pulling power in like she's drinking from a faucet, I'm drinking from a firehose.

"Stop it," Rachel says. "Both of you. You really think they're going to let you get away with having a fight in the casino?"

I know Rachel's right, but I'll be damned if I leave myself open. I won't start a fight but I'm damn well gonna finish it. I feel Nicole stop pulling in power. I keep going for a couple of seconds before stopping. That's right, I can keep this up all night.

They're well aware how much power I was drawing. So is security. I see two men in black suits with maroon jackets step into the bar. They're not the usual walls of muscle you see in casino security, but then those aren't the guys you send to take on mages.

"Are you done?" Rachel says. "How about we all play nice so we don't find ourselves eating fireballs. I have enough problems with the locals without pissing off Bellagio security mages."

"He stops being an asshole, I will," Nicole says.

"You're the one started to draw down on me."

"You're both assholes," Rachel says. "Cut it out. Or we're gonna have ourselves the kind of threesome nobody enjoys."

"I promise to try to not be an asshole," I say, which from the look on her face isn't the answer Rachel wants to hear. "What? You want me to lie to you?"

"Suppose it's the best I can get," Rachel says. "Nicole?"

"Yes," she says. "Fine. I'll stop being an asshole."

"Don't make promises you can't keep," I say.

"Eric," Rachel says.

"Hey, I said I would *try*. So, you lost Jimmy."

"I didn't lose him," Nicole says. "He was stolen."

"Did you know about this?" I say to Rachel.

"Yes," Rachel says. "We've been trying to figure out how to get it back for a while now."

"I thought you hated him."

"I do," she says. She glances over at Nicole.

"Don't say it," Nicole says.

"Why not? It's true. That thing has you wrapped around its fucking finger, or nose, or whatever the fuck it still has."

"It's not that simple," Nicole says.

"And when were you going to tell me it was a severed head? Or that it has a name? I still can't get over that it has a name."

"I wasn't."

"I thought we were past this shit. Jesus, now I'm being the asshole," Rachel says. "This isn't helping. I'm sorry."

"How did somebody get him? Wouldn't he have seen it coming?"

"He did," Nicole says. "He said he couldn't do anything to prevent it, but had taken steps to fix it."

"Let me guess," I say. "He told you this about ten years ago."

"I wish you were wrong," she says. "Almost to the day." Goddammit. Is this why Jimmy set all this in motion? Why he forced me to get involved?

"You think this is why he brought you here?" Rachel says.

"It's completely why he brought me here," I say.

"I knew he was getting somebody to help," Nicole says. "Never told me who. But the timeline's too neat to be anything else. If I'd known I'd have dropped him in a well instead."

She's right about one thing. The timing is too neat. Not that I don't believe her, but there's something to all this that's bothering me. Something Amanda's uncle said, but I can't remember what.

"Let's say I agree with you, and I'm not saying I don't, why me? The hell does he think I can do that somebody else can't? And why does he think I'll help him?"

"Because your friend is—"

"No," I say. "If Jimmy can see what would happen then he knows the sort of person I am. I'll get my answers from him. And then I'll either walk away or feed him to a fuckin' alligator for shits and giggles. He should know damn well that if he wants my help, this is not the way to go about doing it."

"Maybe it's the only way it knew you would," Rachel says.

"Sure. Maybe. But again, why me?"

"Eric, how the fuck should I know?" Nicole says. "But you're here and you're obviously part of this."

"What do they want? Was there a ransom note? Anything?"

"Of course there wasn't a ransom note," Nicole says. "The fuck do you think they wanted? Jimmy's the most valuable thing in this fucked-up town."

Good point. He probably is. And if my conversation at the blackjack table wasn't just to blow smoke up my ass, then his value's skyrocketed.

"Okay," I say. "But why do they want you?"

"I don't know," she says. "It changes things. I—"

A low rumble builds in my head like being too close to crashing waves. Growing pressure behind my eyes. Nicole's head snaps around, looking for what I'm not sure, but it's clear she feels it too.

But Rachel doesn't seem to notice. "What's wrong? You two okay?"

Pain punches through my skull like a spike of ice through my eyes. I barely manage to stay in my chair while Nicole crashes to the ground.

I see a ripple in the world, a shock wave through a far wall like it's rolling through reality itself. The wave passes through me. Screaming in my ears like someone's being ripped apart. An image of white walls and blinking lights. Some sort of device, machine. I don't know what. And then it's gone.

I sink into my chair. It takes everything I have to stay upright. Rachel is checking on Nicole who is waving her off and pulling herself off the floor.

"What the fuck was that?"

"What was what?" Rachel says. "You both just collapsed."

"You didn't feel that?" Nicole says.

"No, I—What are you staring at?"

"Your tank top," I say. "What color is it?"

Rachel tugs at the front of her shirt to see. "Blue. Is there something on it?"

"It was red," Nicole says. "Just a second ago."

"What are you talking about?" she says. "It's always been blue."

I look around the room. The bartender and the two security mages are gone. Either they move really fast, or maybe they were never there.

"We need to move," I say. "An elephant just crashed through the ceiling."

Chapter 7

"I'm not going to pretend to understand what that's about," Nicole says. "We need a way out of here now."

"Follow me," Rachel says. She runs behind the bar, reaches under the countertop. There's a click and a section of the back wall pops open.

"Secret tunnels," I say. "Nice."

"They're not secret," Rachel says. "This is how they restock the bars so no one has to see. The whole place is riddled with hidden hallways, stairs, doors like this. They all have the same sort of setup. Come on."

I take up the rear. Just as I'm closing the door I hear gunshots, screaming, then an explosion. The door slams into me, almost throwing me to the floor, but I stay upright just enough to shove it closed.

I feel the blast in my chest, but more is the old, familiar twist in my gut letting me know there are corpses on the other side of that door.

The lights in the passage flicker, die out, throwing us into darkness. A light winks into existence over Rachel's head. She leads us down the passage until it branches. The only signage is colored lines and numbers, but no words to tell me where we're headed.

"Do either of you want to tell me what the actual fuck is going on?" Rachel says, each word clipped. There's an edge to her voice I remember from the old days. Rachel doesn't panic. Instead she gets harder, already-sharp edges honed like razors. She'll be insufferable for the next couple of hours at least.

"I think maybe talk about it once we're not about to die."

"That bad?" Rachel says.

"That boom you heard took out about a dozen people," I say.

"How do you—"

"Really?" I say. "I thought we covered that. How do you know this place?"

"Worked here," Rachel says. "Needed to know the layout inside and out. Me and David were stealing a thing from a guy whose security was too tight in his room. Decided to hit him on the casino floor instead."

"How'd that work out?"

"Scrubbed it last minute," Rachel says. "We missed our window. Somebody shot him in the elevator on his way down before we could get to him."

"Gotta say, I don't miss this life."

"You loved it," Rachel says.

"Love's a bit strong," I say. "Kill the light." A flare of magic and the feeling of a couple deaths nearby. Nothing like the blast earlier.

"That wasn't a big spell," Nicole says.

"No," I say, "But whatever it was just took out a couple people. Maybe thirty, forty meters forward and to the left."

"Shit," Rachel says. "That's where we're headed. It's a loading bay."

"Guess we're in for a fight," Nicole says.

"I'll be right back," I say and slide over to the dead side. No ghosts right here but there are a couple Wanderers a few blocks over who'll catch my scent before too long.

The passage exists on this side, but the walls aren't very solid. Before the Bellagio there was the Dunes. It was torn down back in '95. It was around only slightly longer than the Bellagio has been. Neither of them have the kind of history that the Ambassador Hotel back in L.A. has, it's an actual ghost, but there's enough that they've both left an imprint on the psychic landscape.

Which is both good and annoying. On the one hand, the architecture isn't entirely solid. I can see and probably pass through the walls with little effort. On the other hand, both casinos are over here, giving it all an Escheresque feel. Walls bisect at strange angles, staircases double back on themselves, elevators from each take up almost but not quite the same space.

Places like this give me a headache. But at least the architecture is insubstantial enough that I can see the loading bay we're headed to.

Navigating the real world based on what I can see on this side is tricky. On the other side there are probably boxes and crates, maybe a forklift. Over here there's nothing. Those things move around too much to settle over here.

But it does make the three people in the bay stand out like mini-bonfires. I can't make out details, but I can see that they're there. Seeing the living from this side is like seeing ghosts from the living side, just not as clearly.

Two of them are standing with their arms in a position that makes me think they're holding rifles, maybe shotguns. The third is crouched down near the floor fiddling with something. I have a bad feeling that something is a bomb.

At least one of them is a mage. Considering how many of us don't use guns because magic does such a great job at solving all of our problems, it's a pretty good bet the two with rifles are normal and the crouching guy is the spellcaster.

Only they're not reacting to me. One reason I wanted to come over here was to see how the mage reacted. Either they're not taking the bait or they're a shit mage or none of them are mages at all.

I slide back to the living side to find Nicole and Rachel staring at me, guns up and in my face.

"I'm glad to see you're armed," I say, keeping my voice low. "I could do without the pointing at my head part, though."

"Where the hell did you go?" Nicole says.

"Nowhere. I slid over to the other side."

"Is this a dead thing?" Rachel says.

"It's a dead thing." That seems to satisfy them at least enough that they lower their guns, making me feel much better about our current situation.

"Okay, so there are three guys," I say. "Two of them look to be armed with rifles or shotguns. The third is fiddling with something on the floor. Could be a suitcase, could be a bomb, I dunno. I think at least one of them's a mage, only none of them seemed to react to my spell."

"Is there another way there?" Nicole says. "A different exit?"

"There are lots of exits," Rachel says. "That's just the most direct."

"I don't think these guys are here for us," I say.

"Why not?" Nicole says.

"They'd have brought bigger guns," Rachel says. "And bigger brains."

"Exactly. There's maybe one mage. And whatever the hell they're doing they don't seem to get that there are mages on security and probably staying in the hotel itself."

"You think they're normals?"

"Mostly, yeah," I say. "There was that one spell, but what if it was a paper charm somebody bought?"

"But where did they come from?" Nicole says. "What? Don't look at me like that. Jimmy can't do that. He doesn't work that way. For something like this he'd—"

"Have to be able to change the past," I say.

"Fuck. No. I'm telling you it's not something he can do."

"You really believe that?" I say.

"I—I'm mostly positive."

"But you do see it as a possibility."

"I still don't know what the hell you two are talking about," Rachel says.

"Which is another point leaning toward this being Jimmy," I say. "Whatever the hell the thing is that made all this happen, Rachel didn't feel it. Or notice anything wrong or different. But we did."

"It's moot right now," Nicole says. "Whatever this is, we need to get out of here."

"You wouldn't happen to have a grenade on you, would you?" I say. Rachel stares hard at me.

"Do I look like somebody who just casually carries grenades around in her purse?"

"Honestly? Yes," I say.

Rachel smiles, opens her purse and pulls out a spherical green grenade the size of a golf ball, with a spoon and pin as big as it is.

"Ya know, I was kinda joking," I say. "Also, that's a grenade?"

"V40," she says. "Dutch. Lethal up to around fifteen feet, but it'll fuck your shit up inside of a thousand or so. Pull the pin, four seconds later 'pop goes the weasel.'"

"Pull the pin, drop the grenade, four seconds it goes boom?"

"Pretty much."

"If this goes off in that loading bay, isn't it going to fuck up the doors?" Nicole says.

"So?" Rachel says. "We got magic. We can get through a busted door."

"Great," I say. "Give it here."

"It'll destroy the whole loading bay," Nicole says.

"Have you even used a grenade before?" Rachel says. "These things are dangerous."

"You do remember who you're talking to, right?" I say.

"Just give it to him," Nicole says. "Worst case he blows himself up. Or maybe best case."

"That's a good point," Rachel says and hands me the grenade.

"Fuck both of you," I say. "You hear the boom, come running." I slide back to the other side.

My last move over got the attention of the nearby Wanderers in the area and now they're starting to close in. They're a little more limited than I am over here. For me the architecture is more diffuse. For them it's more solid. So though I can see them and they know I'm here, they can't run at me in a straight shot.

That should give me a few minutes. I push my way through the insubstantial walls to the loading bay and get behind one of the guys with rifles.

The one who was fiddling with something on the floor still is. Makes me think it's not a bomb. Either way, once I set this grenade off it won't matter. I slide back one hand holding the grenade over the spoon and the other on the pin.

The loading bay's what I expected. Forklift, crates, and boxes. But the three guys are not. The one crouching on the floor is fiddling with what looks like a remote control built into a metal briefcase. Multiple steering sticks, video screen, a dozen or so buttons.

The other two are not carrying rifles. They're carrying

construction spray foam guns. The kind you use for house insulation. They're each attached through a large hose to a tank and compressor on the floor. All three are wearing white disposable coveralls and goggles.

I don't know what they're doing and I don't need to. I can see the three dead bodies in the corner, so they're clearly not fucking around.

I'm about to pull the pin and roll the grenade between the legs of one of the spray-foam guys when I get hit by a bus.

I hit the cement and skid, my head ringing, the air blown out of my lungs. Miraculously I still have the grenade in my hand. Pity I can't seem to actually move it.

Then I see what hit me and think maybe the grenade won't be much help anyway.

It's a golem. About nine feet tall. Made out of construction foam, which is a new one on me. A metal square embedded in its forehead is studded with gems, under which are etched runes I only vaguely recognize.

There are lots of different types of golems. They're usually made out of mud or clay, but no reason that construction foam can't work. I saw one made out of car parts in a junkyard in Detroit one time. The magic that animates them also makes them hard as cement no matter what they're made out of and they're a colossal pain in the ass to take down. It helps to know what sort of golem it is so you know how to approach it.

It reaches down and hauls me up by the front of my shirt to its face. It has green-glowing eyes, an open mouth about the size of a mail slot, and the metal plate in its head. The runes etched under the gems, I count at least four different languages, are words like "Fire," "Death," "Break," and so on. Most important are the three Hebrew letters written in the middle of the metal plate with paint.

These guys probably had their equipment, remote, construction foam, whatever shipped here so it was waiting for them. Then they came into the casino, got down here, spray foamed their golem together, animated it once they put the plate in.

Then they got surprised by the people who came into the loading bay and had the golem zap them with the magic contained in the gems. That's the spell we picked up.

None of these guys are mages. They just know enough about them to buy themselves a Golem-In-A-Box and put it together like flat-pack furniture. Hömünculi by Ikea.

The Hebrew is written in paint. I reach toward it but before I get close enough, the golem throws me against the wall. This time I drop the grenade.

At this point everybody in the room has clued in to what's going on. I understand why they wore the clean suits—they can wear whatever they want under them and not get covered in construction foam, and they're easy to get rid of.

But they don't have pockets and these guys didn't anticipate they would need to pull out their guns. So while I'm getting thrown across the room, they're trying to get their suits unzipped enough so they can get to their pistols.

This all has to be pretty loud. I'm not sure because all I can hear is ringing. I'm not surprised to see Nicole and Rachel run into the room.

Rachel drops one of them before she's more than two steps through the door. Nicole's shot misses and ricochets off a metal shelf, the bullet burying itself in the foam golem. The golem's healing ability pushes the bullet out and seals the hole up behind it.

This type of golem is the easiest type to create. It has the Hebrew word for truth, *emet*, אמת, written on its forehead. That's a pretty common way of doing it. Technically, you could use any word. That one I ran into in Detroit? It had 'BLOW ME' written on its forehead. I basically had to lure it into a car compactor to stop it.

The Hebrew isn't just tradition, it's practicality; golems have their roots in Judaic magic. This method's been around for centuries and it has a built-in off switch.

If you erase the letter aleph, א, you change the word to *met*, מת. Death. The golem dies. Problem solved.

Only whoever came up with this method didn't take into account that most golems are fucking huge and you need a stepladder to reach their goddamn foreheads. Fortunately, there's a way around this.

I jump out of the way of its fist and grab hold of the grenade. Now comes the tricky part. I avoid another swing, instead grabbing the fist as it goes by. The palm's the size of a dinner plate so it's easy to hang on.

Golems are not smart. They don't know how to deal with something coming to them instead of running away from them. It lifts its fist, me hanging off the edge, toward its face to get a better look.

I don't have an eraser to change the letters. But I do have the next best thing. I pull the pin, shove the golf-ball-sized grenade into the open mouth, and drop to the floor. There's no rule says it can't be erased from the inside out.

I run toward Rachel and Nicole, who are in an intense gun battle with the two who are still standing, tackling them and getting us behind a wide metal crate.

The grenade goes off with a muffled pop. A piece of shrapnel punches through the metal crate, dragging a furrow across my arm. Silence.

I raise my head over the metal crate. The golem's head is missing and most of its torso is turning into powder. Turns out unmagicked construction foam is about as ballistic resistant as tissue paper. Aside from destroying the golem, the shrapnel has turned the humans into shredded meat.

"We're clear," I say.

"What the hell was that thing?" Rachel asks.

"Golem. They bought it from somebody. Assembled it here."

Nicole peers over the edge of the crate. "That's . . . juicy," she says.

"I've seen worse," Rachel and I say at the same time.

"Jinx, you owe me a beer," Rachel says.

"Can we leave?" Nicole says. "I'm about to be sick all over my shoes and they're Louboutins."

"You can puke on mine," I say. "They're Payless."

"Don't tempt me."

Chapter 8

Nicole doesn't take me up on my offer, which I can't say I'm upset about. We get out of the loading bay and Nicole casts a net around us, making us invisible to anyone looking.

Good thing, too. The place is crawling with police. While we're heading out of the loading bay, SWAT officers are taking up positions and we're between them and the casino. We speed it up a bit since invisible does not mean bulletproof.

I'm honestly surprised it works so well. I have this theory that the kinds of magic you're good at say a lot about your personality.

For example, I'm good at personal-level magic and talking to the dead. I'm a narcissist with hangups over the past and an inability to connect with other people. See what I mean?

My experience of Nicole is admittedly very brief. But she was willing to sacrifice her boyfriend's life so I'd cut off his head to make the Oracle and then murdered him, presumably when he wasn't able to defend himself, so she could get it.

This doesn't fit with my idea of someone who can cast a single spell over multiple people that actually benefits them. It's kind of a selfless thing to do. So either the theory needs work or I'm just an asshole.

Probably just an asshole.

Fires are erupting all around the building, blowing out windows on multiple floors. Smoke pours through every exit on the main floor. Buses out front are filling with evacuated hotel guests.

"Could be worse," I say. The cupola with the building's sign on it explodes. "I stand corrected. Guess I'm not staying there tonight."

"Room service sucks anyway," Nicole says. "We need to get out of the open. Rachel?"

"I'm not telling either one of you where I'm staying."

"I think that room up there with the window belching flames is mine," I say. "That's two for two."

"Fuck," Nicole says. "Come on."

Nicole has a white Porsche Cayenne SUV. I thought only botoxed Beverly Hills moms with nannies and three houses drove those. It's nice, if a little weird. I'll never get over the idea that a company that made nothing but sportscars moved into making SUVs for yoga moms.

It takes a while to get off the Strip. Nicole casts a suggestion spell that has people moving out of our way but between the gawkers, evacuees, and first responders, just getting out of the parking lot is slow going.

Once we're out of there, though, it's pretty clear. None of us talk on the drive. All thinking whatever the hell we're thinking. Me, I'm thinking Nicole knows more about what's going on than she's telling us. Or at least me.

It doesn't take long to get to Nicole's. We drive into a suburb surrounded by walls of tan brick and pass mansions all built on the same plan. How's that song go? *Little houses on the hillside and they all look just the same.* You'd think they'd do something a little less generic.

"You live in Summerlin?" I say.

"Yeah," she says. "Just because I'm playing second fiddle to an arcane power doesn't mean I can't do it in style."

Rachel said that Jimmy had ruined her life. Destroyed lives look like all sorts of different things, but I'm having trouble lining this one up with Louboutins and a mansion in the most expensive neighborhood in Las Vegas. And it's a hell of a mansion.

"This place is huge," I say when we get inside. Marble floors, curved oak staircase, a grand piano in one corner. And this is just the foyer.

I run a finger across the top of the piano and come away with a thick layer of dust. A questioning look to Rachel, who shrugs. From the way she's looking around it looks like she's never been here, either.

"Five bedrooms, eight bathrooms, wine cellar, movie theater, peristyle, rooftop deck, the works."

"Big space," I say. "You live alone?"

"Yeah," she says. "Don't spend much time here."

"Got that."

"I'm getting a drink," Nicole says. "You?"

"I'll have a beer if you got it," Rachel says. Nicole stops on her way toward the bar in the main room and turns to stare at Rachel.

"Since when do you drink beer?" Nicole says.

"I dunno," Rachel says. "I was at some brewpub a couple weeks ago. Tried a Stella. Liked it. Now I drink beer."

"Ding ding ding," I say. "We have a winner."

"What?" Rachel says.

"You don't drink beer," Nicole says.

"You told me yourself tonight that you hate the stuff," I say.

"Wait. You think what happened changed what I like to drink?"

"Not exactly," I say. "It probably just shifted where you were going a couple weeks ago and unintentionally nudged you to decide to try a beer."

"And that changed the future?"

"I think it was more a side effect of something else," I say. "But let's put a pin in that. I have questions."

There's so much to unpack here my head is spinning,

but this gives me a place to start figuring this shit out. But before that, I want some fucking answers.

Why was Jimmy kidnapped? Why bring me in to help find him? Who hired the mercenaries who hit Rachel's looking for Nicole? Why do they want her? But there's a big one hanging over my head right now that we need to address before we go any further.

"What the actual fuck happened back there?" I say.

"The wave?" Nicole says. "I have an idea. But I don't know for sure."

"Best guess," I say.

"Time out," Rachel says. "You two saw something I didn't. Fill me in."

"At the bar the world sort of . . . rippled," I say. "Once it finished there were some changes. The security guards and the bartender weren't there anymore. Your tank top changed color."

"Don't forget the guys setting off a bomb on the casino floor," Nicole says. "I doubt they were there before that happened."

"Why didn't I see it?" Rachel says.

"Because Jimmy's doing it."

"We don't know that for sure," Nicole says, though she doesn't sound convinced.

"You and I are the only ones who noticed," I say. "Reality changed around us. The only common thing between us is that we made him."

"The only way he could have done that is if he'd changed the past," Nicole says. "That's not something he can do."

"You said something about an elephant," Rachel says. "What was that about?"

"Had a conversation a little while ago," I say. "Somebody pointed out to me that at their core all events are a binary. They either happen or they don't.

"Like the chance that an elephant would crash through

a ceiling. It might be a billion to one, but that's taking into account all the other things that led to that point. But remove the context, it either happens or it doesn't. Before it can, though, you need an elephant up there. Either an elephant's above the ceiling or it isn't. But before that, you need to have an elephant to put up there. You either have one or you don't. A lot of things need to happen the right way in order to arrange for an elephant to crash through the ceiling."

"That's what Jimmy does," Nicole says. "He does things today that will have consequences in the future. One event changes and it ripples out to other events and so on."

"So eventually, there's an elephant in the ceiling to crash through?" Rachel says.

"Exactly," I say.

"But he can't do it retroactively," Nicole says. "He can't change the past."

"And to have what happened tonight happen," Rachel says, "he would have had to have made changes a while back that would affect today?"

"Exactly," I say. "But he didn't. We know he didn't because we saw the changes happen. If he had, those things would already have been reality for us."

"Like my tank top," Rachel says. "I remember it being the color it is. For me that was already reality."

"Right. But not the one we remember."

"Except that Jimmy can't—" Nicole starts.

"Give it a rest, Nicole," I say. "Maybe he didn't, but so far I'm going on the idea that he did or somebody used him to do it. Nobody's going to go to the trouble of kidnapping him unless they have a plan for using him."

"Fuck," Nicole says. "Yes. I know. Okay? I just—I just don't want it to be true."

"Say he can change the past," Rachel says breaking the following silence. "Why? To get to Nicole?"

"I can think of a few dozen other ways to get hold of her that don't involve blowing up the Bellagio," I say. "And that doesn't answer why he would."

"Unless it was a side effect," Nicole says. "It happens a lot when he changes futures. It's not clean. The bigger the change, the more other things shift. I couldn't tell you what they are, only Jimmy knows, but he's told me about it."

"Like Rachel's tank top," I say.

"The color of my clothes is not the same as a bunch of people with a golem burning down the Bellagio," Rachel says.

"He brought down an airliner once," Nicole says. "Killed a hundred and eighteen people."

"What was he changing?" I say.

"The Detroit Tigers were supposed to win the pennant in 2003. Somebody wanted them to come in last." Jesus. Talk about unintended consequences.

"Did he know that was gonna happen?" I say.

"Yeah. Said it was the only way to ensure they lost."

"All those people who died tonight," Rachel says. "That could have happened because somebody wanted to win a bet?"

"How'd he feel about it?" I say. I have an idea, but I only saw him for a few minutes after I finished the ritual, so I could be wrong.

"Jimmy doesn't feel," Nicole says. Pretty much what I thought.

"The thing that worries me," I say, "is if the Bellagio was a side effect of a change, what was the change?"

"Don't look at me," Rachel says. "Apparently nothing's different for me."

"Are you feeling left out?" I say. She answers me with a raised middle finger.

"Anything look different to you?" Nicole says. "Nazi blimps, flying cars?"

"No on the cars," I say. "And the Nazis have always been here. That ripple in reality. You said you had an idea what that might be."

"Jimmy called them reality quakes. He knew about them, but said he couldn't make one happen. He didn't go into much detail. Mostly, I figured he was just talking out his ass."

"Figuratively," I say. Nicole glares at me. Everybody's a critic. My phone buzzes. A text from Amanda.

Heard about Bellagio. U ok?

>   Are you asking if I burned it down?

Yes.

>   Not this time. Know anything about realty
>   quakes?
>   Sorry. Real Realt duck reality quakes

U old

>   Duck you

Will check get back to U

>   👍

How many tries did it take you to get that

>   Three

👍 1

"Everything okay?" Nicole says.

"Peachy." I can see she wants more information, but I'm not giving it to her. She was listening in on my conversation with Rachel. She knows the basics. I don't trust her with anything more.

"Let me make sure I got this," Rachel says. "If the Oracle . . . if Jimmy—Christ, I still can't believe he has a name. If Jimmy had made changes to take place now, he would have had to have made them in the past."

"Which according to Nicole," I say, "he can't do." We both look at Nicole, who doesn't meet our eyes.

"He's . . . not supposed to be able to," she says. "I'll admit I don't know for certain."

"Let's try a different approach," I say. "We know that the change couldn't have been any later than a couple weeks ago. That's when Rachel changed her mind about beer. So what was happening a couple weeks ago?"

"But the changes could have started before then," Nicole says.

"Maybe, but it's at least a starting point. So, any big news?"

"Like plagues? Stock market crashes? That sort of thing?"

"I think it depends on if it benefits anyone," I say. "Or if it just seems weird or unlikely. You're making an 'oh shit' face."

"That's because I'm having an 'oh shit' moment," Rachel says. "David bought a bunch of casinos."

"I thought he already owned a casino."

"Yeah," Nicole says. "The Lilywhite."

"Not casino," Rachel says. "Casinos. With an s. As in more than one. It was in the news because it caught so many people by surprise. Everything just sort of lined up and he picked up five casinos in the space of a week."

"Which ones?" I say.

"Small ones, mostly. Off-Strip. Rio, I think. Tuscany. Orleans. The Gold Rush? And I think Palace Station."

"Wait, did you say the Gold Rush?" Nicole says.

"Yeah. Why?"

"That can't be a coincidence," I say. "The Gold Rush was where Nicole and I met. It was owned by Sebastian McCord."

"The guy you shot?" Rachel says.

"It was him or me," Nicole says.

"I'd say we have a pretty good idea who's got Jimmy."

"And where they're keeping him?" Rachel says.

"I don't think so," Nicole says. "If he's got him at the Gold Rush, we can just walk right in and take him. That place has been shut down since Sebastian died. Should have been condemned years ago."

"Great," Rachel says. "So the fortune-telling head that can change the past is in the hands of a psychopath who's using it to buy shitty Vegas casinos."

"Don't forget that a side effect blew up the Bellagio," I say.

"I'm done," Rachel says. "This is giving me a head-ache. I need sleep."

"You're welcome to—" Nicole starts.

"No. I—Fuck, I'll call an Uber."

"I can give you a lift," I say.

"You have a car here?"

"No. Lot of other people do, though."

"Sure. Stolen, rented, I don't fucking care. Just get me out of here."

"I'll call you," Nicole says.

"Don't. This has been a shit day. My son is trauma-tized. I've got a few dozen corpses on my property be-cause of a literal talking head, and half of them were zombies. And apparently, this is the wrong reality. So, don't. Can we leave?"

"Sure," I say. "I'll meet you out front. Let me know if you see anything you want to steal." Rachel slams the door behind her.

"I don't think she's gonna help us get back Jimmy," I say.

"After all this and you still do?"

"Yeah. He's got shit to answer for. I give a fuck about David's plans to take over the world or whatever the hell he's doing. I need one thing and that means finding Jimmy. Beyond that, I really don't care."

"Can I call you tomorrow morning?"

"Knock yourself out. Provided Jimmy doesn't erase us from existence before then."

Chapter 9

"All right, Rachel, what the fuck?" Not a lot of cars out on the street in Summerlin. Everybody's got a garage and an expensive car. Fortunately, some of them have more than they can fit and I was able to find a BMW on the curb.

"What?"

"You said Jimmy ruined Nicole's life. Louboutins, a Porsche, and a mansion in Summerlin don't really look like ruined."

"You've never known a coke addict who couldn't keep themselves put together? That fucking thing keeps her alive. She needs it and if she doesn't find it soon the magic linking them will break and that's it." That puts a new spin on things.

"How so?"

"I'm not sure exactly. Before, I thought it was like a drug addiction. Like she needed exposure to it or she'd go into withdrawal or something. She acts like it sometimes."

"Before? How about now?"

"I think it's bullshit," she says. "Not that it isn't fucked up, but if there's a spell keeping her connected, it looks an awful lot like just a really toxic relationship. That's what seeing her in that house feels like. I got a view of the kitchen. It's filled with cartons and wrappers from delivery and fast food. And you saw the dust in there."

"She doesn't have time to clean?" I say and then

realize how stupid that is. "So why doesn't she hire someone to come in and do it for her?"

"And then there's the front of the house," she says.

"What about—Ah. It's well maintained. She has gardeners. So why not get a cleaner? Too much chance they'd bump into Jimmy?"

"Maybe," she says. "I don't know. I just like this even less than I did before." She grinds the heels of her hands into her eyes. "I can't do this right now. I need sleep."

"Where do you want me to drop you off?"

"Outside Fremont," she says. "I'll grab an Uber from there. How about you? I doubt they're letting people back into the Bellagio for a while. You don't blow up a place that pulls a billion-and-a-half a year and just shrug it off."

"I gotta go see somebody," I say. "If things work out, I'll crash at his place."

"Where's that?"

"Jail."

———

I stop at a high-end liquor store and buy the most expensive whisky I can find, a three-thousand dollar bottle of Pappy Van Winkle 15-year bourbon, and a flask. When I tell them to put the bottle into a paper bag they look like I just took a shit on the Mona Lisa. In the car I fill the flask with the whisky because fuck if I'm not gonna drink some of it.

I take the Freeway up to Eastern, over to Stewart, and then it's hello, North Las Vegas Detention Center. Long time, no see. Looks like you've put on some weight.

When I was here it was a small police station with a handful of holding cells. Now it's a sprawling complex of multiple buildings of cell blocks, the whole thing surrounded by razor wire. They kept the cell block I was in, a stark white building with narrow, wired-glass windows looking out onto more stark white buildings with narrow, wired-glass windows.

I park across the street under a No Parking and a Do Not Stop For Hitchhikers sign. Someone will probably tow the car by morning. There are plenty more to steal in a nearby parking lot.

It's weird being back here. A little bit like going home. A little bit like failure. When I left, I didn't just expect to never come back, I planned on never coming back. But then, I said the same thing about Los Angeles and look where that got me.

I've been asking myself a lot whether coming out to Vegas looking for Jimmy is worth it and then feel like an asshole. Of course it's worth it. Gabriela's worth it. To say my feelings are conflicted is a bit of an understatement.

I didn't want to be brought back from Mictlan. I particularly didn't want to be brought back a little bit and have the rest of me left behind. Fucking my wife.

I have to admit, though, it was a good thing. Having humanity at the core of Mictlantecuhtli was a bad idea all around. My leaving was like having cancer cut out of a body. And Santa Muerte is happier. Mictlantecuhtli is more who he's supposed to be. And since he's still kind of me, it's hard to be that pissed off at him.

Gabriela, however. I was really pissed off when I found out what she'd done. She yanked me out of the closest thing to happiness I've ever had.

At the same time I understand why she did it and I have to respect that she did it even knowing how angry I was probably going to be. She does what needs doing. At least what she thinks needs doing.

So am I here because I respect her as a mage and an

ally, as a friend, or as something more? I still don't know what's going on between us, but I'd kind of like to find out.

I pull out a HELLO, MY NAME IS sticker and write I'M THAT IMPORTANT GUY YOU SHOULD LISTEN TO AND CAN'T REMEMBER ONCE HE'S GONE on it with a Sharpie and slap it onto my coat like a badge. I pump some magic into it and head to the fence.

Cameras on poles, bright lights, razor-wire. Prison guards are on patrol. I used to sneak in and out before I figured out the Sharpie trick. Even then I had to be careful. Getting it to hide me from cameras was always a little iffy.

I could go through the front door, talk my way in, but my tolerance for the living right now is pretty much nonexistent.

It's a simple matter of popping over to the dead side, through the fence, and back. I have to make it quick, though. The place is crawling with ghosts.

Jails, hotels, hospitals. The three places you'll find the most ghosts outside of a battlefield. Everybody says graveyards, but if they'd stop long enough to really think about it, they'd realize nobody dies in a graveyard. Cemeteries are nothing but underground meat storage.

And this place has got a lot of ghosts. Haunts, mostly. Not a lot of Wanderers. I guess if you die imprisoned your ghost pretty much stays there.

Some cells have five or six crammed in together, ghosts who all died at different times, sometimes years apart. They must figure they don't have anything to lose, so they do a lot of screaming. I can hear them over on this side of the veil. They never shut up when I was here before, and it sounds like they're still going strong.

A quick blip and I'm on the other side of the fence. I'm

walking toward my old building and bump into a two-man patrol with a German Shepherd who does not like me.

Dogs are harder to fool. I haven't figured out how to stick a scent on a sticker that tells them to calm the fuck down. But the guards get one look at me and stand up a little straighter.

"Evening, sir," one of them says. I nod and walk by, forgotten by all but the dog by the time I turn a corner. The rest of the walk is easy enough. I'm not feeling any other magic in the area, which is good. I don't really want to deal with another mage right now. I've had my fill for the evening.

Same trick to get past the door of the cell block, the guards, the gates, the checkpoints. Takes me a second to find the right cell. They've re-numbered them. Now it's number eighty-seven. Back in my day it was six.

I know I'm at the right place when I can feel a powerful ghost in one and absolutely none in any of the adjacent cells. Now I need to be careful. Popping over to the other side here is a really bad idea. Instead, I pop the lock with a spell, short the alarm sensor, and step inside.

The cell's occupied. One guy in a dark blue two-piece jail uniform. I'm trying to remember if that means they're low-risk or suicidal. I can never get the colors right.

He pops his head up, eyes bleary, struggling to get out of his bunk. Probably thinks it's one of those spot inspections.

"Go back to sleep," I say. I pump some magic into the words and after a second he's back out. This is where I prefer Sharpies. Speaking a spell takes more energy than just writing it down on a sticker.

"As I live and breathe," says a voice.

"You don't do either of those, old man."

A cackle, a face from the shadows. Weathered, cracked,

fading. A moment later a ghost, probably the most cohesive and powerful ghost I've ever met, fades in.

His name is Herbert Cruikshank. He was an alcoholic necromancer—pretty common coping mechanism for most of us—who got so incredibly shitfaced one night that he passed out and the cops tossed him into this cell, where he proceeded to have a massive coronary.

Dying of a heart attack won't normally leave behind a ghost. But we're talking about a powerful necromancer who'd been born some time in the early 19th century and died sometime in the late 1960s. If he wanted to leave a ghost, he was damn well gonna leave a ghost.

Though he acts like a Haunt most of the time, rarely leaving the area where his original holding cell was, he's a Wanderer. Probably the most together, most powerful one I've ever met. I might be willing to risk sliding over to the other side with other Wanderers nearby, but I doubt I'd survive if I had to go up against him.

"What the hell you doing here, kid?" he says.

"I was in town, thought I'd stop by. Brought you a present." I pull the bottle out of its bag and twist off the cap. I take the razor and cut my arm, letting a few drops of blood into the bottle.

"I appreciate the thought, but you know it doesn't work like that, right?" he says. "I can't exactly grab a bottle over on your side. Or did you forget everything I taught ya?"

"You're not the only one who's got a few tricks up his sleeve, ya know," I say, and send the bottle to the dead side. The look of surprise on his face is priceless. I've never seen him speechless before.

I can't see the bottle, but I can see his hands as he picks it up, looks it over. Then he raises it to his lips and takes a swig. His eyes pop.

"Damn," he says. "That is some potent shit."

"Thought you could use a drink," I say.

"I did not teach you that trick," he says.

"Learned that one all on my own," I say.

"How long's it been?" he says. "Couple years?"

"Not quite thirty," I say. "Lot's happened. I died, turned into an Aztec death god, got brought back to life. You ever meet Darius?"

"The djinn? Couple times."

"I killed him," I say. "Collapsed a universe on him."

He takes another swig of the blood-infused whisky. "You been busy. So, what do you want?"

"You wound me," I say. "What makes you think I want anything?"

"Because you're you."

"Can't really argue against that. Couple things. I missed the old homestead and I need a bunk for the night. My hotel blew up."

"Nice to see your penchant for property damage remains undiminished. And the other?"

"You ever hear of the Oracle of Las Vegas?"

"I'm dead, not deaf," he says. "I hear plenty. Even the dead talk about it. What about it?"

"Apparently it's been stolen. I need to find it."

"Feel sorry for whatever poor bastard got their hands on it. Those things are what you get when a monkey's paw fucks a hand grenade."

"Pretty accurate, yeah," I say. "You ever deal with one?"

"The fallout from one, yeah," he says. "Killed a lot of good people."

"How'd you stop it?"

"Didn't. One of those good people grabbed it and teleported them both somewhere. Don't know where, but it wasn't for a luxury weekend in the Catskills."

"Great. The only pocket universe I had I collapsed on Darius."

"They're complicated machines," he says. "They'll figure out the path of events they can influence that'll lead them where they want to go and then kick off the first one."

"And the rest topple like dominos, I know," I say.

"Divination's easy when you make the future happen. What's your interest?"

"Friend of mine got hit by a spell by one of his clients. Need to reverse it. He's the only one who knows how."

"Interesting choice of pronoun you got there."

"Yeah, well. He was a person before I cut his head off."

He looks at me to see if I'm joking. "Jesus, kid. You made an oracle? You really know how to fuck yourself, don't you?"

"Hey, I learned some impressive magic making that thing. Also how much blood spray you get when you saw a person's head off."

"Uh huh. Why do you think it knows how to fix your friend? Or does Daddy just want to reconnect with his little boy?"

"I think it might be the other way around." I give him the highlights of why I'm there, what it looks like Jimmy can do now. The more I talk about it the worse it feels, but then I rein it in. I'm out here for one reason.

"And you think all this is him forcing you to come to his rescue?"

"Fuck if I know. Whatever it is, it looks like I'm part of his plan. There's something bothering me about this whole thing that I can't put my finger on."

"You mean besides a being with almost god-like powers to shape the future having its eye on you?"

"That's nothing new," I say.

"Here's what I don't understand," Herb says. "I get how creating him was a necromancer spell, but how come there wasn't a chronomancer involved? You're talking some pretty heavy time magic there."

"Don't say that. This shit's complicated enough as it is. I figured it was because of the ker I shoved into Jimmy's head. They can sense future death."

"That's a big leap to being able to manipulate future events," he says.

"Is it, though? It's a matter of degree, not type."

"You know much about time magic?" Herb says.

"Beyond having a pocket watch that ages shit fast and that thinking about it gives me a headache, not really." Though I've used the pocket watch plenty of times, I have no idea how it works.

"It's more common than you'd think," he says. "Any divination is time magic. Not far off from what the Oracle does. You're right in that it's a difference of degree. If a ker is a fart in the wind, the Oracle's a bullhorn. Biggest difference with things like that is power."

"What, you saying Jimmy's got a battery?"

"Maybe," he says. "Take your pocket watch. You wave it around and it just does its thing, right? Don't feel a spell going off or anything like that?"

"Yeah. Though I'll be honest, when I've used it I've been a little too preoccupied to pay attention," I say.

"That's because whoever or whatever made it put all that power into it while it was being created. Maybe it slowly recharges and you've never noticed because you've never had to use it so often. Could be all sorts of things. Point is that power's coming from somewhere."

That's a good point. When I finished the ritual that made Jimmy, I wasn't paying much attention to anything but my own exhaustion and needing to get the hell out of there before the drugs wore off Sebastian and Nicole and they shot me.

"You'd think somebody would have noticed," I say.

"Not if it was a power nobody knew about or how to

look for it. Hell, maybe it runs off the dreams of little children. Maybe it feeds off time itself."

Now that's an interesting thought. "Or like, say, the emotional energy of a bunch of horny Las Vegas strip bar patrons?"

Herb shakes his head. "You're thinking erotimancers. Nah. The kind of energy they tap is easy to track if you got the eye for it. And if you're generating that much energy you're getting attention. Lotta leeches are gonna come by to fill up their tanks. You can't hide that shit. Too many erotimancers around, especially in a place like Vegas. And again, we're talking hardcore time magic here. It's making changes to the past. Whatever's powering that is something different."

I'm not sure I buy it, but I don't think he's far off the mark.

"You sure this David guy has the Oracle?" Herb says.

"Reasonably sure," I say. "Probably in one of his casinos." Wish we'd figured out he probably had it before that fucking reality quake hit, before one casino turned into six.

"I'd say whichever one he's living in," Herb says. "Unless one of them has a better vault. He's not gonna want it far or unsecured. And if he's screwing with it, trying to make it do shit it's not supposed to, it's gotta be big enough to hold some kind of ritual space or a lab. Something."

"And people to work on it," I say.

"Don't think he's got the chops to do it himself?"

"Oh, hell no," I say. "David's an idiot. He's got somebody doing the work for him for sure. Or did and he got rid of them."

I didn't think any of this shit was gonna be simple, but I thought it was a hell of a lot more simple than this. I'd like to just say it's not my problem, that all I need is an answer from Jimmy on how to reverse that fucking spell, but there's a reason he wants me here and I can't imagine it's a good one.

"I can't think about this anymore, tonight," I say. "I need some sleep." I pull out a sticker and my Sharpie and write THERE'S NOBODY HERE SO LET THE NO-BODY WHO ISN'T HERE SLEEP OR THE NOBODY WILL CUT SOMEBODY'S NADS OFF. Pretty wordy for a sticker but I'm looking for something with a little more nuance than FUCK OFF.

"You're still using those fucking things? All this time and you can't come up with something better?"

"Sorry, gramps, but I got rid of my sandwich board sometime in the thirties."

"You kids and your new-fangled ways," he says. "Grab some shut-eye. I'll just sit here and stare at you creepily while you do it."

"Just like old times."

I lay my head back onto the paper-thin mattress and just as I'm almost asleep, the world starts bucking around me like a really pissed-off bull.

It twists my head up as it passes and when it does I can see the ripple of the reality quake disappearing out into the distance. This one wasn't as bad as the Bellagio, but it wasn't fun.

"Problem?" Herb says.

"Yeah," I say. "But I'm too fucking tired to worry about it."

"Glad I don't have to deal with any of that shit anymore."

"Lucky you."

Chapter 10

"You're alive," Amanda says when she picks up the phone.

"More or less," I say. I had woken up to the alarm clock of my impromptu roommate's farting. Jail food'll do that to you. Herb had been nowhere to be found, which was just as well. At this point I don't know that I have anything to say to him.

It was weird seeing him after all these years. Things have definitely changed. For me if not for him. He was, I can't call him a mentor, he was too much of a pain in the ass for that, but a tutor.

I was nothing but raw, undirected talent. Everything I knew about necromancy was through trial and error, usually with disastrous or at least disgusting results. Don't try to animate a bloated dead possum for example. They tend to pop.

I found a decent looking Kia in the jail parking lot, popped the lock, and headed out. I need to see Nicole. Ask her some pointed questions. And if she's not at the Summerlin house, so much the better. Might give me a chance to poke around.

"So, the Bellagio?" Amanda says.

"Place really knows how to put on a party." It doesn't take long to give her the highlights of the evening.

"Jesus," she says. "How do you end up in the middle of shit like this?"

"Just lucky, I guess."

"Have you seen the news?"

"Not yet." I can't imagine it's going to be good.

"They're treating the Bellagio like it's a criminal arson investigation. Nobody wants to say 'terrorist' in a place like that. No details yet."

"Any idea who's selling golems out this way?"

"I know an information broker who might be able to get some answers," she says. "Think you can meet with her?"

"Yeah, though the golems probably aren't important anyway. What I could really use is where David's keeping Jimmy, provided he has him."

"The broker should be able to help with that. We've got a family account with her. I'll ping her then send you a meeting place. She doesn't sleep, so might be able to get you in now."

"Let's do it." There's a pause where neither of us says anything. I don't want to talk about this because it gives me a headache to think about it, but this might be the most crucial piece in this bullshit puzzle.

"Reality quakes," I say. "You find anything about that?"

"Yes," she says. "It's not good. They're also called time quakes. They're changes in the past snapping into the present. Not a lot known about them. When they happen, most people don't know it. They change along with everything else. I'm trying to track down a chronomancer who might know more."

"What does it mean that Nicole and I saw it happening and it didn't do anything to us?"

"The ones who can perceive them either know how it happens and they're attuned to it, or they're part of it."

"Shit." I suspected as much. "Well, that's confirmation they're because of Jimmy, then. If they weren't, I'd be swept up in them, too."

"Time magic is not something to fuck around with," Amanda says. "The way my dad's . . . my house can freeze time in various rooms is pretty simple, and even that takes an insane amount of power to do."

I've wondered about the pocket universe Amanda's estate is in ever since I saw it. Whoever owns it can change its layout, configuration, style, contents, everything. When we fought her uncle, he'd managed to get some control over it. Suddenly there's empty halls, upside-down rooms, doors that opened back in on themselves. Real pain in the ass.

"Where does your house get its power?" I say.

"You know I'm not going to answer that," she says.

"Fair enough. Better question, then. Where's *Jimmy* getting the power?"

"I've heard of some things, artifacts, creatures, long-lasting spells, that sort of thing that use an external source like a battery. Or they're just insanely powerful relics. I found a reference to a timepiece that occasionally changes form to match its present time, though apparently it never quite gets it right. Nobody seems to know why, or what it actually is, just that it can twist time in ways even chronomancers can't figure out."

"What's it look like now?" I say, suspicion gnawing at the back of my mind.

"No idea," she says. "Disappeared around World War I. Looked like something called a Henlein watch. Copper sphere about the size of a golf ball. Why?"

"Curiosity," I say. I've always known the family pocket watch I'm carrying around is insanely dangerous and has shifted with the times, but I didn't realize it was a tactical nuke.

"Whatever's giving him this power, he couldn't do it before," I say.

"Maybe he could have, but just didn't have enough power till now," she says. "He does do time magic, even if it's only in one direction."

"Don't even go there," I say. "It's bad enough he can influence the future on his own. Any luck on figuring out how to get Gabriela and your dad back?"

"Not yet. Spatially, if your soul-tracking gadget works right, Dad's somewhere around Union Station, but I can't get more specific than that. And Gabriela, all I can get is that she's somewhere. It can't seem to lock onto her."

When their souls were shunted out of their bodies they stayed connected via a glowing gold thread. When I touched the thread connected to Attila, Amanda's dad, I got a lot of information from it, but not on where his soul might be or how to get it back.

I haven't tried that with Gabriela's because when the souls were kicked out the bodies died. We got Gabriela into a room of Amanda's house and had it freeze time right away. We didn't understand what was happening with Attila at first, so he was dead and rotting for a few hours. Bringing him back might prove problematic.

When we pull her out of the room, Gabriela's body will have only been dead for about ten or twenty seconds. I'm confident that we can get her back. Attila not so much.

I was still able to find the thread connected to Gabriela, but the magic that froze her body did something like that to the thread, too. I couldn't get anything from it when I touched it. Needless to say, we're hesitant to unfreeze her.

"Do you really think we can do this?" Amanda says.

"Get the spell reversed? Yes," I say. "Jimmy wants something from me. If he can't deliver, he has to know I'll find a way to fuck him up. When he was alive he was kind of an idiot. But that's clearly not the case now. As to getting your dad back . . ."

"Yeah, I know," she says. She hesitates. "Is it bad that I don't know if I want him back?"

"No," I say. "And it's not bad if you do want him back. There's no right or wrong here. Whatever you decide to do, you'll have to live with the consequences. Can't say I envy the position you're in."

"Well, at least I know you're not telling me this to make me feel better," she says.

"Haven't lied to you yet," I say. "Don't plan on starting now."

"Thanks. I guess. Let me check to see if the broker can fit you in today. I'll text you if I get anything."

It doesn't take long to hear back from Amanda. Her information broker has a slot open. I pull up the address and head over. The area's all light industrial. Warehouses, mostly, some manufacturing and . . .

"You sure this is the right address?" I say when Amanda answers her phone.

"Yeah, why?"

"Because it's a roller rink."

"Oh yeah. Forgot that bit. That's where she has her office."

"Your high-powered information broker has an office in a roller rink?"

"Actually, she has an office and an apartment in a roller rink. She owns the place. Likes roller derby."

I've never really been into roller derby. Kind of surprising. The only sports I like to watch are the really violent ones. You'd think roller derby would be right up my alley.

"Okay, how do I find her in a sea of derby queens?"

"First off, her name's Diane. She won't be on the track. She's probably watching practice. Sometimes she coaches. Look for a woman about four-and-a-half feet tall with long, black hair in a braid."

"Four-and-a-half feet?"

"She's a Nimerigar. The Shoshone and Paiute named

them. I don't know much about her. They feed on human flesh and drink their blood."

"So, kind of like a leprechaun?" I say.

Silence. Then, "Leprechauns eat human flesh and drink blood?"

"All the ones I've met. Nasty little fuckers. Almost as bad as gremlins. Stupid as a box of hammers, though."

"Yeah, don't, uh, don't tell her that. I don't think she'd like the comparison."

"Hey, I'm stupid but I'm not that stupid."

"I'm going to leave that one alone," she says and hangs up.

I head inside, the sound of skates clattering on wood echoing through the building. Most of the bottom floor is taken up by the track with some bleachers set up on all sides. A short woman with black hair in a long braid down her back stands at the track railing yelling at the players like she's Burgess Meredith in Rocky.

The women on the track are not fucking around. They zip around like they're on rockets instead of skates, slamming into each other by some set of rules I can't quite suss out. Hitting each other seems to be the only constant here.

I keep my distance. I don't see any reason to disturb the flow. It's nice to see people who aren't me getting the snot kicked out of them.

Also, Diane's kind of terrifying. There's no doubt she's not human. I don't know if she's got a glamour I can't see or if all her derby dolls know what she is. Either way she radiates menace like Axe body spray off guys in a Hollywood club.

After about ten minutes she calls for a break and heads over to me. She's short, but it's not dwarfism. Everything's normally proportioned. She's just really small.

"You're Amanda's friend," she says. Her voice sounds

like a gearbox with sand in it. Her serrated teeth look like a miniature bear trap.

"Close enough," I say. "You're Diane?"

"Yeah," she says. She narrows her eyes at me. "I don't think I like you."

"That puts you in excellent company," I say.

"You even human?" she says.

"More or less. Depends on who you ask. Mostly I'm just some guy."

I assume she's picking up whatever's left over from being Mictlantecuhtli. Besides my memories there shouldn't be anything, but then, I shouldn't have been able to see through the glamour on Rachel's kid. The only thing I'm sure of anymore is that I can't be sure of anything.

"Fine. Whatever. Keep it to yourself. Come on." I follow her upstairs to a small office made out of a tacked-together drywall cube with no door. There's a particle board desk with a couple chairs and a laptop.

"All right, Mister I Don't Want To Tell You What I Am," she says. "We're on Amanda's dime, so what do you need?"

"There's a guy in town, David Jewel—"

"If you've come here to ask if he's an asshole let me save you some time and money. He is and then some."

"Believe me, I know. No, I need to find out where he might be keeping something. I figure it's going to be in a pretty heavily protected vault, but I can't be certain."

"How big is this thing?"

"About the size of a bowling ball," I say.

"Magic?"

"Very."

"Okay. That gives me a start point," she says. "When do you need the information?"

"Soon as I can get it."

"All right. I got your number from Amanda."

"If you can't get me, call this number." I jot down Rachel's number on a folded over HI, MY NAME IS sticker and hand it to her.

"You carry these things around with you a lot?" she says.

"Never leave home without 'em."

"Awright, I hear anything or have any questions I'll let you know. Anything else?"

"Golems," I say. "Ran into one the other night that was made from a kit. Looking for the seller."

"That'd be Rudy Cunningham," she says. "Only one in town deals in shit like that. I deal in information, Rudy deals in pretty much everything else."

"Know where I can find him?"

"He jumps around a lot. He's a human mage with a talent for knowing where he needs to be."

"Must be handy," I say.

"Not as much as you'd think. A few times where he needed to be was on the receiving end of some guy's fist. I can track him down."

"Appreciate it."

She leans forward and takes a big sniff. "I know that smell."

"It was a long night and I haven't had a shower yet."

"I'm gonna figure it out eventually, you know," she says. "I always do."

"Smell like death?" I say.

She snaps her fingers. "Yes. I knew there was something I didn't like about you."

"Get to know me and you'll find all sorts of things you won't like about me."

She peers at me, eyes narrowed, then, "Get the fuck out."

So I get the fuck out.

Chapter 11

I really don't want to spend another night sleeping in a jail cell. I drive around town looking for a motel with any available beds. Considering how many tourists were displaced by the Bellagio disaster it's not surprising that the number is none and zero. I finally find one place off the Strip that's so ratty I'm surprised they have anybody staying there at all. Even I'm not sure I want to be there.

"Room 17," the kid at the desk says. He's got too many pimples and a lisp from so much orthodontia you could build a bridge with it. He starts to hand me the key and his face goes slack and his hand freezes inches from mine.

"You okay there?"

"You should go play some blackjack at the Luxor," he says.

"Beg pardon?"

"The Luxor. You should go play some blackjack."

"Really? This is how you try to get hold of me? Do you even know what a fucking telephone is?"

The kid blinks and finishes handing me the keys. "Have a nice day." There's no point asking him what that was all about. He doesn't know and won't remember it. Assuming this is the same sort of invitation I got at the Bellagio. They probably want me over straight away. Fuck 'em. One thing gods have in spades is time. I get situated into my room and take a shower before heading over to the Luxor.

The Luxor is, I wouldn't say the strangest themed casino, fuck knows there are a lot of them here, but it's definitely up there. As the name implies, it's designed to evoke Ancient Egypt. The building is an enormous black pyramid with a huge spotlight at its spire beaming straight up, so bright you can see it miles away.

Instead of elevators it has funiculars designed to move up and down the pyramid's structure at an angle. They're kind of trippy.

I make my way past sphinxes, obelisks, massive façades of ancient tombs that reach up into the hollow pyramid. The casino floor is like every other casino floor in that it's a labyrinth of blinking, screaming slot machines that'd give Theseus a headache. It doesn't take long for me to find the right blackjack table.

Shait is sitting alone at the table drinking a glass of wine.

"I see you got my message," she says.

"Yeah. You know you could just give me a call."

"Actually, I can't," she says. "It's part of who I am. It was this or a falcon flying in different patterns that you'd have to interpret. Or I could have you kill a ram and read the entrails."

"Okay, yeah, I can see that being a problem. So, what do you want?"

"You'll notice I'm alone," she says.

"I do. Is there a problem?"

"Your friend Mister Freeburg is about to destroy the entire idea of fate and luck and uncertainty in this city and no one will know it's happening," she says.

"That's what you said last time."

"Things are a little more dire. Of the other three only one still exists and that's only because they are powerful enough to push back, but it's going to get harder."

"The dealer," I say. "Are they luck?"

"In a way," she says. "Have you heard of the gambler's fallacy?"

"Yeah, it's a misunderstanding how probability works. If something happens enough times in one direction, then it's more likely to hit the other direction. I roll shitty dice twenty times, I'm due to start getting good rolls. Doesn't work that way. At least it's not supposed to."

"Exactly. Well, the gambler's fallacy does exist and you had a conversation with them last night. They skew probability so that it works in favor of whoever they've attached themselves to. They become something of a patron. For a little while, at least."

"What about the other two? Frank and Bugsy?"

"The idea of them still exists, but they've changed so drastically they might as well not. It's like they have amnesia. Things shift here so much that they're not the most stable of avatars. It wouldn't take much to change them into something else."

"Are we talking bad something else?"

"Not necessarily. Just, they might look more favorably on different people than they would have before. Like Robin Hood going from stealing from the rich to give to the poor to suddenly beating up the poor to give to the billionaires."

"So just like real life," I say. "Was this some kind of attack?" Is Jimmy going after the avatars of Las Vegas? And why? What is he hoping to accomplish?

"I don't think so, no," she says. "I think they might be a side effect of the Oracle's new powers."

"You mean the reality quakes," I say. "Yeah, I ran into two of them the other night. Nicole and I can't be the only ones who can see them."

"I think you might be, besides those things that exist

outside of its effects. Right now Jimmy can reach about two weeks into the past and has a range that covers most of the city."

"So instead of someone having to be in the same room with him to affect them he can hit anybody in Vegas."

"Most people here aren't from here. Do you understand?"

"Shit." If he can start toppling dominos with anyone in Vegas, he can arrange things possibly all around the world.

"The elephant," I say.

"I was thinking more like a plague, but okay," Shait says.

"No. That example. Jimmy can't make an elephant drop out of the ceiling ten minutes from now because there would have had to be an elephant there in the first place. But now that he can do things in the past and can influence people potentially all across the world . . ."

"Yes," she says. "I imagine you're going to see a lot of elephants."

"And you think what's happening is a side effect?" I say.

"Do you think the Bellagio burning down was an attack on the Bellagio?" she says.

"No," I say. "It felt off. Lots of criminals are stupid, but these guys seemed more stupid than most. And if that was the case how the hell did they get that far?"

"They weren't really much of a threat to you either, were they?" she says.

"Not really, no. More of a nuisance."

"This feels the same way. I'm not sure what has changed. You felt the one last night?"

"Oh yeah," I say. If I were in L.A. and felt a typical earthquake I'd have probably ignored it because that's what we do out there, but reality shakes, damn right I noticed it.

"I'm a little surprised," she says. "Most people attuned to them will only feel them if the present time they're experiencing has significant changes."

"And it didn't feel like that to you?"

"It felt—"

"Weak," I say. "I was thinking that after it hit that it sucked but that it was a lot better than the earlier one."

"I think he did something small," she says. Okay, what the hell could that be? Figuring that out's going to be like finding a needle tied to a rock and thrown into the ocean.

"Any idea what?"

"No. But it was something that inadvertently changed the nature of Las Vegas to some degree. Or maybe a power balance. I'd think that would be something much larger. The death of a headlining star, new gambling laws, things like that. Even the burning down of the Bellagio didn't change much."

"For want of a nail?" I say. Little things can have surprisingly severe consequences. "Maybe something that hasn't happened yet, but it's been started? Or something that happened two weeks ago? I hate this shit. Why are you even talking to me about this? Near as I've been able to tell I can do fuck-all about it."

"You're wrong about that," she says. "First, I only have so much power here. I'm not a goddess as much a godling? Godette?"

"Demigod?"

"More than that but less than most. My constraints keep me from doing a lot."

"You said first. What's the second?"

"The Oracle can't see you."

It takes me a second to process this and when I'm sure I heard what I think I heard, I say, "Come again?"

"Jimmy can't see you," Shait says. "You're his father. Like it or not, he's part of you."

"He can see me just fine."

"With his eyes, yes. But otherwise you're a blind spot. He can't see you, what you're doing, what you're going to do. And not just sight. Once you get involved in a situation it's like somebody flips a light switch."

"That makes no sense. How the hell was he able to do what he did at the Werther house if he couldn't see me or anybody in the situation?"

"Because he did it ten years ago," she says. "He can extrapolate. Set events in motion he thought you'd be involved in. Probably set up half a dozen other things that would have got you here if that hadn't. Probably knew you were hooked when that whole branch of the future disappeared to him."

"I show up and he can't see the future of whatever I'm involved in?" I say. "No. If—" Then I remember. If. Sonofabitch.

"I know that look. Something interesting just happened," Shait says and takes a sip of her wine.

"When I talked to Liam Werther, he said Jimmy's payment was for him to mention Las Vegas to me. Basically drop a hint at my feet that only I'd understand. But the way he said he was to do it 'if he happened to see me.'"

"There you have it," she says. "If Jimmy sees a future and moves things around so it happens, there shouldn't be any uncertainty involved."

"Fuck. Fuck fuck fuck." Jimmy knew he was going to be kidnapped, but he couldn't do anything about it. But he had an ace up his sleeve. Me.

"You seem very upset about this," Shait says.

"Because I am," I say. "I knew I was being played, just

not how. Fucker can't see me but baits a trap hoping I'll fall for it. The only way I get what I want is to come to Vegas and break him out of wherever he is."

"If he doesn't know what you'll do, he can't warn whoever has him that you're coming for him."

"Exactly. I'm his goddamn camouflage."

When he was alive, Jimmy's knack was this subconscious negative space around him that would seep into the places he spent most of his time. It's why I became his roommate. I didn't want people to find me and a casual look with scrying wouldn't see me because of my proximity to him and his apartment.

And now the fucker's using me as his camouflage. He's pissing me off, but I have to respect the irony.

"What now?" Shait says.

"Get him back and, I dunno. I guess nothing's really changed. I need to find him, I need my answers. I don't suppose you could twist my fate around so I already did it."

"I probably shouldn't tell you this," she says. "What the hell. Predestination 101."

"You need a whiteboard for this?"

"Hush. First, understand that both fate and free will exist. They don't contradict one another even though it might seem they do. They complement each other.

"This is a horrible simplification, but one is like a town you drive into and the other is all the different roads you can take to get there. Some points in a person's life are pre-destined. Everything will lead to that choice. But it's very flexible and not fixed. Say you're destined to eat a sandwich. Where, how, with whom, and so on are all free will."

"Sandwiches are pre-destined?" I say. She laughs.

"Yes," she says. "For some people. Fate isn't some grandiose thing that creates Chosen Ones who go on to fight evil. It does sometimes, but mostly it's small, banal things because most people have small, banal lives. And some people are more destined than others."

She looks around the casino floor. "Him," she says, pointing at a man at a slot machine. "He has billions of pre-destined events in his life. Tiny things. He'll wear a particular belt or eat a particular meal. He simply doesn't have a lot of free will. The universe decides for him."

She nods toward a woman coming down the escalator. "She, on the other hand, has only a few thousand. She has a lot of free will. Most of those pre-destined events are simple, but a few of them are fairly profound. She's working on her PhD in physics and right now her work will lead to a breakthrough in fusion technology."

"What do you mean by right now?" I say.

"Caught that, did you?" she says. "Yes, right now. There isn't always just one destiny and there isn't just one way to fulfill it. Hers isn't necessarily to create that breakthrough in physics. It could be or it could be something she's done, a paper she writes, a conversation she has that will inspire someone else. Say you shot her right now. The same thing might still happen and in fact you shooting her might be part of it. Or it could, pardon the pun, trigger a different fate. One in which she's simply destined to die and her legacy never occurs. That sort of outcome is less likely. It has to push against all the other possibilities to fulfill her fate."

"Predestination isn't predestination."

"Like I said, it's flexible. Each destiny, each town on that road of free will? There's more than one. There could be dozens all stacked up on each other. Or maybe there's just one. Make enough of the right choices and you can bend toward one destiny or another."

"How is that different from just having free will?"

"Because there are only so many variations," she says.

"They're not infinite. One of them will happen. This is how the Oracle changes things. It's not looking for a vague sort of future, it's looking for those predestined milestones."

"Then steers things toward the ones he wants."

"Yes," she says, "except that it doesn't just see one person's fate. It sees what triggering a particular fate will do to someone or something else. Nothing exists in a vacuum."

"If I shoot the physicist," I say, "I'm not just altering her life. I'm altering the lives of everyone she's touched. Mother, father, friends."

"As well as the people they interact with. A grieving brother misses an important meeting to attend his sister's funeral. Someone else gets a job meant for him. Both of those people's lives are altered forever."

"You're giving me a headache."

"Isn't destiny fun?"

Something about this is gnawing at the back of my mind. And then it clicks. "He works backward," I say. "Finds what he wants and then follows it back to see what changes he needs to make."

"I thought that was obvious," she says.

"It is, but the implication is that if you know what he wants, you can backtrack to him. Know what he'll need to do to make something happen. Get in his way."

"If you could see all the destinies of all the people someone might interact with, maybe. I seriously doubt you could."

"Could you?"

"No. I don't see fate like he does. I see *a* fate. One person's at a time. He sees all of them all at once. As well as the consequences."

Nicole's words echo back to me. Jimmy doesn't feel. He doesn't care what happens to anything outside his goal. If he needs to down a passenger plane so somebody could win a bet, then that's what he does.

"Somebody I know called him what happens when a monkey's paw fucks a hand grenade."

"Apt. In a way, he grants wishes, and they spread out in a wide area. They come with dangerous consequences, though I suppose they're only good or bad depending on what they are and who they happen to. Like most things."

"You said you can only see one person's fate at a time."

"I'm a god and as such I am beholden to my believers. They shape what I can and can't do. Anubis measures the weight of one's heart against a feather. He will never weigh it against, say, a microwave oven.

"They see—saw—me as a very personal god. A god who knew a person's fate and cared about that fate. I can see yours because you're here. And though I'll remember it, I don't see it side by side with another."

"You can see my fate?" I say.

"I've ever only run into its like a few times over thousands of years."

"Great. That does not sound good. My fate is like having a rare kind of bone cancer."

"It's actually rather fascinating. Do you want to know what it is?"

"Not particularly, no," I say.

"You don't have one." And she's gone.

Chapter 12

To say I knock on Nicole's door would imply a level of ci-
vility I'm not feeling. I damn near blow it off its hinges
with a spell before she finally opens it. I shove my way
past her into the foyer with its dust-covered piano.

"Hello to you, too," she says.

"Can Jimmy see you?"

"He sees just fine."

"That's not what I meant and you fucking know it. Can
he see you?" A silence that draws out just a beat too long.

"Sort of," she says.

"I am done with cryptic bullshit. The fuck does that
mean?"

"If I weren't his Keeper, no, he wouldn't be able to see
me. As it stands I'm . . . a little blurry."

"Blurry."

"He can sort of see the shape of my future and events,
but not very well."

"Anything else you want to tell me about?"

"No," she says. "I swear. I'm not—"

"He also can't affect you with his powers."

"Goddammit. No, he can't. Not as much as with most
people. And if I'm directly involved in a situation—"

"He loses all visibility to it, period."

"Not entirely. Like I said, I'm blurry. How do you
know all this?" she says.

"A better question is how come you didn't tell me

about it? This is why we weren't affected by the reality quake last night, isn't it?"

"Probably, yeah," she says. "Eric, I hadn't seen you in almost thirty years and we spent most of last night escaping a burning casino and fighting a spray-foam golem. When the fuck was I going to tell you?"

"Are you in on this? Is this whole thing bullshit?"

"What? No."

"I don't believe that for a second," I say. "Convince me you're not working with Jimmy."

"Or what?"

"I'm leaning toward beating you to death, but a bullet to the head's a good option, too."

"Finish what you started thirty years ago?" she says. "Go ahead. You'll just speed up the inevitable. I'm already dying."

"Welcome to the club. We all are."

"Fuck you, Eric. This is lung cancer. It's been in remission since the night we made Jimmy. Now it's exploded. If I don't find him soon, I'm fucked."

Now that I know what to look for, I can see it through Mictlantecuhtli's sight. Tumors in her lungs, down her intestines, liver, stomach. It's eating away at her bones, carving divots out of her spine. Most people I'd wonder how they're even walking around, but she's a mage and we can be stupidly difficult to put down. Then the vision fades.

"Shit. Fine. You have lung cancer. So fucking what?"

"You think I'd be okay with this death sentence if I was working with Jimmy?" she says.

I want this to be simple. I hate this town. I hate these people. I want someone to blame so I can beat the shit out of them and call it a day.

"No," I say. "You're too much of a narcissist to do that."

"And fuck you too. Eric, I need to find Jimmy. I've only got a few months left." It's more like a couple weeks, but she doesn't need to know that.

"I'm working on that," I say. "Assuming David has him, I've got someone looking into where he might be holding him."

"Good. Now who told you about how Jimmy can't see you?"

"I have sources," I say. In other words I'm not about to tell her what they are. "What else should I know?"

"Oh, *sources*. You mean your sources didn't tell you about all the other stuff? The powers of flight and the extra five inches it adds to your dick?"

"Okay, yes. I'm an asshole. But I have a history of shit with you in case you don't recall. So if—"

A flare of magic out on the street stops me cold. Someone's pulling power from the pool. Nicole feels it too. She spins toward the door and I can see in her eyes she's about to do something stupid.

"If you cast a spell right now, we're fucked," I say.

"What?"

"That's bait. Whoever's out there knows we're in here, but they don't know where in here. You do that and I guarantee a lone mage on the street will be the least of our problems. You got a back exit?"

"I've got an exit to the garage through a safe room," she says. "If we have to we can hole up in it. It's through the kitchen. The fridge pulls out. The door's behind it."

I'm not crazy about safe rooms. Just means you're stuck in one place while people are outside trying to get in. Give them enough time, they will. Having an exit is good, but it also means we're not sneaking past anybody.

I draw my gun and chamber a round. "We're gonna go old school on this. You got a gun?"

"Not on me. I don't normally need one."

"Fair enough. Come on." I have Nicole hang back as I crouch-walk my way through the den. The kitchen's around the corner. I can't see anyone, but I hear a click and the scrape of a window opening.

I break into a run, clear the corner, and put two bullets into a guy who's just gotten through the open window. His partner behind him starts firing at me.

I dive for cover behind the kitchen island, glass showering the floor with glinting shards. A crunch of glass behind me. I turn and almost shoot Nicole and have a split-second pang of regret when I don't.

"They know where we are now," I say. "Go ahead and let loose."

She nods then closes her eyes. I can feel her drawing a lot of power from the pool. I've never known how strong a mage she is, but if this is any indication, a fight with her would be all sorts of not fun.

"There are three left. At least one mage. One's coming around to the patio door, one's upstairs heading down. The mage is still on the street."

"Let me know when the patio guy's almost there." I aim at the sliding glass door. The curtains are drawn and I don't know whatever locator spell Nicole's using. I'm probably going to go through a lot of bullets.

"Now," she says. She tugs the curtain to the side with a spell and I see him. Two shots. One hits him in the head and he goes down.

"There's another—" she starts, but doesn't get a chance to finish. Our sidewalk mage does something, Nicole's eyes roll into the back of her head, and she hits the floor.

They know where we are, me roughly, Nicole specifically. But this works both ways. I can tell they're in the foyer. I hear footsteps. I'm just a tic too slow getting my shield up. My gun turns red-hot and I toss it away before it can do more than singe a little. By the time it hits the floor it's glowing white and melting.

The mage steps into the kitchen. A man wearing goggles, a bandana around his face, and black BDUs like the rest of these clowns.

I bolster my shield and duck. He looks a little amused as to why I would duck if I have a shield up, but finds out very quickly when the ammunition in my gun cooks off, blowing out bullet fragments and hot brass like the world's stupidest grenade.

He drops, clutching his face and screaming. A familiar weight appears in my hand, the straight razor already open. The fact that it always has a better idea when I need it than I do is starting to get a little creepy.

I take the opportunity to finish off the mage with a slash at his throat. Since his hands are in the way I take them off at the wrist.

Two down, two to go. One of them comes in through the shattered patio door. Without Nicole spotting targets, I don't know they're there until they're shooting at me.

The shield absorbs the kinetic energy of the bullets, bouncing them harmlessly to the floor. I wait for him to reload, then drop the shield and run at him.

He backs away at just the right moment and instead of catching him, the razor just takes off the entire front end of his gun.

Guy's fast, I'll give him that much. He's got a Ka-Bar combat knife out before I complete the swing. He jabs, hitting me in the chest. A flare of magic from my tattoos, and instead of sinking into a lung the blade slides off a rib. I fucking hate that, but I hate the alternative more.

I hit him with a push spell, but he's a beefy guy and I don't put in enough power to do more than push him back a foot or so. Still, it's enough to give me the room I need to take another swing at him.

He brings up the knife to block and the razor goes through it like it's made out of paper, leaving only about an inch of blade left.

I can't see his face, but his body language tells me he was not expecting that. Turns out he's not expecting the next bit where I swing up, catching him in the belly, and draw the blade up through his abdomen, sternum, and halfway up his throat, either.

There's a bit of flailing as his guts spill out onto the floor. Turns out when you slice through a guy's heart and a lung they don't last very long. Who knew?

Now where is number four? I get my answer before I can even finish the thought when a bullet zips by my ear, nudged away just enough by the protective spells in my tattoos.

I spin and get the shield reoriented in time to stop the next couple of rounds. This assassin is standing with his back to the counter where his buddy who tried to get in through the window is leaking all sorts of fluids into the sink.

Far be it from me to look a gift corpse in the mouth. I animate the body, puppeting it to reach out and wrap its arms around the guy's neck in a sleeper hold.

Sort of a sleeper hold. I have the corpse snap the guy's neck with a thought, then release the body, letting it fall back onto the counter.

Nicole is coming around, blinking and dazed, but she's alive. I help her to her feet. She wobbles a bit.

"Where are they?" she says, her voice groggy.

"Far as I can tell they're all dead. You happen to have a first aid kit?" I say.

She lifts her arm toward the fridge. "Safe room. Push in that edge and it'll pop away from the wall." I do, it does, and we're closing the swinging fridge behind us and lowering a security door.

It's less a saferoom and more like a safeapartment. Kitchenette, bathroom, bed. Shelves along one wall hold food, supplies. This place is built for a longer haul than a couple hours waiting for the police to arrive.

"You okay?" I say.

"Yeah, I think so. But you're not."

"Common occurrence. That first aid kit?"

"One second." Nicole goes to a shelf and pulls down a fully stocked EMT case. I clot the blood in the knife wound with a spell. I find a couple packs of QuikClot gauze and wrap that around my chest. If it starts bleeding again, the QuikClot should take care of it and I won't have to think about it too much.

It takes a minute to get the dressing secured because I don't trust Nicole enough to get anywhere near me to help. It's not ideal, but I've done it enough times to know it'll hold.

"Who the hell were those people?" Nicole says.

"Not the same sort of weekend warriors that hit Rachel's place, but I'll bet the same people are behind it."

"You think they were compelled?"

I think about that for a second. The one's at Rachel's place all thought they were there going after something they weren't. Not mind control so much as mind nudging.

"Maybe," I say. "Possibly by the mage out front?"

"Shit," she says. "And you killed him."

"And then some," I say, irritated. I just saved her ass and this is the shit I get. Hell, I saved her ass from me wanting to kill her, too. I deserve a fucking medal.

"We can go out there and try to ask him, but I'm betting he's got bullet shards in his brain. We're going to have company soon if we don't get the hell out of here."

"I—"

"You want to stick around, knock yourself out. I don't particularly want to be here when reinforcements show

up. Stay here or shut up and grab whatever you need so
we can get the hell out."

———

Turns out Nicole travels as light as I do. After she scans
the house with her vision spell and we're clear no one's
still alive inside, we leave the safe room, grab her stuff,
and take off, ditching the Porsche in a parking lot for an
E-Class Mercedes.

None of the men who came for us left ghosts, and their
bodies were all too messed up to get them to talk otherwise. Getting a dead man to speak when you've eviscer-
ated it with extreme prejudice is a bit of a challenge. I
really need to find a less messy way to kill people and a
faster way to get them to talk.

I wish it were as simple as calling up somebody's soul,
but with everyone going off to who knows where when
they die, I don't know how I would even find them. I'll
have to work on that.

I question a lot of my life choices, but the one I regret
most, even more than leaving L.A. and my sister, is taking Nicole and Sebastian up on their offer to make the
Oracle.

All I had to do was say no. But could I have? Maybe
today, but maybe not. And back then? No way would I
have passed up that opportunity.

Nobody has stupid ideas like mages have stupid ideas.
That's how we learn magic, grow our power. It's also
largely how we die. You have no idea how many of us
burn to death because we were teaching ourselves how to
create a fireball in an enclosed space.

Mage kids are just as stupid as normal kids. They just
have more ways to blow themselves up.

Just figuring out how our knacks work, or even what
they are, is a huge pain in the ass. I got lucky. I happened

upon a dead frog when I was an infant and made it get up and dance around. I thought it was awesome.

My grandfather, who was watching me at the time, did not. He'd had a bad experience with German necromancers in World War II. Seeing what I could without even breaking a sweat brought all his PTSD screaming back to the surface. Almost killed me. Probably would have worked out better for everybody if he had.

"Where are we going?" Nicole says. That's a good question. I get an answer from a text.

"How do you feel about roller derby?"

Chapter 13

"Diane, Nicole. Nicole, Diane."

"We've met," Diane says in a voice you could flash-freeze half of North America with.

"This is your information broker?" Nicole says. "You have got to be fucking kidding me." Nicole does a one-eighty and heads for the exit.

"Don't let the door hit your ass on the way out," Diane says. Nicole comes back, crouches down, and gets into Diane's face.

"I do not forget and I do not forgive," Nicole says. She turns to me. "And you better watch your ass around her. She'll stab you in the back."

"Kinda like you, then," I say.

"Oh, fuck you," Nicole says and stomps out of the building. Diane and I watch her go.

"You and Nicole, huh?"

"Me and never Nicole," I say. I really don't care what their beef is with each other. Not my circus, not my monkeys. "You have something for me?"

"I do," she says. She hands me a flash drive. "Everything's on there. Which casino, which vault, most of the security. Only thing I could identify on the magical side is a couple alarm spells. There's more, but I couldn't get anything else exactly."

"Jesus. I can see why the Werthers work with you."

"Still tracking down Rudy," she says. "Elusive fucker. One more thing. Really, don't trust Nicole."

"I don't," I say. "Didn't trust her years ago. Don't trust her now." She cocks her head like a dog trying to figure out a math problem. Then she finally gets it.

"Holy shit. You're the guy."

"If you mean the guy who fucked up and didn't shoot her when I had her trussed up out in the middle of nowhere, then yeah. I'm the guy."

"Wow. She really hates you."

"Most people do."

"You don't get it. I mean *really* hates you. Now get outta here. I don't want to be in the blast radius."

———

"Got what we need?" Nicole says when I get into the car. She's in the driver's seat with her arms crossed and looking pissy.

"All right here. Or most of it, anyway."

"Good. We're meeting Rachel at the club."

"Candyland? You roped the Twins into this?"

"Not me," Nicole says, pulling the car away from the curb. "Rachel. She trusts them."

"You don't?"

"Not as much as she does. You gonna ask?"

"Nope."

"Diane and I dated," she says. "Few years back."

"What part of 'Nope' was open to interpretation? I really don't care, Nicole. Stop trying to act like we're friends. We're not. We never will be."

She doesn't say anything and we spend the rest of the trip in silence.

———

It's weird seeing Candyland in the daytime. Even weirder once we're ushered inside by one of the Twins' bouncers, still as immaculately dressed as he would be in the evening.

All the lights are on, revealing those dim corners filled with mystery as just more matte black wall. We follow the bouncer through multiple locked doors to a back hallway lined with more private rooms like the ones upstairs. These feel more exclusive, somehow. Certainly more private. The rooms for the really high rollers.

"They're down in front, sir, ma'am," the bouncer says, opening the last door at the end of the hall. I catch a glimpse of what I'm walking into before I step through the door.

"They have a movie theater back here?" I say. It feels beyond extravagant or even tacky. It's not a big theater, but it's not small. We're not talking a widescreen TV here. This is a full-on movie screen.

"I suddenly want popcorn," Nicole says as she heads down the aisle to the front, where Rachel and the Twins are standing around a table looking at a laptop.

"The couple of the hour!" Ken or maybe Kendra says. "I understand you have a gift for us." I toss them the flash drive.

"Should have most of what we need in there. Not much on the wards other than that a few of them are alarms."

"Mademoiselle, would you be so kind?" They hand Rachel the drive. She slots it into the laptop, hits a key, and the movie screen comes alive with row after row of files.

"Assuming it's not all bullshit, I think we're in business," Rachel says.

"What's that one? Research," I say. Rachel opens the folder and a stream of files listed Iteration_1, Iteration_2, and so on, all the way down to thirteen. Rachel opens number thirteen and the plans for a device that looks like a cross between a helmet and a birdcage, sitting on top of something like a flat game console, appear.

"You thinking what I'm thinking?" I say to Nicole.

"That this is what's letting him change the past and causing the quakes?" she says. "Maybe. Looks big enough to hold him."

"I was thinking more that I could really use a drink, but yeah, that too. Can you scroll down?" I say. There's a drawing that shows a wiring diagram with leads going toward a rectangular hatch on the bottom of the device, connecting to a slightly kidney-shaped space beneath.

"It runs on batteries?" Rachel says.

"I've never seen batteries shaped like that," Nicole says.

It reminds me of something. When it comes to me, it takes everything I have to not let on that I know exactly what that space is for.

Gabriela's got a dead friend, Joe Sunday, who's animated by an opal in his chest. It's one of a group of four, five? I don't remember, but they've gotten plenty of people murdered over the years as mages the world over all tried to get their hands on any one of them like it's the Maltese Falcon.

The stone in Sunday's chest is insanely powerful and nobody, at least nobody I know, really knows what it does. The rest of the stones have all disappeared, sunk to the bottom of the ocean, landed in warehouses boxed up like the Ark of the Covenant. They have a very long and very bloody history.

Herb said Jimmy would need a lot of power to do his revisionist history bullshit and I can't think of anything more perfect for it than one of the stones.

I weigh telling the others about it, but decide to keep it to myself. If anyone else knows, it would be the Twins, and they're not talking. I decide to let them think I'm as clueless as anyone else in this room.

"We can cross off him being powered by AAs," I say. "Maybe D cells?"

"This isn't what we need," Nicole says. "What about the vault? The alarms?"

"Gimme a few minutes." Rachel goes searching for the files we need to look at. The Twins take a seat in one of the extremely posh, wide leather chairs that have plenty of arm and leg room. A really unusual amount of legroom.

"What do you show in here?" I say.

"Eric, I'm disappointed. You're usually much more astute than this. What do you think we show in here?" they say.

Of course. "Seems a bit excessive for porn."

"My boy, you haven't lived until you've seen a fifteen-foot penis."

"I'll put it on my bucket list."

"Got it," Rachel says, and brings up a few different diagrams.

"Pretty standard stuff," she says. "Doesn't mean I like it, but I'm not seeing anything out of the ordinary. It's a strong vault, that's for damn sure. Twenty-five-inch steel reinforced concrete panels, stainless-steel cladding. Same for the door. Thirty locking cylinders, dual-locking mechanism, four timed mechanisms. Jesus. More I look at it the more I don't like it. This thing is a class-5 vault door sealing a class-3 vault."

"None of that means a goddamn thing to me," I say.

"Vaults aren't designed to be impenetrable," Rachel says. "They're just to slow you down. The longer it takes, the more likely you're going to get caught before you break in.

"A class-3 vault's guaranteed to take two hours of drilling to get through any one side. A class-5 door is guaranteed for twenty hours of drilling or ten minutes of sustained blasting if you try to blow it open."

"Ten minutes doesn't sound bad," I say.

"You start setting off a bunch of high explosives and, believe me, ten minutes is a long time. And it's not just one blast," Rachel says.

"Other options?"

"Torch and a drill will take forever. And it's iffy. It's got a copper plate sandwiched in between different layers. You burn through, the copper melts, reseals the hole. And behind that is a glass plate. You can drill through that carefully, but you'll likely crack it. That happens and it triggers more bolts to engage. Then you're not getting through without a week of working it with heavy equipment."

"How about a pyromancer?" I say.

"Tough," she says. "Just burning through the vault door before you even reach the copper and glass is gonna take a lot of power. And that glass plate's tough. You don't heat it up slowly enough, the temperature differential will crack it. But if we can, then we can fill the cavity with foam and prevent the bolts from firing at all. You know anybody that can do that?"

"No," I say, "but maybe Bridget does. Why are you all staring at me?"

"Bridget's been dead for years," Rachel says.

"Not what David told me. Said she's in prison after burning herself out on a job. He said he had one teleportation charm to get you all out and couldn't get to her. When he got back she was already surrounded by cops." Silence.

"You are fucking kidding me," Rachel says, voice quiet.

"Let me guess," I say. "David was being less than truthful? I am shocked." By the look of fury and red climbing her face, I'd say I'm right.

"That sonofabitch," she says. "That was the last job we

ever did. He told us she'd died. We had a funeral for her. I'm going to fucking kill him."

"She got a funeral?" I say. "I didn't get a funeral." Nobody's paying any attention to me.

"He said she burned herself out?" the Twins say. "That doesn't sound right."

"Didn't sound right to me either," I say. I pull out my phone and start typing. "I've seen her cut through heavier vault doors without breaking a sweat."

"I can't believe he told us she'd died," Rachel says. "And that I believed it."

"Bridget Connolly," I say, reading off a Nevada Department of Corrections website. "Offender ID 633392. In for armed robbery."

"She should be out by now," the Twins say. I scroll down her record.

"Might be the fifteen assault charges she racked up over the years in lockup." Bridget rarely gave any fucks. I can't imagine her losing her magic and being locked up would help that at all.

"Where?" Rachel says.

"Florence McClure Women's Correctional Center," I say. "Where is that?"

"It's up the fucking street." Rachel shoots out of her seat, heads to the doors. Stops halfway there. "Well?"

"Well, what?" I say.

"We're breaking her out," Rachel says. She cuts me off before I can say anything. "Do not fucking argue with me."

"Fine," I say. "But at least hit a drive-through. I haven't eaten all day."

———

Florence McClure Women's Correctional Center is a series of three squat, connected, white buildings north of the Strip and just west of Nellis Air Force Base. As you can guess there's not much around it and nowhere to hide if you broke out. The land it's on is all flat, empty desert.

Normally it can take weeks to arrange a prisoner meeting, but we've jumped the line with a little magic. Rachel and I showed up about an hour ago posing as Bridget's lawyers and charmed the guards into thinking we were already scheduled.

I've got a HI, MY NAME IS sticker slapped onto my chest telling the world that I'M A SHIT HOT ATTORNEY WHO YOU TOTALLY CAN TRUST and Rachel has a charm bracelet that's doing pretty much the same thing.

"You guys new?" the guard walking us to an interview room says. Older guy. Probably been here for years. "I don't think Ol' Fireball's ever had any visitors."

He's leading us past rows of locked doors with wired glass inserts to look in on the prisoners. Half of the doors are open with guards going through doing cell searches.

"You call her Ol' Fireball?" Rachel says. She glances at me. If we're lucky maybe that actually means something.

"Yeah," he says. "Sets somethin' on fire at least once a week. Least that's what people keep sayin'. She's never been caught doing it. I have my doubts, but somebody called her Ol' Fireball a while back after somebody else's head burst into flame when they were working the kitchens. Don't know why they blamed her. She was in solitary at the time."

"Not exactly a model prisoner?" I say.

The guard laughs. "Oh, that's a good one." He stops in front of a large green door. "She's already in there. I need to prep you on her. Don't get too close. She's chained up, but she's a biter. Anything goes to shit just holler. I'll be just out here. And pardon my saying so, but I really hope things go to shit. See these scars on my neck?"

They're ugly scars. Like he was mauled by a tiger, the marks going from the bottom of his jaw on the left side to the hollow of his throat. "She did that, huh?"

"Couple years ago. I still need an excuse for some payback. So, like I said, anything goes weird in there you just holler. I'll take care of the rest." I'm sure you will.

"Appreciated," Rachel says, her voice tight with rage.

He bangs on the door. "Comin' in." A loud buzzer sounds and he pulls the door open, ushers us through.

"The fuck is this about, Murphy?" A woman in orange scrubs sits handcuffed and tethered to a stainless-steel table bolted to the cement floor. She's thin to the point of being gaunt, hair shaved in a dirty blond buzz cut, skeletal fingers nervously tapping the table. She has fresh bruises on her face.

"Your lawyers are here to see you," the guard says.

"I don't have—" Her eyes go wide and she shuts up the second she sees us.

"Miz Connolly," Rachel says. "We're here from the Carter and McManus law firm to talk to you about your upcoming parole hearing."

"Parole? Her?" Murphy says. "That'll be the day. She's gonna die in here."

"Fuck you, Murphy. And get the fuck out. These are my lawyers. I don't need you listening in to my shit."

"I hear more than enough of your shit already. Seriously, you two. Don't trust her. She'll probably try to shank one of you."

"We'll be fine, but thanks for the concern," Rachel says. She casts a small spell and Murphy's eyes glaze over for a second.

"Sure. Yeah. Have fun." He's all smiles as he walks out the door. It locks behind him.

"You motherfuckers," Bridget says. "If I wasn't chained to this table I would fucking gut you both."

"Bridget—"

"You left me to fucking rot in here, Rachel. And you're here now to, what, gloat? Fuck you. And what the hell are you doing here? I figured you'd never come back to this shitshow of a town after you fucked us on that last job."

"I'm not here because I want to be, Bridget," I say. "And don't blame Rachel. She didn't know you were alive until a couple hours ago."

"No," Bridget says. "That's— How—?"

"David told us you were dead," Rachel says.

"And he told me the other day that you'd burnt out and got sent to jail," I say. "We compared notes. Before we go any further." I cast a silence spell over us. Bridget reels back as if she's been slapped.

"You felt that?" Rachel says.

"Of course I fucking felt it," she says. "I just can't do it."

"No, that's not right," I say. Rachel nods agreement.

"That was a nothing spell," she says. "If you were burnt out, you wouldn't have even noticed he was casting it."

"I—No. I don't know why you're here or what the hell you want, but I am not doing this. Murphy, we're done here." She pulls on her chains like it's going to help.

"He can't hear you," I say.

"We're here to break you out," Rachel says. Bridget freezes.

"Don't fucking say that," Bridget says. "Please. I finally accepted I wasn't ever getting out of here. Don't dangle that shit in front of me."

"We're serious," Rachel says. "We can walk you right out if you want."

"Can you see this?" I say. I'm looking at Bridget's chest. "There's something here."

"They're my tits," Bridget says.

"No," Rachel says. "I don't. What is it?"

I didn't see anything at first and then, like one of those magic picture images that suddenly turns into a 3-D whale, I do. There's something inside her chest the size and shape of a small starfish, just under the skin.

"Unless your tits are shaped like an Old West sheriff's badge and stuck to your sternum, I don't think that's what I'm looking at," I say. It's giving me a headache, which hasn't happened with Mictlantecuhtli's sight before. I figure out why when I blink and it turns out I'm seeing the same thing twice.

One is with this freaky leftover god vision and the other is less sight than it is a sense of something dead inside Bridget's chest.

"I don't know what the hell it is, but I think it's encased in, I don't know, a cyst? Whatever it is, it's dead flesh. Or the thing itself is. Hard to say."

"Any idea what it is?" Rachel says.

"I don't even know what you're talking about. There's something in my chest?"

"Yeah," Rachel says. "You don't have any weird surgical hardware or anything, do you?"

"No."

"You think it might be something that's blocking her ability to channel?" Rachel says.

"Probably, yeah," I say.

"Wait, what? There's something inside my chest? Can you get it out?" She unzips her jumpsuit, yanks it open. There's no surgical scar or anything that would indicate some sort of implant. The skin isn't even raised, which I would expect considering how thin she is.

Bridget starts to claw at her chest. "Fuck, get it out. Get it the fuck out of me. I need a knife, I'll get it out myself."

"I think I can do it a little more cleanly than that," I say.

"Just fucking do it."

This one's tricky. I just can't rip the thing out of her chest. I don't know what it would do. But I can pass the dead flesh through the living. Theoretically?

"I think this is gonna hurt," I say. "A lot."

I concentrate on the object. No, on what's surrounding the object. But I can't quite get a hold on it. Then I will Mictlantecuhtli's sight to come and there it is, the thing stuck in her chest clear as day. That's the first time I've been able to call the sight on command. I have no idea how.

I get a mental grip on the object and start to pull it through. Bridget screams. I keep pulling. Damn thing does not want to go. Crap. This isn't working.

"I'm really sorry about this," I say, and yank it out of her. It doesn't tear away from her skin so much as from her soul, leaving no scar on one and a massive hole in the other.

Bridget slumps forward against the table, unconscious. A bloody wad of pulsing flesh the size of a silver dollar hovers in front of me before falling to the table with a bloody, wet splat.

I peel bits of already drying and desiccating flesh off the mass while Rachel retches and holds on to Bridget. She might regret that once Bridget wakes up and starts losing her shit.

The skin peels off the item like an orange, leaving me with a thin metal star two inches across with the words "Fac potestatem eius se ipsum ligare" carved into it.

"Jesus, what the hell is that?" Rachel says.

"I think it's a curse in Latin," I say. "I think the grammar's fucked up, but it's something like 'Bind her power to itself'? Thinking David managed to get this into her and it blocked her ability to channel any magic."

"I am so going to fucking kill him," Rachel says.

"No," Bridget says, sitting up and groaning. "Motherfucker's mine. Holy shit. I'd forgotten what this felt like." She puts her hand out, palm up and a flame appears. It twists into the shape of a ballerina and jumps from fingertip to fingertip.

Bridget starts laughing and then crying.

Rachel folds her up into her arms. "I'm so sorry," she says. "I didn't know." Soon Rachel is crying, too, Bridget hanging on to her as if to a life preserver thrown out to her while she's drowning. She's been drowning for thirty years.

Thirty years. Fuck. So much time locked up in here with your entire identity gone but just out of reach. I've lost access to my magic before. More times than I care to think about, honestly. Enough that when it happens I know to ride it out. But the longest I've been without has been a week at most.

"It's okay," Bridget says, her voice hitching. "You came as soon as you found out. And Eric, fuck I hate you."

"Everybody keeps telling me that," I say.

"Well, you're a prick," she says. "But goddammit, thank you." She wipes her eyes and nose on her sleeve. "Now what was this about breaking out of here?"

"Give the word," I say. "We've got a car outside."

"Good. Good. But I need a little time. I got some shit to do here."

"I thought as much. We'll meet you in the car when you're done." Rachel and I get up and I drop the silence spell when we get to the door. Bridget's already out of her cuffs. They're nothing but a little puddle of slag on the floor.

"Hey, guard," I yell, banging on the door. "We're done here."

"She didn't bite you or anything, did she?" Murphy the guard says. "She can—holy shit." He tries to back out of the room and go for an alarm button on the wall, but I grab him and haul him back inside.

"Have fun, you two."

"Oh, we will," Bridget says. Her eyes are bright and her smile makes her look like a rabid hyena. Flames engulf both her hands. "Won't we, Murphy?"

I close the door on the guard's screaming and throw a silence spell at it. That should buy her some time. We breeze through the checkpoints and get to the car before the alarms go off.

"Was this a bad idea?" Rachel says. We stand at the car and watch the spectacle start.

"Oh, hell yes," I say. The roof of the main building erupts into flames a couple stories high. Somewhere in the distance there's a muffled explosion.

"Is she going to—you know."

"Kill everybody and burn the whole place to the ground? What do you think? Bridget and restraint are not two things that go well together."

I should have regrets. A lot of people are about to die. But strangely, I can't bring myself to care. Bridget's a shark, but she was thrown into the shark tank after having all her teeth pulled out. I'm amazed she survived this long. Then I remember Murphy's scars and realize it was more a case of everybody being locked in with her, not the other way around.

"We should have said something," Rachel says.

"Like what? 'Mind not taking thirty years of rage out on the people who made you feel like you were less than human and destroying the torture chamber it all happened in?' Yeah, I don't see that working."

The flames draw inward and begin to spin turning into a tornado of flame. I feel flares of deaths that, even at this distance, are giving me a sour stomach. Chunks of the roof, air vent ducts, aerials, pipes, anything that isn't bolted down, and quite a few things that are, tear off the building to be swept up into the maelstrom.

"I suppose," Rachel says. We watch the flames for a moment. "It is pretty, though." Can't argue with that.

The tornado drills into the building and when it breaks through it start to suck out whatever's inside. Tables, chairs, beds, people. The place holds over nine hundred inmates. No idea how many staff. I can barely hear the screams over the roar of the flames. The pain is starting to crawl up toward my head.

I felt the deaths of hundreds during the L.A. firestorm. At one point I got hit with a batch of five hundred or more. Knocked my ass out for a good twelve hours. Glad it did. I don't know that I would have survived the experience otherwise.

"This is gonna take a while," I say. "And I'd really rather not be here while it happens. Wanna grab something to eat? We never did hit a drive-through."

"Sure," Rachel says. "Sushi work for you?"

Though I can feel all the deaths happening inside, the rate seems to be slowing down. The punches of death feel less like getting slammed into by a hundred baseball bats and more like a hundred golf balls. It's not pleasant, but at least this I'm kind of used to.

I can tell she hasn't killed everyone in there, which means she's being selective. Good. Might make me feel less like a bastard for letting her out of that place.

I wonder if everyone Bridget's killing deserves it. But then what the hell does that even mean? And does it even matter? People die all the time. Good, bad, deserving, undeserving. When it comes down to it death is the only thing that ties us all together. Still, this whole spectacle is making me nauseous.

"Yeah," I say. "I could do sushi."

Chapter 14

Normally, mages try to avoid massive displays of magic. If the normals know what we can do, they'll get all pissed off at us—many not because we're heathens to burn at the stake, but because we won't share.

Fortunately, most people have a hard time accepting big magic. Small, yes. Rabbits out of hats, card tricks, blood curses against your enemies for every vile thing they've done to you. Seriously, have you seen how many revenge spells you can find out there?

But those are easy to shrug off. Yeah, people might believe in small magic, but most of them don't take it seriously.

Now big magic is a different story. On the one hand you can't exactly hide it. The L.A. firestorm, for example. Or the toxic cloud that's turned South L.A. into a wasteland.

People have a lot of theories about both of those. None of them are anywhere near the truth. Sure, magic's in some of them, but it's either Satan or Sexy Witches and not "Some dipshit necromancer pissed off a god and called a world of fiery shit down on the city."

I do like the Sexy Witches one, though.

Where this becomes a problem is when you land in the middle of the Venn diagram between big and small. Big enough to be noticeable, small enough that people ask questions. Mages get a little worried about those.

"And you let her do this?" Nicole says.

We've been back at Candyland for about an hour. Nicole, Rachel, and I are sitting at a table setup near the movie screen while the Twins handle Bridget, who cried all the way over from the prison. I'm assuming tears of joy, but whether it's for being out, getting her magic back, or destroying the nightmare funhouse she's been stuck inside for the last thirty years, I'm not entirely sure.

"We didn't 'let' her do anything," Rachel says. "Do you honestly think we could have stopped her?"

"People got her on camera hovering over the parking lot blowing up police cars."

"She can hover?" I say. "Did you know she could hover?"

Rachel ignores me. "People are gonna ask questions," she says. "Especially the police. Oh god is Jeff gonna be pissed. But this is not the epic fuck-up you think it is. Yeah, it's not great, but there have been far worse and we're fine."

"She's talking about me," I say. "I burned down one of the biggest cities in America and no torches and pitchforks. No pitchforks, at least. Vegas has to have a clean-up crew. Every big city does."

"That's not the point," Nicole says. "Now David is going to know she's out of prison and has her magic back."

"Oh. Huh."

"Yeah," Nicole says. "This wasn't just a jailbreak. It was a jail-pull-the-pin-out-of-the-grenade-and-hand-it-to-the-baby-break."

"Didn't really think this one through, did we?" Rachel says.

"Welcome to my world," I say. "We can figure out some way to counter it. Hell, it might even work in our favor. He doesn't know we have anything to do with this. He's gonna focus on keeping Bridget from killing him, not on somebody trying to rob him."

"Which means he'll be watching for her," Nicole says.

"Then we just make sure he doesn't see her until we want him to see her," I say. "We don't even know what we're going to do. If we want to freak out over anything, freak out over the wards and alarms on that vault door."

"I actually have a thought on that," Rachel says.

"Does it involve burning down another state prison?" Nicole says.

"Lucas."

"Seriously?" I say. "I vote for burning down another state prison."

"I thought you got along with him," Rachel says.

"I did," I say. "Until we ran into each other when he was trying to steal an artifact for himself and I was trying to steal it for somebody else."

"Who's Lucas?" Nicole says.

"How'd that turn out?" Rachel says.

"I got the artifact and left him hanging upside down over the display case. I heard he was still around so I figure he got out of it fine."

"Jesus Christ. Is this gonna be a problem?"

"Hope not."

"Who the hell is Lucas?" Nicole says.

"He's a wardcracker," I say. "One of the best. Thirty years ago, at least."

"We've worked with him before," Rachel says. "I haven't talked to him in a few years, though. We exchange the occasional Christmas card."

"He's clearly not in Vegas because he hasn't shown up to stick a knife in my chest," I say.

"No. He's in Reno last I heard. He's got a kid now."

"No shit?"

"Yeah. Cute as a button."

"Setting aside that he might have an issue with me, why would he show up?" I say. "I know why Nicole and I are doing this. I think I know why you're doing this. Pretty sure Bridget'll do anything as long as she can get a crack at David. But Lucas will want something to make it worth his time. And for the cost of putting up with me."

"You're forgetting us, my dear boy," the Twins say, coming down the aisle. "We're involved in this too, now."

"Okay, what do you two want?" I say.

"Nicole?" Ken or maybe Kendra says. "Would you be so kind?"

"We didn't just get vault plans from Diane," Nicole says, almost spitting out her name. "We have vault contents, too. He keeps everything cataloged for insurance purposes."

"He has a painting," Ken says.

"Reading Girl in White and Yellow by Henri Matisse," Kendra says. "It was stolen from the Kunsthal museum in Rotterdam some years back."

"You just want the painting?"

"It holds sentimental value," Ken says. "Henri was a dear friend."

"Okay," Rachel says. "We grab the painting, too. What about Lucas?"

"Send him a copy of the catalog," I say. "There's gotta be something in there he wants. Tell him it's like Christmas shopping."

"Before or after I tell him it's David's vault?"

"Tell him at the same time," Kendra says. "One of those two things will hook him and the other will reel him in. But maybe hold back Eric's participation at first."

"What's the deal with Lucas and David?" I say. "I know why he'd be pissed off at me, but David was really hostile when I brought his name up."

"Lucas fucked him out of twenty million bucks," Rachel says. "It was glorious."

"Holy shit. I need to buy that man a drink."

"First time David tried to buy a casino," the Twins say in their weird harmonic resonance. "Some run-down shack of a place out by the border. Lucas brokered the deal. Only the client didn't exist.

"Of course, David didn't find out about this until after the wire transfers had all gone through. And he couldn't exactly call the police because most of that money wasn't legally acquired."

"David must have shit a brick," I say. "He ever go after Lucas?"

"Oh, hell yeah," Rachel says. "A bunch of times. Everybody he sent came home in a body bag or not at all."

"Nice to see Lucas hasn't lost his touch."

"Can you trust this guy?" Nicole says. It's a little weird having her in this conversation. The Twins, Rachel, me. We're not family or even friends. More like a group of alcoholics at an AA meeting where we've all fallen off the wagon and stopped giving a shit. She's an outsider all the same.

Which makes me wonder again if we can trust her. I check myself. When did this become a "we"? I'm here for one reason. If I didn't think it'd get me killed I'd walk into the vault and grab Jimmy myself.

"With my life," Rachel says. "And I have. A few times. The question is whether or not he'll trust us."

"Why?" Nicole says.

"Besides me?" I say. "He's a little paranoid."

"Almost as much as Eric is," Rachel says.

"Almost," I say.

"Then what do we do?" Nicole says.

"Eric apologizes, for one," the Twins say.

"I did. Several times."

"Do it again."

"Jesus. Fine. Whatever gets him out here."

"I'll give him a call," Rachel says.

"Do we have a backup plan?" Nicole says.

"A lot of explosives?" I say.

"I can get that," Rachel says. "If, you know, we decide to go that route."

"Have you given any thought to how you're going to get away?" Kendra says. "Las Vegas police take a dim view of casino robbery. People tend to get caught and get dead."

"I think the police are going to be the least of our worries," I say.

"Yeah," Nicole says. "Once David figures out what's happening, there's gonna be a lot of people with guns and spells."

"First off, you all need to figure out how you're getting out of town," Bridget says, stepping into the room. She looks a lot better than when we got her. She's got some color in her cheeks, some of the tension has bled out of her shoulders, and she's wearing real clothes.

"What about you?" I say.

"I'm staying to kill David." I know that sort of phrasing, that tone. She's not planning on leaving, period.

"How about you two? I know you're not leaving. You gonna be shielded enough when the shit hits the fan?"

"We will be perfectly fine," they say.

"For me it depends on Jimmy," Nicole says. "If he wants to stay, we stay." I can see Rachel is about to say something that she's probably going to regret. I cut her off at the pass.

"Rachel? What about you?"

"What?"

"You've got a lot to lose out here."

"I don't know yet. I have to check on a couple things. But if I have to disappear, I'm good to go." She runs a prepper school. Of course she's prepared.

"And you?" the Twins say. "How will you be getting away?"

"Not sure yet," I say. "Depends on what I get out of Jimmy. Figure I'll burn that bridge when we get to it."

"Don't you mean cross?"

"No," I say.

I've been running on adrenaline since I got into town and my body's finally cashing all those bad checks I've been writing. Sleeping in a jail cell does not do wonders for one's back.

"But I can't think about this shit anymore tonight," I say. "I'll talk to you all in the morning." I get up, grab my messenger bag.

"Where are you staying?" Ken says.

"Shitty motel," I say.

"At least it's not that filthy jail cell," Kendra says.

"That was last night."

"Dear god. With that horrid ghost of yours. No, you're staying here tonight," Ken says. "We have plenty of rooms. And yes, before you say anything, they are immaculate, and I am insulted at the insinuation."

"I didn't say anything."

"You thought it very loudly. In fact, you're all staying here. Aside from the fact that you all look like you've been sat on by an elephant, you're also safer here."

Ugh. Elephants. Which reminds me. "Nicole, did Jimmy ever say anything about fate?"

"Not that I recall? Why?"

"Oh, just something I heard," I say. "You know, I'll be just fine in my shitty motel."

"If David knows about Bridget," Kendra says, "he may very well be on the lookout for both her and you."

"Why Eric?" Nicole says.

"Playing the odds," I say. "Trouble follows me around like a brain-damaged puppy. Fine. You made your point. I won't say no to a place to crash." Bridget leans in close to Kendra and whispers in their ear. Kendra's eyes pop.

"My word, where are my manners," they say. "Of course. I'm sure we can find someone who would be happy to indulge."

"Thanks," she says. "It's been a while."

"And on that note, I'm going to bed," I say. "I will talk to you all once I'm conscious."

"We would be remiss if we did not offer other hospitality," Kendra says. "Or company."

"I'm good," I say.

"Same," says Rachel.

"Yeah, I'm, uh . . . No. But thanks," Nicole says. "Which way to a room?"

"Pick any one you like. These are the private quarters and we can guarantee no one will disturb you."

"Fantastic," I say. "Happy to not have another night of prison farts."

"Word," Bridget says.

———

"She burned down the whole prison?" Amanda says on the phone. The music upstairs isn't loud, but I can hear it growing as the club opens. The fact that it's not slamming into my temples with a jackhammer is a testament to how well sound-proofed this place is.

"What I saw was impressive. But I guess I missed the real show, because she hovered over the place and spun in a circle spewing fire."

"Did she kill everybody?"

"I don't think so. The news reports made it sound like a lot of the inmates escaped. I'm sure they're still tallying up the dead. I felt a lot die, even when I wasn't close. But that place held like nine hundred people and I didn't feel nearly that many die."

"Hell of a jailbreak," she says. "I feel sorry for the Cleanup Crew."

"If they catch up with Bridget they'll try to hit her up for some of the cost. They will if they're stupid, at least. After all this time, she gives less than zero fucks about anything."

"I heard the casinos pay for a lot of that out there."

"They used to. Not sure about now," I say. "Doesn't mean they didn't send around leg-breakers to recoup the loss. How you holding up out there?" I sit down on the bed and everything hurts the second I start to bend any of my joints.

"Me? You're the one getting stabbed and shot at," she says. "Plus, I'm not the one making old man noises."

"I am not making old man noises. I'm making young beat-up man noises. I'm only a month old, remember?"

"I hate it when I'm the adult," Amanda says.

"Nobody's tried to shoot you yet?"

"It hasn't gotten that far," she says. "I only had to turn a few of them to glass to get most of them to back off."

I would expect her to be dealing with a higher number of assassins than usual since she's got more people gunning for her than just her family. But I doubt many of them know what they're going up against, yet.

People have been trying to kill Amanda her entire life. Sure, her family technically couldn't lay a finger on her because some twelfth-century patriarch cursed the family so if any of them killed any other, they'd suffer the same fate. But apparently, it took only a few years before they started to realize why family heads kept exploding. If the killers were indirect enough about it, hiring assassins through multiple cutouts, they usually survived. And the Werthers got really good at it.

But it also meant that they had to get really good at surviving, too. That's made Amanda one of the best.

"This plan to get back your friend's head . . ."

"Whoa. Jimmy's not my friend."

"Fine, your 'one-time roommate whose head you just so happened to have cut off to turn into a carnival fortune telling machine.' Better?"

"Yes, thank you," I say.

"You think it's going to work?"

"I honestly don't know. I know the direct approach won't. David's too much of a stuck-up prick to say yes if I ask him nicely."

"Blow up the vault?"

"Something that big and noisy brings the rest of the city's casino mages down on our heads. An attack on one is seen as an attack on all. Make one of them look weak in public and it reflects on all of them. I had to contend with some of that crap in Atlantic City a while back. It's a pain in the ass to deal with."

"How'd you fix it?"

"Killed a lot of people."

"Why did I even ask? So why not do that to David?"

"Easiest option, actually," I say. "The other mages won't give a fuck since it won't make them look bad. I'm all for killing him, but only after we get in the vault. Beforehand is just going to make it more complicated than it needs to be."

"So, a heist."

"This isn't a heist. This is slapping candy out of a baby's mouth. This is his private vault. It's not going to be as secure as the casino's and we don't necessarily even need to be all that quiet about it. He's gonna know it's us as soon as he finds out about the theft. We just need to slow that down enough so we can get out of there."

"But then he's going to come hunting you."

"That's the hope," I say. "Bridget and Rachel both want a piece of him. I think Bridget's claim trumps Rachel's, but they'll have to work that out between themselves."

"You know some really fucked-up people," Amanda says. "Not judging. I mean, you've met my family."

"I don't disagree with you." We share a moment of silence for how jacked up our lives are.

"Heard from Diane," she says. "Got a lead on the guy selling DIY golems and the opal."

"Don't tell me they're linked."

"Those two, no."

"I'm not gonna like this, am I?"

"Let's start with the opal."

"Oh yes, let's."

"Smart ass. One of the opals was with a collector in Belarus. About three years ago he got gunned down in his home. Only one thing was stolen."

"Let me guess," I say. "An opal?"

"It went on auction about a year later. I don't have the buyer's name, but I do have a manifest that shows it was heading to— Come on, that's your cue."

"Las Vegas."

"I haven't been able to narrow it down any further than that," she says.

"I don't think we really need to," I say. "Seems pretty obvious."

"This is my OCD, goddammit. Don't take that away from me."

"You know what would be useful? Finding out who built that device. It sure as hell wasn't David. He can barely tie his own shoes."

"Shouldn't be too hard," she says. "Artificers aren't all that common. They might not still be in Vegas, though."

"Anything will help," I say. "The golem?"

"This is a fun one," Amanda says. "Rudy Cunningham is one of the biggest providers of magic reagents for the entire Western United States."

"No shit. I always wondered where that shit got sourced."

I had a friend back in L.A. Kind of guy you go to when you need something you can't buy in a regular store. I'm not talking clean guns, though he did sell those. I mean magical reagents, devices, favors. He worked in volume. You wanted half a ton of mugwort, five thousand hands of glory, he was the guy to talk to.

But he got all that from somebody else. From what Amanda's saying, sounds like that somebody else was Rudy Cunningham.

"I'm told he sold a golem kit two weeks ago," Amanda says.

"Do you know who he sold it to?"

"No, but I know something better," Amanda says. "I know Rudy's address. And I know something even better than that. But it's not even the best part."

"Can we maybe lump them both together and make the better-best part so I can go to sleep?"

"Fine. He lives in Vegas. I'll text you the address. He also contracts out magical assassins and small unit mercenary teams."

"Like the ones who hit Rachel's and Nicole's places," I say.

"He usually gets good talent."

"Not based on the assholes I dealt with," I say. "And how do you know—oh. This is the guy your family uses to hire their assassins in the U.S."

"The very same. Or one of them, at least."

"I think I'll be paying Rudy a visit tomorrow," I say.

"Hey, something I wanted to ask you. This has been bugging me all day. Have you figured out what David wants with Nicole?"

"From what I could tell, kill her," I say.

"You sure about that? That mage at the house knocked her unconscious. Sounds more like they were shooting at you."

"Honestly, with everything else going on I haven't had a chance to think about it much."

"They said they were looking for the Keeper at Rachel's camp," she says.

"Okay. Where you going with this?"

"I don't know yet," she says. "Something about it bugs me. What does David get with Nicole that he doesn't already have?"

"That's a good question."

"Maybe it's leverage against Jimmy?" she says.

"That would make sense," I say, "except the way Nicole tells it he doesn't give a damn about her or anyone else. If anything, Nicole needs Jimmy more than the other way around. But you're right, he's gotta have a reason."

"Maybe some sort of synergistic effect from having the Oracle and its Keeper together?" Amanda says.

"That's a thought. I'll—hang on." A piercing cry echoes through the room. It doesn't take long to figure out what it is.

"I gotta go," I say. "Need to find a new room."

"What's wrong?"

"Bridget's next door enthusiastically making up for the last thirty years."

"If you want to sleep, a sex club is not the right place to try it," Amanda says.

"What the hell else am I gonna do?"

"Well . . ."

"Everything here is too athletic and I'm bruised enough as it is, but thanks for the thought. Besides, last night was jail. Trust me, this is an improvement."

Gotta admit, though, jail was quieter.

Chapter 15

The best thing to ever happen in modern architecture is the strip mall. I know. What the fuck, right? At least I didn't say Brutalism.

Here's the thing about strip malls. You can stick anything in one and no one will bat an eye.

When's the last time you were surprised seeing Mexican food, frozen yogurt, acupuncture, laser hair removal, and vaginal rejuvenation all in the same strip mall? Never.

Give you an example. Back in L.A., the largest church of Santa Muerte is in a strip mall next to a nail salon on Normandy near Eighth. People go by it every day. They park next to it to get their nails done, pass it as they're taking their laundry out of the car. No one even notices. It's just one more shop.

Strip malls are also great places for magical shops to appear. Not shops that sell magic crap. I mean shops that are magic. People go by and see a new place, it doesn't occur to them that it wasn't there an hour ago. They figure they just missed it.

If you see one, don't go in. They're usually predators and you'll never come back out again.

I'm not surprised that Rudy Cunningham's computer repair shop in a strip mall on Tropicana is the front for a guy who handles the assorted material needs of the modern mage. But I am surprised that they actually seem to be repairing computers.

I walk in and see a completely normal scene. A woman

helps a customer who's dropping off a hard drive while a kid barely old enough for high school uses a cordless screwdriver to take a computer apart.

Neither of them looks out of the ordinary. They're both wearing loose shirts, jeans, sensible shoes. Nothing expensive. The woman has a frizz of brown hair pulled back in a ponytail. The kid looks like he could be her son.

At first I think I might be in the wrong place, and then I see the wards etched into the doorway, around the windows, on the back of the register. The woman catches me looking but finishes up with her customer and waits until they've left the store before walking past me, locking the door, and turning the sign to "Closed."

She turns to me and leans back against the door, arms crossed, a look on her face that says she's going to give me a stern talking to or, worse, maybe a piece of her mind.

"Hi," I say. "I'm—"

"I know who you are," she says. "And we don't want a damn thing to do with you."

"I get that a lot," I say. "If you really didn't want anything to do with me, why'd you lock the door?"

"Because she's very protective," the teen says. "Since I don't see a laptop in your hands, I imagine you're here looking for Rudy."

"Yeah, I'm not really the laptop type. Hey, is she gonna try to hurt me?"

"Not unless I tell her to," he says.

"Good to know. I take it you're Rudy?" The fact that he looks like a sixteen-year-old kid means nothing. Attila Werther was over two-hundred years old and looked like he was in his seventies. Probably could have looked like he was sixteen if he wanted to.

"You caught me," he says. "And you're Eric Carter. Who shouldn't be alive, much less inside my shop."

"Yeah, I'm wacky that way. Look, I'm not here looking for trouble."

"You never are," he says. "But trouble seems to always be looking for you." I can't deny that, so I don't even bother.

"Kind of exposed here, isn't it? I mean, it wasn't hard to find you."

"That's because I'm not hard to find," he says. "I don't keep any of this a secret. Just most people don't bother to come here. Besides, no one's going to do anything to me. I'm too valuable."

"Plus, he's got me," says the woman, giving me a glare that would strangle me if it could.

"Sister?" I say.

"Construct," he says. I look back at the woman at the door.

"No shit. Excellent work."

"Thanks. I got a guy in New Orleans who does them."

"I'm right here," the woman says.

"Gretchen, be a dear and shut down for a few minutes," he says. Gretchen's posture doesn't change, but she freezes and her eyes go milky white.

"Hope you got a back door out of here, 'cause I don't think I can move her."

"She's just off so I don't have to deal with her glowering at everything while we talk. You're here about the Bellagio golem."

"You know a lot for somebody who's never met me before."

"People tell me things. And they talk about you a lot. You want to know who bought it."

"That would be nice," I say. "What's it gonna cost me?"

"This one's free. Same person hired a few people for a couple hit jobs."

Jackpot. "Now you really have my attention."

"I thought that might intrigue you."

"What's a name gonna cost me?"

"I need—"

But he doesn't get a chance to tell me what he needs, because the shop's front window explodes and he takes a rifle round to his skull, popping it like a rotting canta-loupe dropped from a great height.

I drop to the floor and roll over to Gretchen, using the construct as shitty cover. Three more rounds through the window. Two hit Gretchen, blowing her left arm off at the shoulder and her right leg at the knee. The third punches into the cash register, blowing it into a cloud of scrap plastic and metal.

I crawl toward the back of the store. I have to stop twice as more rounds explode through the drywall over my head.

There's something bothering me about this. I mean be-yond the fact that somebody just blew the head off the guy I came here to talk to.

With the kinds of holes these bullets are making, I'm guessing .50s? Maybe an M82 or an M107. Pretty heavy ordnance. Never used anything like that myself. Closest I've come is using an old Dragunov.

Fortunately I only needed one shot, because I was hor-rible with it. You gotta be good to use one, especially from a distance. Fuckers kick like a mule. This asshole sucks.

No. Wait. If they were crappy shots, they wouldn't have gotten Rudy and his construct. They're not bad, they're missing me on purpose.

I stand up, give them the finger and wait. Man, I really hope I'm right.

From here I can see half a dozen spots a sniper could have been, but I don't hear a gunshot. They could be over a mile away if they're using an M82. Or with some magic on top of a building even farther away, and I'd never see them.

One last gunshot explodes the wall less than a foot to my right, as if they're just trying to get across the point that they could kill me if they wanted to. I wait another couple of minutes. Nothing. Doesn't mean they're gone, but I think it's a good bet.

What worries me isn't so much that Rudy's just been taken out by a sniper who it would seem wants me alive, it's that the bullet punched through heavy-duty wards on a window that would have made it stronger than an Abrams tank.

Any regular round probably would have bounced off the glass or just stopped dead before it got close. A normal sniper might have been given the job, but I doubt whatever mage ordered this hit was going to trust a normal to get the job done with magical bullets.

I pick a piece of meat off my shirt and drop it on the floor. One entire wall looks like what would happen if Jackson Pollock had painted with shotguns. And that means police are going to be here soon.

I wonder what they'll make of Gretchen. She's still standing on one leg, her eyes just as dead as before. Instead of blood, she's dripping a viscous blue gel. Yeah, they're gonna love this one.

Rudy's a dead end, in more ways than one. Not only did he not leave a ghost, I can't get anything out of a headless corpse. Charades, maybe.

It's all moot anyway. I can hear sirens in the distance and the looky-loos are starting to come by. My cue to leave. I head out the back, writing out a sticker with I'M NOT HERE and slapping it on my chest as I step into the alley.

Good thing, too. Because there are already police

heading toward me. I give them as wide a berth as I can in the alleyway. Bumping into someone while I'm wearing one of these isn't disastrous, but it can get awkward.

I consider stealing one of the cop cars, but if I'm trying to avoid being awkward, that's a non-starter. Instead I find a Civic a couple blocks away.

Jesus Christ, I had .50s flying next to my fucking head. I stood up and dared them to shoot me. How fucking stupid can I be?

Amanda should probably know about this. So I pull over and call her up.

"Hey," she says.

"Rudy's dead," I say. "Sniper round through his window. Popped his head like a zit. Seems they don't want me dead, though, because they intentionally missed me with something like eight hundred bucks in ammunition."

"The fuck?"

"Yeah, I pretty much feel the same way. But I did get some interesting information. The golem and the two hit squads were hired by the same person. I'm betting it's the same person who was shooting at me just now."

"Are you all right?"

"Don't have any holes in me," I say. "No new ones, at least. One hand's a little cut up from shattered glass, but it's pretty much nothing. Gonna be interesting to see what the Cleanup Crew does with this one. He had a construct that looked really human, but is very clearly not, that the cops are gonna have some questions about."

"Fuck. A lot of people are gonna be pissed." The tone in her voice is like a teenager who's just crashed the car and is worried daddy's gonna be mad.

"This isn't going to blow back on you, is it?"

"No. Honestly, nobody will be surprised. A lot of people have known about his setup for years and thought he was an idiot believing he was too valuable to kill."

"He was violently disabused of that notion, believe me."

"You said the people who hired the hit squad were the same ones who bought the golem?"

"That's what he said before his head popped. He didn't get around to telling me who, though."

"Jesus. The fuck did you step in up there?"

"Don't know, but somebody really likes me or I'd be splashed on Rudy's back wall, too."

"Or they really hate you and they're lining you up for something messier."

"Great pep talk, coach," I say.

"Just returning the favor, pops."

"Oh, don't call me that. Given the reason I'm out here, it sounds weird."

"Why would— Oh. Ew. Yeah, I won't do that anymore. Seriously, though, are you okay?"

"Need to get these cuts handled, but they're more annoying than anything else."

"What are you going to do now?"

"Head back to Candyland," I say, "and—huh."

"What?"

"Not tell them about it. Not all of it, at least. About the attack, sure, but not what he told me."

"Why?"

"Because I know someone who could have made those shots and has access to that sort of weaponry."

"Rachel?"

"Rachel."

Chapter 16

Rachel and I met about six months after I got to Vegas. Not so much a meet-cute as a meet-shoot. She was acting as lookout for the group, who I had not been introduced to yet. I was looking to talk to a ghost in the house next door to see what I could find out for a "Talk to Your Dead Mom" scam and was doing it in the alley where hopefully no one would see me.

Rachel saw me. Rachel shot at me. Rachel missed.

Not realizing that if she really wanted to, she could have popped zits off my nose with a bullet, I did what I always did when threatened. I rushed her.

I would like to say I held my own, that my time street brawling and learning how to fight down at Quick-Change Alice's MMA barn meant I was able to meet her fist-to-fist on equal terms.

She thoroughly kicked my ass.

I was on the ground in about ten seconds with the wind knocked out of me and her standing over me calling me a bawbag or something else suitably Scottish.

That's about the time the rest of the crew came out. David, thinking having witnesses was a bad idea, decided to try a memory wipe on me.

I slammed him through the window of the house they just robbed with a push spell. I made the mistake of fighting fair with Rachel. Wasn't about to make the same mistake with David.

It got messy from there. David came out of the house

and I tossed him back in. Bridget thought it was the funniest goddamn thing and told me to do it again. So I did. Rachel was standing back, looking at me like she didn't know what to make of me.

Lucas is the only one who intervened. And he did it in a very Lucas way.

"Would you please stop beating the shit out of my colleague? I'd really like it if we didn't all have to take you on at the same time because, and I think you know this, you'd lose."

It was the "please" that did it. I brushed dirt off my clothes and walked out of the alley with my dignity, if not my pride. That pretty much set the tone of my relationship with these people.

Three months later I was doing what I always do— necromancy—giving them intel on safe combinations and which relative was the most loaded. David was a dick, but we worked well enough together.

But Rachel and I got along great. Nothing sexual. Not even a hint of it. We simply weren't into each other. It was fun. One time she showed me how good she was by shooting the pasties off a showgirl's tits from the rafters backstage with a slingshot. Never forgot that night.

So yeah, she could have made that shot today.

———

Candyland is still closed when I get back. I have a couple ideas to check if it was Rachel who shot at me. They're all dumb. They're not flat-out ask-her dumb, but they're close.

But that all goes to hell when a six-and-a-half-foot tall black man in a button-down short-sleeved shirt and glasses steps in front of me with a scowl on his face and, before I can shoot him, pulls me into a hug that threatens to pop my ribs.

"Not the reaction I was expecting," I say. "Also, my ribs hate you and I think I need to change my bandages."

"Did you get beat up again?" Lucas says.

"I'm always getting beat up," I say. "You don't expect me to just give that up, do you? It's my raison d'être. How come you're not trying to kill me for what happened in St. Louis?"

"Kill you over a trinket? Dude. The hell kind of people you hang out with?"

"The kind who believe in disproportionate response."

"You might want to reconsider some of your relationships. I understand you need a thing stolen."

"Right to the point," I say. "Yeah, it's a severed, talking head." Lucas stares at me, not quite sure what to make of that.

"David Byrne?" he says.

"No. A real talking head. Tells the future by, well, manipulating the future. He was stolen a while back and I need to ask him some questions, and Nicole—have you met Nicole?"

"About ten minutes ago when Rachel and I got here from the airport."

"When did your flight get in?"

"About an hour ago, hour-and-a-half."

"And Rachel picked you up?"

"Yeah."

"Shit."

"Problem?"

"No," I say. Only there is a problem with my only theory so far. A big fat one. There's no way she could have been shooting at me and picking up Lucas from the airport at the same time.

"Okay, so . . . talking head?"

"Right. Nicole's the head's Keeper," I say. "She and he

have a connection, and she's been away from him too long. It's causing problems."

"That's two. What about everybody else?"

"Money, glory, an opportunity to fuck over David in as thorough a manner as possible."

"Oh, I like that one. But the first one's good, too."

"Anything that's not nailed down is all yours."

"I saw that he's got a few choice pieces in his vault," Lucas says.

"I have no doubt," I say. "But first we gotta get into it."

"Oh, I can get into it. Especially now that Bridget's back. Did David actually do something to her to block her magic?"

"Yeah. Used a charm and, I don't know how, planted it inside her on her sternum. She went to jail, he told everybody she was dead."

"Fucking hell." Lucas takes off his glasses and pinches the bridge of his nose. "I hate that man so much."

"From what I saw he hates you, too. Twenty million?"

"Twenty-six million, eight hundred forty-two thousand, four hundred and twenty-two dollars," Lucas says. "And eighteen cents."

"That's a lotta hate."

"And yet not nearly enough."

"Word. What now?" I say. "Seems we've got the gang all here."

"Jesus, we do, don't we?" he says. "I never thought I'd be out here doing this sort of thing ever again. These days I run a hedge fund. I mean, yeah, I steal the occasional rare diamond, but that's recreational."

"Ya gotta have hobbies."

"What about you?" he says.

"I was dead for five years and my soul was used to regrow an Aztec death god, until I got peeled out of him and dumped into my grandfather's mummified corpse so I could destroy an eight-thousand-year-old djinn. That was about a month ago."

"You always were an overachiever."

—————

We've gathered in the theater to go over the plans Rachel's pulled off the drive. The Twins are upstairs managing their business. We used to do this sort of thing in a tiny little office space, little more than a broom closet.

"This is where David keeps his loot," Rachel says, tapping a button. A photo of his casino, or rather his first casino, the Lilywhite, appears on the movie screen.

"As casinos go, it's pretty modest," she says. "There's a hotel with a pool, a small theater that books D-list acts, an attached restaurant that won a Michelin star back in 1992. And it has a 75% slot machine payout."

"Isn't that the minimum for the state?" Nicole says.

"Yes. Making it one of the least popular casinos."

"I hope he didn't pay a lot of money for it," Bridget says.

"About twenty-six million," Rachel says.

Lucas barks out a laugh. "Ooh, that must have stuck in his craw," Lucas says.

"I understand the temper tantrum went on for days," Rachel says.

"Weren't the two of you, you know." Bridget mimes a hole with her hand and slides the index finger of the other back and forth through it.

"We'd broken up by then. And how the hell did even you know?"

"'Cause you were fuckin' like rabbits before everything went to shit."

"Wait, what?" Lucas says. "Really? You and David?

Oh, sweetheart. I am so sorry. You know all you had to do was ask."

"I thought we were being discreet," Rachel says. "And can we get back on task?"

It's weird to see this easy banter between them. Even Bridget seems to be enjoying herself. Was a time I was part of that and every so often I could forget who I was and why I was there. Just not often enough.

"The casino vault is here." The blueprints of the casino appear on the screen. They're a little hard to read. Like most architectural blueprints, they show a lot more than walls. Pipes, conduits, ventilation ducts, everything needed to actually build the thing is on there. Fortunately, Rachel has circled the vault in red ink.

"I don't understand any of that," Bridget says. "Just tell me what to burn."

"We will," Lucas says. "Don't you worry."

"That's not the one we have to hit, anyway. This is the one we want." She points out a much smaller vault. For reference she displays a set of photos of it alongside the plan. It might be smaller but it is by no means small. The door is massive with bolts inside as thick as my arms to seal it in place.

What's interesting is that there's no pretense at hiding that it's a mage's vault. Wards have been stamped inside the door, outside the door, on the walls, the floor, the ceiling, and all the lockboxes.

"Jesus Christ," I say. "Dude's loaded for bear."

"Enh," Lucas says. "I know all of these. The real heavy hitters aren't going to be there, they'll be in the elevators and stairs, the entrance to the room the vault's in. If you can get a burglar before he even reaches the target you save yourself a lot of headaches and money."

"Can you crack them?" Nicole says.

"Oh yeah. A couple will take a little time, but he's not gonna have anything I haven't seen before."

"Bringing us to the vault itself," Rachel says. "This thing is a beast. Twenty-five-inch steel reinforced GSA compliant concrete panels, stainless-steel cladding. Same for the door. Thirty locking cylinders, dual-locking mechanism, four timed mechanisms."

"Did you memorize all that just so you could sound like you know what you're doing?" I say.

"You didn't understand a word of it, did you?"

"Not a bit."

"I did," Bridget says. "This is bigger than anything else I've burned through."

"Think you can do it?" I say.

"Oh yeah," she says. "I just need to figure out how. Do you have lock details? I think I'm going to need to burn through five or six places at the same time. I just need to know where."

"We got wards, we got vault," I say. "What about physical security?"

"This is where we might have an easier time of things," Rachel says. She brings up another architectural drawing with helpful photos.

"David and I did a job a long time back," Rachel says, "where we needed to get into a cardkey-controlled system. We found that that model had a bug where if the controller got two simultaneous signals it would go into an unsecured override state.

"Spoofing it is stupid easy," Lucas says. "And David decided to install that very model of cardkey system."

"Cameras, guards?"

"We're still working on getting that," Rachel says. "There isn't enough information here to plan for them."

"Using someone besides Diane," Nicole says.

"Sounds like you're on top of it," I say. "Glad to hear it. Who's doing what?"

"Lucas, Bridget, and I are working on the wards and vault," Rachel says.

"I've got my contacts looking into guards, cameras," Nicole says.

"What do I do?" I say.

"Hang out with the Twins?" Bridget says.

"I do that and I'll be walking funny for days. Seriously, there's gotta be something I can do."

"Sit there and look pretty," Rachel says.

"I would get the impossible job," I say.

"Oh, please," Rachel says. "You love a challenge. Okay, let's get started."

Chapter 17

I have nothing to do.

I'm sure this has happened before, but I honestly can't remember when. Even when I was dead, I had shit to take care of. Hell, I was busier as Mictlantecuhtli than I ever was as Eric Carter.

You'd think going on to your afterlife would be simple. Mine actually was. Being married to Santa Muerte had me halfway there already. Second I popped into Mictlan I got to work.

All the souls coming into Mictlan—and there were a surprising number—plus the souls already there, stuck in the mists leading to Chicunamictlan, had to be led through the place. I didn't take them. I didn't even really guide them.

I was more like the pal who keeps you upright when you're drunk and trying to find your house keys. Souls don't really make mistakes on their road to the end. But people get distracted. Sometimes they're supposed to get distracted.

The point of all the crap they go through, from the entry at Mitla all the way through the mountains, the winds, and the mists, is to help them clear their shit. Come to terms with their mistakes, accept what they never wanted to in life.

Kind of like visiting a really angry therapist who used to be a drill sergeant. By the time they got to the end they were a hell of a lot better adjusted than I was.

It's not always pleasant. A lot of the time that was because I made goddamn sure it wasn't. Rapists, human
traffickers, cartel assholes, all sorts of really unsavory
types. Murderers, even, though I gave a pass for folks
who killed somebody because they needed killing.

Anyone who took their abusers out permanently, I
sped through the process. They'd had enough shit in their
lives, they didn't need it when they were dead.

Mictlan doesn't really have a hell. It just has a lot of
unpleasant pit stops on the way to the end. Sometimes I
made a point of parking a few . . . okay, a lot of people in
some of them. They won't be getting out of those holes
any time soon.

I miss it. More than I expected. I get hit with these
waves of, I can't call it nostalgia—longing? Let's go with
longing. I miss the place, I miss Mictecacihuatl. I miss
ushering souls through all the shit they suffered and
made others suffer through.

I miss redemption. Las Vegas is a far cry from redemption.

So, what do I do? Wander the Strip? Play some slots?
Being a tourist in Las Vegas is almost as appealing as
nailing a tambourine to my nutsack and shaking out "Jin-
gle Bells."

This whole time I haven't had a moment to really think
about what I'm doing and why I'm doing it. I could find a
dark corner in the club, get drunk, and think about my
sins.

Fuck, that'd take all night. Instead, I go back to lie on
the bed in my room and think about Gabriela.

She spent years figuring out how to bring me back from
the dead. Or at least the human part of me. The rest of
me is still playing tour guide in Mictlan and keeping the
flow of souls from backing up.

Why? I know some of it was because only I could do

anything about Darius's bottle, though not as much as either one of us had hoped.

We fought about it. Not a huge fight. We'd had worse. Nobody was bleeding at the end of it, no cracked ribs. And when I told her she didn't need to bring me back for that shit, she caught me off guard.

"I needed you."

We've always had a complicated relationship. I doubt any mage anywhere has had simple. We've tried to kill each other, save each other, watch each other's backs. It just never occurred to me that it could be anything more.

Or did it?

"Hey," I say once Amanda picks up the phone.

"Did you drunk dial me?"

"No. Yes. Actually, I don't think it counts unless it's calling an ex, and we've never dated. And I'm certain of that because you have not come at me with a knife or tried to eat my soul."

"I'd say you need to pick better romantic partners but that would be kind of hypocritical, wouldn't it?" she says. "Oh, god. That's why you're calling, isn't it?"

"Do you love her?"

"It is why you're calling. Okay, hang on." She puts the phone down and I can hear her rummaging around in the background, a clink of glass.

"I was going to mix up a cocktail," she says, "but I have a lot of catching up to do to get where you're at. So I've got a bottle of Jägermeister and a straw."

"Why do you hate yourself so much?"

"Hey, you don't have a monopoly on self-loathing, bucko."

"Fair enough," I say. "Back to my question. Do you love her?"

"No bullshit? I don't think I even know what that

means," she says. "I've had fuckbuddies and a couple longer term girlfriends, but Jesus. I'm twenty-three, Eric. Most of the people in my life have been over a hundred. Not exactly the best examples. I don't know what I'm doing."

It's easy to forget that. Amanda seems to have her shit together, but she's just like the rest of us. She's just playing it by ear best she can.

I remember after the fight at Quick-Change Alice's how she wanted to celebrate with pie. Her energy, her sheer enthusiasm, that felt like the real her. A kid excited to get pie. And then somebody blew her car up and getting pie pretty much went to shit.

"I'll let you in on a secret. Even the old folks don't know what the fuck they're doing."

"Does that include gods?"

"Even more so," I say. "If you meet any who tell you otherwise, know that they're full of shit. Have you slept? Like more than twenty minutes at a time?"

"Have you?"

"Maybe twenty-five," I say. "Then the nightmare clowns show up."

"Same. My dad, my uncle, my whole goddamn family. I'm in charge now. I don't know how to be in charge. I'm already getting emails and phone calls requesting audiences. Audiences. Not 'hey, can I pop by for a chat,' but actual fucking audiences.

"I'm alone, Eric. And I'm scared. And I got nobody to talk to except you. How fucked up is that? My aunt's too Machiavellian to let out of her cage, I can't kill my uncle or my head will pop, and my girlfriend is dead and frozen, waiting for her soul to come back into her body. And I don't even know if that's going to happen."

"You're not alone," I say.

"I know you've got my back," she says. "If nothing else, with the fight and everything you've done for me and my family, I know that."

"I'm not talking about me. You have friends at USC. People who care about you. Holt, Jordan. The other students."

"No," she says. "I tried. It's different now. I was a fucking princess and now I'm the queen. Everybody's, shit, I don't know. Like they feel they need to respect me or I'll set them on fire or something. I'm getting calls from people all the way from Castaic down to Laguna."

"I know that feeling," I say. "For me it's not that weird respect as much as 'stay away.' I've always had a rep, but now? I actually scared a bunch of mage bouncers the other night when I told them my name."

She laughs. "Oh my god. That would have been something to see. Is it because of the fight? I'm sorry about that."

"Don't be. It was my idea."

"Do *you* love her?" she says, turning the question back on me.

"Kind of," I say. "I trust her, which I never thought I'd say about anybody, and I respect the hell out of her, but I know that's not the same thing. But, and this is where it gets weird . . . weirder . . . I'm still getting over my ex-wife. It feels like I walked into my house and found she'd moved all her stuff over to her new boyfriend's place while I was out getting groceries or something. It's only been a month."

"I honestly can't imagine what that's like."

"Hurts," I say. "Though not as much as it did. My leaving or being ejected or whatever you want to call it was the best thing that could have happened in that situation. Now she's with a proper Mictlantecuhtli. Something without all that pesky humanity. Still sucks, though."

"And Gabriela did it."

"Yeah. That's a bit of a wrinkle on things. Not as much as I expected. We *are* going to get her back, you know."

"I do," she says. "But then I forget, get overwhelmed, and it just feels like another loss."

"I get that. Probably more than you realize. Hanging onto hope is not my strong suit. But you know I've got your back no matter what happens, right?"

"Yes," she says.

"I know I don't know you that well," I say, "but over the last few days I've come to realize something."

"What's that?"

"You are very much your father's daughter. You are going to be fine." The silence goes on so long I start to wonder if she hung up.

"Thank you," she says, voice quiet. "I really appreciate that. Please don't get yourself killed."

"Not gonna happen. Death is a lot like seeing the Grand Canyon. Did it once, no need to go back. I'm sobering up, so I'm gonna go crash in an empty bed at the sex club. Or an occupied one. At this point I don't think I care."

"Might do you some good," she says. "All, right. Goodnight, King of the Dead."

"Goodnight, Queen of Los Angeles."

———

As a general rule, never eat the food at a strip club. Considering what's going on in the place—and I don't mean with the dancers or the staff—you can't trust it. Don't go waving around a blacklight if you want to keep your appetite, is what I'm saying.

Fortunately, Candyland is as far away from that as a Michelin-star restaurant is from a cockroach-infested dive bar. The Twins will never skimp on quality, and they wouldn't be caught dead in a place that wasn't immaculate.

I'm eating hangover food out on the main floor. Eggs, bacon, coffee—very strong and very bitter. You know, like I like my women.

There are a couple dancers practicing on poles over in one corner while the place is being cleaned by a small army, vacuuming the carpet and polishing brass and chrome.

They do this every day to get ready for the evening. Years ago, I couldn't wrap my head around something about it. Yeah, people were getting paid. Quite a lot, actually. But there was a different vibe I couldn't quite understand. Now I do.

Everyone here is family, or as close as people like us get. Scratch that. They're just family. It's like one big, magical hippie commune. It feels like a great idea. I'd last about ten minutes trying to be a part of it.

When I saw Lucas, I expected him to take a swing at me, not give me a hug. I expect everyone I've met before to take a swing at me. Which might be why they do it.

Am I the problem? Or is it my perspective? Can I not see the possibility because I just can't see it? Tautological dog is tautological.

I feel like I'm blind and people are trying to describe color to me. If I can't imagine something good, will it ever happen? Or if it does, will I even recognize it?

"You're alive," Lucas says, sliding into a chair across from me. I grunt something that probably sounds vaguely like assent. "Hmm. No, alive might be stretching it a bit."

"Rachel says you got a kid now," I say. Not sure why, because I know exactly what's going to happen next.

"Bradley," Lucas says, all smiles. He's almost giddy. He pulls out his phone and before I can tell him I'm allergic to children in any form he's waving it in front of my face.

Have to admit, the kid is cute. Looks like his dad, only with chubby baby cheeks. Again, before I can stop him, he's swiping picture after picture by my face.

I don't get the appeal. They're all pretty much the same. Baby smiling. Baby smiling and looking like it's got a concussion. Baby smiling and looking like it's got a concussion but covered in what I hope to god is food. Half of these smiling baby photos I have to assume are just the kid having gas. I mean, who doesn't feel better after a good fart?

"Enough," I say. "The cute is seared into my eyeballs. You're gonna make me go blind."

"Say it," he says. "He's a cute kid."

"He's very cute. So are koalas. They'll still fuck you up."

"Sure you're not thinking wolverines?"

"Wolverines, koalas, tomato, tomahto."

"You're very strange," he says.

"Says the guy who has a child. I only hope he grows up to understand the error of humanity's ways and stays blissfully child-free."

"Come on. You can't be serious."

"About having children? Lucas, my life is a fucking reality TV show where the contestants play Russian roulette for fabulous prizes and trips to Cancun that never happen. I'm not bringing a child into that shit."

"Ever come close?"

"Once," I say. "Then they saw me for who I really am and bailed."

"Sorry to hear it, man."

"Enh. She was a normal. Never would have worked. Aren't you supposed to be in the porn theater planning our Italian Job under a waving, fifteen-foot penis, or something?"

"Should be, yes. But instead I'm out here talking to you. Was hoping you could do me a favor."

"I don't kill people before eleven if I can help it."

"This is just moving some gear. Rachel asked me to come out to her murder-hut compound and help her load her truck."

"But you don't do manual labor?"

"Not if I can help it."

"Sure. Let me finish my coffee and I'll head over there."

"Thanks," he says. "And for what it's worth, I think you might make a decent dad."

"Don't go flingin' around curses like that, man. I got enough problems."

Chapter 18

The air around Rachel's double-wide is still and heavy, and though the bodies have been carted away a hint of death lingers. Those bodies were out in the Nevada sun long enough to get plenty ripe, their juices seeping into the earth. It's going to smell this way for a while.

There are only two cars in the small dirt lot, an F-150 and a Las Vegas cop car. It might be her ex-husband. I grab a sticker and a Sharpie, but before I can so much as get the cap off the pen, the door bangs open.

Rachel steps out of the trailer. Then Rachel steps out of the trailer right behind her. After a brief moment of confusion I realize that the first woman is the ex's girlfriend I saw the other day.

The woman who isn't Rachel, I never got her name, is wearing a Las Vegas Metropolitan Police uniform. Similar build, similar height, a strand of red hair poking out from under her cap. It really is uncanny how much they resemble each other.

The Rachel clone marches down the steps, a scowl on her face. I get out of her way, because something tells me she's not going to stop if I don't. She ignores me, gets into the police car, and drives away.

"She didn't look happy," I say. "And you look even less happy."

"She must have pissed somebody off, because she got assigned to come out here and take another statement. Or maybe I pissed somebody off. One of those."

"Has it occurred to Jeff that it might be cheaper to just hire redhead escorts for the full GFE?" I say. Rachel glares at me. "Yeah, you're right. That shit's expensive. No way he could afford that on any kind of regular basis."

"Shut up," she says.

"Was there a cat fight?" I say. "At least tell me there was a cat fight. I'd pay to see a good cat fight."

"How about I just stab you in the face," she says.

"Seem a bit touchy. So what's this thing Lucas was supposed to come help you load into your truck?" I follow her behind the trailer.

"That," she says, pointing at a cart loaded with something that looks like a high-tech jackhammer. It has to weigh a good couple hundred pounds. Another cart has a portable drill press, except the base is missing legs and there's a vacuum pump attached to it. Then there's a generator.

"The fuck is that?"

"Safe drill," she says. "The drill part's obvious. That other bit is a vacuum plate. Holds it onto the side of the safe. Drill attaches to that arm and you use the press to control the drill."

"I thought Bridget was going to burn her way through," I say.

"She is. But there's one spot where she can't. It's that glass plate holding back an additional set of locking cylinders I was telling you about. If you break it, the cylinders engage, and the only way we're getting in at that point is blowing the whole thing up.

"If Bridget tries to burn through it the glass will contract unevenly and shatter. We need to drill through one exact spot carefully enough that we can get through the plate without destroying it. After that we can fill the whole thing with expanding foam to keep the glass from breaking at all."

"Jesus fucking Christ."

"Yeah," she says. "This one's going to suck. Fortunately we'll be able to use some magic to help, just not a lot."

"Why not?"

"Something about the wards," Rachel says. "Lucas knows more about it than I do."

I can't imagine how we're going to get this thing to the safe, much less turn it on without attracting attention. This is turning out to be a whole lot more complicated than I'd realized.

"Those high explosives are looking better every minute."

"Aren't they? I'm bringing some along just in case. Hell, when we're done I might just set them off out of spite."

"Do you really think we can pull this off? I got a lot riding on this, sure, but Nicole's got a hell of a lot more."

"What do you mean?"

"If she hasn't told you, I don't think it's my place to say anything."

"Except you already did. What's going on?" If Nicole really wanted to keep something a secret, she probably shouldn't have told me.

"She's dying. Cancer. Went into remission when she became Jimmy's Keeper. Now that he's been gone, it's exploded. She thinks she has a few months. I give it two weeks, tops."

"You're fucking kidding me."

"Nope. Saw it myself. I don't know what spells she's using, but magic's the only thing keeping her upright. She doesn't get Jimmy back soon, she's fucked. Might even be too late."

"Goddammit, Nicole," she says. "Why did she tell you and not me?"

"Because I confronted her on a couple things and that

was the only way she convinced me she wasn't jerking me around."

"You wouldn't just take her word for it?"

"I think you don't have a really good grasp on what her and my relationship was like," I say. "The fact that I haven't shot her yet says a lot about my growth as a person."

"I forget you met her at a . . ."

"Low point?"

"An ambitious one," she says. "We were all young and stupid."

"Ambitious. Yeah. That's what magic does," I say. "It's not the power that's the problem, it's the people who can use it."

"Magic just fucks everything up, doesn't it?"

"We're not exactly superheroes," I say. "Or if any of us are, we're really dysfunctional ones."

"My dad thought he was one," she says. "He was just an idiot who couldn't see his own shit."

"Bad?"

"Misguided," she says. She sits down on the edge of the cart, wipes sweat off her brow with the back of her hand. "He actually thought he could make the world a better place at gunpoint. Mercenary work suited him."

"But not you."

"I never told you what happened to him, did I?"

I sit down in as much shade as I can find against the edge of the trailer. "You never talked about it. It wasn't any of my business."

"Back in the, shit, nineties? Sierra Leone hired these mercenaries to guard diamond mines from rebels. Only instead of guarding, they took them over. I don't remember exactly what happened to them, but years later we were in a team hired to do the same thing. I was fifteen."

"I can't see that going well," I say.

"It didn't. You'd think they'd have learned, but of course different people were in power and panicking because the same shit was happening.

"Inside of a week everything goes to hell. We're the only people in the team who don't want to steal the diamond mines. I try to convince my dad to leave. He wanted to fix things."

I can see where this is going and it's nowhere good. "Fuck. I'm sorry."

She shrugs. "He made his own choices. He and I both had pretty much the same knack. He was better with explosives than I was. Saw him shape a grenade blast into a needle one time and take a tank out with it."

"How long did you last?"

"Longer than I expected," she says. She smiles at a memory. "Gotta understand, he was good. A lot better than me. Sneaky. Taught me a lot about misdirection and guerilla tactics. We took out a lot of 'em."

"Just not enough?"

"Just not enough," she says. "You know what separates places like the U.S. from hot spots like Sierra Leone? The size of our families. You see yourself as an American first, or as a mage?" These days I don't know what the fuck I am, but I know where she's going with this.

"Mage. Kind of hard not to."

"Right. We're your people whether you want to admit it or not. Doesn't matter what country we're from, we're all mages. Normal Americans mostly see themselves as American, right?"

"Suppose so."

"The people we were fighting didn't see themselves as Sierra Leonean. They wanted to, but their world wouldn't let them. They saw themselves as Revolutionary United Front, or Mende, or Temne people. Even the fuckers who hired us didn't see themselves as part of the country. We were fighting for De Beers, the National Diamond Mining Corporation, an incompetent leader who let corruption run rampant. Sierra Leone is a place, but it's not a people."

"And we're any better?"

"No," she says. "That's the point. Whether we think in terms of country, family, culture, whatever, it's all the same bullshit. We tell ourselves the same lies everybody else does. The only reason we aren't out in the streets murdering each other over here is that we're too fucking scared to."

"Or lazy," I say.

"That, too."

"So what do we do, then?"

"Nothing," she says. "There's nothing to do. Nothing gets better. Everything just keeps sinking. Until there's nothing at all."

"I can't believe I'm being the positive one here," I say, "but I can't agree. You and I have seen a lot of death and a lot of pain. You know necromancers almost never commit suicide?"

"Really? I figured you'd all have a revolver-shaped exit plan in your back pocket."

"There's no point. It doesn't end. Your soul's gonna keep on keepin' on whether you like it or not. Might not be pleasant, but it'll still be around. Your nothing that you're talking about? It doesn't exist. Or if it does, I haven't seen any evidence of it yet."

"You saying we have to keep trying to make it better because there's no void to escape to?"

"I don't fucking know," I say. "I just know it's not that simple. What you do is up to you. Most of us get one shot at this. I guess make it count?"

"Jesus. All right, we've already used up our allotment of maudlin for the week," she says.

We haul the drill into the back of the truck and secure it with cargo straps. Rachel goes into the trailer for a couple bottles of water and I open up the passenger door to try to vent a little heat out of the car.

And that's when I see it, a spent .50 cartridge on the floor. It's rolled under the passenger seat along with a crumpled piece of paper with a rune written on it.

"Problem?" Rachel says, coming out of the trailer. I pocket both before she gets to the truck.

"Too goddamn hot in there," I say. I roll down the passenger side window. It's an older truck with a crank handle that sticks.

"Welcome to Vegas," she says. "Good to go?"

I want to say, "Why'd you shoot Rudy? Why'd you miss me? Did you hire the teams to kill your customers? Take out Nicole? Set things up at the Bellagio?"

Instead I say, "That I am," and get into the truck.

Chapter 19

We drop the pickup off at a maintenance yard filled with utility trucks. Nobody's going to notice it there, but Rachel puts a camouflage spell on it anyway.

Rachel heads back to the club, but I bow out, saying I'll be there in a little while. I've got to think.

I steal a truck and park it off the Strip. I wander into one of the casinos, the Venetian I think—everything looks sort of Italian, more kitsch than anything else. At least it's air conditioned. They have a gondola ride you can take in a loop, sort of a Tunnel of Love thing, next to a café. I grab an espresso and get a seat near the faux-Venetian canal.

This might be the calmest place I've been in Vegas yet. No slamming bass, gunshots, clanging slot machines. Just a seat next to a quiet fake canal. Until a very large man in a light gray suit slides into the chair opposite me.

It was fun while it lasted.

"Eric Carter?" he says.

"If you have to ask, you're in the wrong line of work," I say. "Working for David Jewel?"

"I am. He'd like to speak with you, and he's asked me to escort you to his casino."

"Did he now? Did he happen to tell you anything about me?"

"Just that you and he are old friends and he'd like the

pleasure of your company." I can feel the looming presence of more of David's thugs collecting behind me.

"I would love to," I say, "but I'm enjoying my espresso and then I was going to take a stroll through the casino. This seems like a nice one."

"You can take just as nice a stroll through Mister Jewel's casino."

"See, the problem there is that it's Mister Jewel's casino," I say. "And Mister Jewel is an asshole. So, thank you for the kind offer and implied threat, but I'll have to pass."

"I'm so sorry, sir, but I really must insist."

"Wow. He really didn't tell you anything about me." Since this man sat down, the area has been quietly clearing out. Now there's no one here but me, Light Gray Suit, and—three? No, five at least—of his cronies behind me, looking to rumble.

"Enough," he says.

"Enough to only bring that much backup with you? Shame. You really need to work for somebody better."

"He pays very well," he says.

"Not for this he doesn't." I push back from the small table, shoving it up into Light Gray Suit's face and rolling off the chair as it tips over to face the rest of the gang.

Five people, three men and two women. Light Gray Suit didn't give off much of an air of menace, but these people sure as hell do. They're wearing tailored clothes, and it's clear that underneath there's more muscle than fat on their bodies.

One of the men has had his nose broken so many times that it's almost flat. One of the women has scars on her face that tell me she's seen more than a few knife fights.

I'd be worried, but I've done this dance before. Nice of them to clear out all the civilians. I'd feel awful getting blood on an innocent bystander.

Killing them would be easiest, but it seems rude to make other people clean up my messes. Not killing them still gives me a lot of leeway.

One of the men comes at me with an extendable baton. I must be getting used to it because I'm not surprised to see the razor is already in my hand as I move to block the baton. The baton and the blade connect and the baton cleaves in two. He's not expecting the sudden shift in weight and starts to stumble. A foot in the right spot and he's in the canal.

The two women are on me before I can blink. One of them tags me in the side with a baton. I move away from her but that opens me up for the other to swipe at my mid-section with a knife.

I manage to get the razor in her blade's way with the same result as the baton. I pump a lot of power into a push spell and slam all four of them back a good ten feet.

I turn to head toward the exit and Mister Gray Suit is standing there wearing my coffee and a furious glare with a gun in his hand.

"He want to talk to me or gloat over my bullet-ridden corpse?" I say.

"I'm sure he won't mind that much either way," he says.

"You know, I really didn't want to do this," I say.

"What, die?"

"That too." I dive at him. The gun goes off, the bullet grazing my side. I take him down in a tackle and before he can throw me off I score the straight razor crosswise through his face from temple to jawline, digging in half the length of the blade.

It takes him a second to realize he's dead. The cut's so sharp that his brain keeps working until the connections physically slide out of alignment. He shudders once and then goes limp. There's surprisingly little blood.

The whole fight has lasted less than thirty seconds.

I get up, ready for round two with the rest of his squad, but they're standing far back. The guy in the canal, which is only a few feet deep, stands staring at me like I'm the Devil.

"Get your buddy outta here. And let David know that if he sends you after me again, I'll kill all of you." I wipe the blood off the razor on Light Gray Suit's jacket. It's his blood, after all. He should have it back.

———

It's nice to know that David still cares about me. I should send him a fruit basket. The question is, why does he want to see me? I can think of a few reasons. I don't think any of them have to do with what we're planning. Not directly, at least.

With Bridget out of lockup, he might think something's going on but not know what. Probably assumes I helped get her out. It's not like I won't admit it. If I'd known the details about the situation, I'd have gotten her out with or without Rachel's help.

Now, did he send his goon squad to pick me up for a chat? Or to kill me? Either way I don't see him being all that happy when his people show up with a corpse that isn't mine.

Nobody bothers me as I make my way out of the casino. Either security was in on it or they don't really care about David. Either is possible.

Fuck this town. Should have skipped it altogether once I left L.A. I wonder how different things would be right now if I'd moved north instead of east?

My phone buzzes. A text from Nicole.

Come on back ready to talk the plan

I send her what I think is a thumbs-up emoji but turns

out to be some sort of purple dildo looking thing. Whatever. I'm sure she'll get the idea.

I stop the bleeding and clot the wound in my side with a spell. Not great, but it'll hold. My suit jacket's dark enough to hide the blood. Not that any of them will be surprised if they see it.

Everyone's down in the theater at the table. Printouts of guard schedules, photos of ID badges, what look to be alarm codes are pinned to a corkboard sitting on an easel.

I take my time walking down the theater aisle. Partly because I'm figuring out if I should say anything about the bullet and the paper charm I found in Rachel's truck. But mostly because my side feels like it's on fire.

I've gotten a good look at the paper charm, but I'm still not sure what it was for. It's clear the spell's spent, but what sort of spell was it?

If I'm going to confront her, now's the time for it. With everyone here it cuts down on the likelihood that there's going to be a knock-down drag-out with her.

But it might also blow the only chance I have of getting Jimmy. If it was her who shot Rudy, it doesn't necessarily mean it's going to be a problem. After all, she didn't shoot me.

I sit down in the front and feel like I'm at a high school presentation where one of the other kids is going to show us pictures of clouds and talk about the rain cycle.

"You all right?" Nicole says as I slide into the seat next to her with a wince.

"Oh, the usual," I say.

"The plan's pretty straightforward," Lucas says, bringing up a building plan of the casino. "The Lilywhite is an old casino. One of the oldest. As such it has a lot of structural weirdness that was grandfathered in so they didn't need to change it.

"Tunnels between casinos aren't new. All the MGM

properties have that so they can move cash easily from one to another, for example. The tunnels for the Lily-white, though, are a closed system with only a few entry and exit points."

"Why?" Bridget says. "Tunnels to nowhere?"

"Calling them tunnels is a bit of a stretch," Lucas says. "They're labeled that way, but they're really just base-ment hallways to move food, drinks, cash, towels, that sort of thing."

"These tunnels are where David has his personal vault," Rachel says, pointing at a section of the map walled off from the rest. "It's closed off from the rest of the tunnel system. It has an elevator, three ID checkpoints, and a guard station before you get to the vault itself.

"We've got maintenance credentials that'll get us as far as the vault. The story is that we're doing pressure checks on the HVAC system. That gives us an excuse to bring down our equipment and to make a certain amount of noise."

"I can get us through the wards," Lucas says. "I know how David thinks. And he's not that imaginative. And I know he didn't hire the best to build it for him. Because that's me."

"Nice to see you've become so humble," I say.

"What can I say? Perfection's timeless. Getting through most of the wards isn't the problem."

"The alarms?" Bridget says.

"Right," Lucas says. "David's not going to want anyone else to get into that vault, so most of his magical alarms are designed to notify him and only him immediately."

"Why not have them notify a security team? He's got mages on staff." I say.

"You can learn a lot about a ward by what it does when it's set off," Lucas says. "David's going to hire good people."

"Good enough to reverse engineer the wards?" I say. I could see why you wouldn't want to let somebody else in on those particular secrets.

"Exactly."

"So how are these any different from any other wards?" Nicole says.

"If they're tampered with, he'll know," Lucas says.

"That sounds like a problem," I say. "How do we get it so David doesn't get that alarm?"

"I'm glad you brought that up," Rachel says. "We do it by drowning them out." She pulls a gold money clip from her bag and tosses it to me. It's pretty standard for a money clip except for a rune etched onto the back. "Once the rune is triggered, it sets off a sort of magical white noise. It grows gradually so it shouldn't be noticed, at least not for a while."

"How long are you expecting this to take?" I say.

"Once we get to the first layer of wards, about an hour."

"An hour," I say. "Alarm goes off, but he doesn't hear it. How close do I have to be? I suspect you mean closer than on the sidewalk outside."

"A few feet. No more than ten, maybe less. If it stays within five that should do the trick."

"I'm really leaning toward just killing him," I say. "We'll already be past everything we really need him for." Silence.

"Wow, you have changed," Lucas says.

"Told ya," Bridget says. "Kinda hot."

"Been a rough few years," I say. "Still doesn't answer my question."

Lucas points to a photo where a rune carved into the vault door has been circled in red. "Because that is a dead man switch. He dies, and something happens."

"Something?"

"No idea what. I recognize the switch, but I don't know

what it's connected to. Probably triggers something inside the vault. I don't know what could destroy the Oracle, but I can tell you whatever that is, it's gonna try."

"Yeah, that sounds like David. 'If I can't have it, no one can.'"

"I'm still gonna kill him, ya know," Bridget says.

"After we hit the vault," Lucas says.

"I'll even help you out," I say. "How do we get this thing close to him? Slip it into his pocket?"

"Nope," Rachel says. "We slip it into yours."

"You have got to be kidding," I say. "I walk into that casino, he'll know something's up."

"That's the beauty of it," Lucas says. "He already knows something's up. He's gonna take one look at you and wonder what the hell is going on. You just need to keep him talking for an hour as I burn through the wards and Bridget burns through the vault door."

"I'll be lookout," Rachel says. "Anybody comes to check on us gets shot."

"You set off a gun in there and this whole thing's botched," I say.

"That's why I'm using an airgun with tranquilizer darts. Etorphine Hydrochloride. Enough in one dart to knock out an African bull elephant inside of ten minutes."

"And people?"

"It's lethal to humans at 0.03 micrograms," she says. "Each syringe is 17 milligrams. You do the math."

"Slight hitch in that plan," I say. "You want me to spend an hour hanging out with someone who, if he didn't want me dead before, sure as shit wants me dead now?"

"Eric," Rachel says. "What did you do?"

"Existed? Half a dozen of his people ambushed me in the Venetian right before I came here. One of them's dead. And in a way that he's going to think conveys a message."

"Are we talking a pinkie finger in a candy box message?" Lucas says.

"More a horse head in the bed when you wake up message."

"Oh, for fuck sake," Rachel says. "Goddammit, Eric."

"What are you pissed off at me for? They're the ones that wanted to kill me, not the other way around. If it had been, none of them would have walked out of there."

"No, this is good," Nicole says.

"You and I might have slightly differing ideas on what counts as good," Rachel says.

"This way you're guaranteed to get an audience with him. Being around him for an hour shouldn't be a big stretch."

"Yeah, as he's gutting me," I say.

"You'll figure something out," Nicole says.

Fuck. Can I do this? Do I want to do it? It's not like I'm going to be any good down at the vault with them. Hell, this is the easy job. All I have to do is walk into the casino.

"How will I know when the job's done?" I say.

"I'll text you '1111,' " Rachel says. "If things have gone to shit, I'll text you '0000'. Chances are if that happens I'll be dead, though. And David will know what's up."

"I either get a signal that everything's cool, or David tries to kill me."

"He's probably gonna try to kill you anyway," Rachel says.

"But don't you kill him," Bridget says. "That motherfucker is mine."

"I'll do my best," I say. "But I'm not very good at nonlethal."

"Okay, time out," Lucas says. "I know years change a man, but what the fuck? Every time this topic came up years ago you asked—fuck, demanded—that nobody died. The fuck happened to you?"

I've wondered that question a lot over the years. When I first got to Vegas last I had only killed one person, Jean Boudreau, after he murdered my parents. Before I left Vegas that went up to two, sort of, when I turned Jimmy into the Oracle.

There's a big difference between knowing death and making it happen. Taking someone's life isn't easy the first time you do it. Even as rage focused me to a laser intensity to take out Boudreau, I still second guessed myself.

The second murder's a little easier, especially when you can convince yourself it isn't really murder. Then the third one is maybe self-defense or at least justified. The fourth and fifth, well, it's not as big a deal.

Once you get into triple digits, though, you really have to ask yourself if you need to rethink your life choices.

"I got over it is all," I say.

"Drop it, Lucas," Rachel says. She looks at me and there's a flash of sadness in her eyes. She knows what it's like. There was a time she didn't want to kill anybody either. But when you're tailor made to do it, it's kinda hard to deny.

"Fine," Lucas says. "But I gotta say, I don't like this new you."

"At this point, it's old me," I say. "I don't much like it either. We get through this, I'll tell you all about it."

"What exactly am I doing?" Nicole says.

"Sticking with us," Rachel says. "You know the Oracle. If there's anything weird going on with it, we won't know, but you might spot it."

"Okay, yeah. That makes sense."

"Rendezvous point?" Bridget says. "Job like this we're gonna need to scatter as soon as we're done."

"Jimmy and I will be at the Gold Rush," Nicole says. "David hasn't done anything with the place, yet. We'll hole up in the safe room on the first floor. I went out there yesterday. Little dusty, but still intact."

"He won't think to look there?" I say.

"He might," Nicole says, "but if he does he won't find us. Sebastian was a cheapskate on a lot of things, but he threw a lot of money into that room. Nobody's touched it since he died."

"Rachel and I are going to hole up in a suite down at Caesar's," Lucas says. "Once we're all in our respective spots, we'll connect and twelve hours later we meet up at the Twins'."

To say this all feels rushed is an understatement. But then that's how we always did things. We'd come up with a plan and execute it the same day. We weren't thieves, we were thrill-seekers.

"What's our timeframe on this?" I say. Knowing Lucas, he's got the details all worked out with enough wiggle room to improvise. And there's going to be a lot of improvisation. At least on my part.

Nobody wants to wait on this. I sure as hell don't. The sooner we break Jimmy out of there the better I'll feel. I hope I don't have to kill David. I really want Bridget to get some closure.

"Six hours," Lucas says.

Nicole's eyes pop. "Uh . . . Don't we need to, I don't know, prepare anything?"

"Strike when the iron's hot," Rachel, Lucas, Bridget, and I all say in unison. There's a surprised pause and then we're all laughing.

"The hell was that?" Nicole says.

"Something David used to say," Lucas says.

"Lucas came up with all our plans," Rachel says. "But he let David think they were all his idea."

"Cut down on pissing matches," Lucas says. "So once we had the details, he wanted to move. Got in the habit of getting everything worked out so after we talked about it, we could move on it right away."

"Isn't this a slightly bigger job than you've done before?" Nicole says.

"Maybe for Eric," Rachel says.

"I was more intel and recon," I say. "By the time we moved, my job was pretty much done. I usually hung back with Rachel to watch our backs. Speaking of, you need me to set up any watchdogs?"

"Please don't," Rachel says. "The spell to see those things always made me want to throw up."

"Watchdogs?" Nicole says.

"Ghosts," I say. "Basically, I'd bribe a bunch of them to hang around. They couldn't see much on our side of things, but they'd know if somebody was coming. If I wasn't there, I'd give Rachel the ability to see them."

"I fucking hated it," she says. "You always got the most fucked-up-looking ones. There was a guy with an axe in his head the last time. Kept staring at me."

"Probably thought you were pretty," I say. "Or lunch." Rachel glares at me.

"We still have a couple of details to work out," Lucas says, "but we'll have those ironed out by tonight. Anyone have any questions?"

"I do," I say. "Rachel, why'd you shoot the guy I was meeting with yesterday?"

Chapter 20

Talk about a conversation killer. Rachel looks at me, face a blank. The rest of the group are looking between Rachel and I. Will she deny it?

"I had a shot so I took it," she says.

"What the hell are you two talking about?" Nicole says.

"I got a bead on who sourced the mercenaries who hit Rachel's camp and the assassins who tried to kill the two of us in Summerlin. Oh, and he supplied that golem at the Bellagio, too."

"The hell?" Nicole says. "Why?"

"Because the fucker needed to die," Rachel says. "He sent those murderers to my home."

"Fuck, Rachel. He was about to tell me who hired him. You couldn't have waited thirty seconds?"

"You know what that sonofabitch does?"

"Yeah," I say. "Wholesale."

"I've checked up on him," she says. "Half the shadiest shit that goes down on this side of the continent funnels through him. But then you wouldn't really care, would you, Mister Aztec sun god over here, who's taking out djinn and sleeping on silk fucking sheets in a mansion in L.A. Yeah, I fucking checked up on you, too."

"The fuck does that have to do with anything?"

"He's the man who makes it possible for people like you to get shit done."

"You think I'm some sort of one-percenter badass?"

"Because you are," she says. "Nobody's taken him out because he's too fucking valuable. I was not going to take a chance that you would try to stop me."

"I didn't even know who the hell he was until the night before. Jesus, you really think I'd have tried to stop you?"

"You're no better than anybody else, Eric," she says. I can't help but laugh at that.

"Anybody else want to weigh in?"

"You do act like it," Nicole says.

"Don't look at me, man," Lucas says. "Y'all's drama, not mine. I haven't seen you since you left me hanging in Saint Louis."

"Maybe he does act like he's better than everybody else," Bridget says. "I mean, he sure as hell used to. And so what if Rachel shot a guy you were talking to. Like she said, she had the shot, she took it. None of this fucking matters.

"We're not here to piss on each other's parades. We're here to fuck over a guy and then kill him. That's my goal, at least. So fucking drop it. We've got shit to do."

I don't think I've ever heard Bridget say that much at one time. If I'd been in Rachel's position, I'd have taken the shot, too.

"She's right," I say. "This doesn't matter. What happened happened and I can't say I wouldn't have done the same thing."

"Thank you," Rachel says. "And I'm sorry."

"It's not like I would have learned anything new," I say. "David's fingerprints are all over this goddamn thing."

"We done?" Lucas says. "Anything else? Like the lady says, we got shit to do."

"Okay," Lucas says when none of us answers. "Enough of the circle jerk. Let's get to work. Nicole, can I talk to you? We're going to need you to help us figure where exactly the Oracle is in the vault before we start drilling."

"Hey," Rachel says, stopping me as I'm heading up the aisle. I need to talk to the Twins. I need a better suit than the wrinkled, torn-up shit I'm wearing now. And maybe they've got something for the pain. I don't care how little a gunshot might be, it's still really fucking painful.

"What's up?"

"I—I'm sorry," she says. "Not for killing him. But for not trusting you. I know you were trying to get to the bottom of this thing."

"Neither one of us works well with others," I say. "We do what we have to do. Like I said, can't say I wouldn't have done the same in your position." By and large people try to do the right thing. We just don't always have the same idea of what's right. "Hey, how'd you get from the airport to the strip mall and back again?"

"Teleportation spell," she says. "My dad showed me how to inscribe them as paper charms. They're useful."

That would explain it. But there's still something gnawing at the back of my mind. Knowing me, I'll realize it at three in the morning and wake up from a dream where clowns are throwing wombats at me or something.

"Yeah, they would be."

"We cool?" Rachel says.

"We're cool," I say.

"Then let's go steal ourselves a talking head," she says.

───

The Lilywhite is a casino and hotel done up to look like an antebellum mansion. Between the name and the setting it's more than a little bit racist, and it makes me hate David that much more.

The Twins have a doctor on staff, because of course they do. She patched me up well enough so that I wouldn't start bleeding again. And the Twins also insisted that I not leave their fine establishment in a suit so torn-up it looks like I just had a fight with a woodchipper.

I shouldn't complain, the new suit's fit is fantastic, but I do anyway because it's navy. I swear, everybody's trying to get me out of basic black.

I've gotten so sick of the noise of Las Vegas. Its klaxon ring of slot machines, the cries of angry losers and ecstatic winners, the shuffle of cards, all blending together into one solid wall of noise you can barely think through.

Kind of makes this next bit easier, though. Rachel's texted me a five-minute warning. Time to get this party started.

I walk into the casino and head over to the nearest black-globe-covered ceiling camera, plaster a big shit-eating grin on my face, and wave into the lens.

Security's on me in less than thirty seconds. My record is having armed police in Belize coming after me inside of ten. But then, one, I was in one of their jail cells, and two, I was holding a flaming sword in my hand and screaming something about frogs. Not one of my better days.

"Sir, would you come with me, please?" says the large man in a blue-and-white jacket and black slacks who has just come over to me. It really is an unfortunate combination. Every casino has its own colors. Some might be similar, but if you're in the know, the colors and patterns can tell you what casino a chip came from. The casinos tend to dress the staff in the same colors, and the Lilywhite's are—well, let's just say it's a look.

"You look like a sailor for the world's stupidest navy," I say. "I hope they pay you a lot just for wearing the uniform."

"I really must insist, sir."

"No," I say. "I don't think so. If David wants to see me,

and I know he does, he'll have to come down here to do it."

"Sir, I—"

"And if he doesn't, I'll just have to start trashing the joint. Hurt a few customers, maybe. Accidentally, of course. I'm willing to bet he's more interested in preserving his customer base than I am." I look up at the camera. "Isn't that right, Davey-boy?"

The security guard's eyes dart to the right. He's getting an update in his earpiece. He looks a little confused, then mumbles something I can't hear.

"Sir, where would you like to meet Mister Jewel?"

"Remembers how stubborn I can be, eh? Or how destructive, if I decide to be an asshole." I look around the casino and see a set of poker tables cordoned off by velvet ropes. Far enough away from the hoi polloi to hear each other talk and close enough to cause a ruckus if I have to.

"That'll do, pig," I say. I walk over and sit at one of the tables with my back to the wall. From here I can see a bank of elevators, the front door, and five security guards dotted around the floor.

Nobody's casting or pulling power so I don't know how many of them are mages. I'm going with none of them because even the most self-loathing mage wouldn't be caught dead in one of those jackets.

Of the five guards, there are two in particular I'm a little concerned about. There's a wiry one who looks like he'd be faster than the average bear and a twitchy one who looks one missed dose of clozapine from climbing a bell tower with a hunting rifle.

Strength is fine and all. If you hit somebody and you're built like a truck, it's gonna hurt like a motherfucker. But speed and crazy beat brute strength every time. You can't kill what you can't hit or what doesn't fucking care.

And then there's David's knack to consider. If he feels cornered, would he sacrifice his customers? There are a lot of people in here. I don't know how many he can control all at once or how well, but one is one too many. If David and I come to blows here I will definitely be outnumbered and outgunned.

One of the elevators dings and David steps out wearing khakis and a blue button-down like some Silicon Valley middle manager. Guess you can project whatever image you want when you're the boss. He comes to the table with two bodyguards in tow and sits down across from me. We sit there, neither of us saying anything for a long moment. Finally, David breaks the silence.

"Eric," he says. "Given the message you gave my people at the Venetian, I wasn't expecting you."

"Minor miscommunication," I say. "What I should have said to your man was, 'I can't come with you now, but I'll swing by later,' instead of splitting him in half like an anatomical model."

"Ned was a friend of mine," he says.

"Bridget was a friend of mine," I say.

"Shit. I knew it had to be you. My fault, really. I shouldn't have said anything. But keeping that secret for so many years, I just had to tell someone. Stupid of me to think you wouldn't get all uppity about it."

"That's me, Uppity Carter. Why'd you do it?"

He smiles. I thought I knew the type of man he was, someone who throws around casual cruelty, but in that moment I realize I'm wrong. There's nothing casual about his cruelty at all.

"Because I could," he says. "And fuck her. She's nobody."

"You hit on her and she turned you down," I say.

"You know, this is nice and all," he says, "but I don't really trust you."

"Smart of you," I say. He glances at one of his body-guards, who comes around behind me. I know what happens next and there's no reason to fight it. I stand up and let him perform an uncomfortably thorough search.

"Since you're already crawling up my asshole back there, mind checking my prostate?" I say.

The bodyguard finishes finding the only things I have on me: the money clip surrounding about five thousand dollars in hundreds, the black poker chip, my phone, and the metal star I took out of Bridget. He totally misses the ring on my finger. It's just some piece of jewelry, right?

"So, doc, am I gonna live?"

"That remains to be seen," David says. He picks up the poker chip, turns it in his fingers. "What casino is this from?"

"A poker club in Hawaiian Gardens in L.A.," I say. "I liked the color."

He flips it back to me. I catch it and slide it into my coat pocket. I pick up the money clip, trigger the rune with a touch of my thumb, and slide it into my pocket, too.

Either it doesn't work at all, or it's doing what it's supposed to and charging up slowly. A second later I feel it. If I wasn't looking, I never would have noticed it.

I leave the metal star on the table. It's flipped over so the inscription is hidden, but David knows exactly what it is.

"Pretty sure that one's yours," I say. He slides it over to himself and flips it over.

"It's true. She's actually out."

"What, you didn't see the news?"

"News is fake half the time," he says. He flicks the star and it slides over to me. I pocket it.

"Not this time it isn't. What the hell do you want, David? You send a small gang to take me out at the Venetian. I know I've pissed off a lot of people, but I didn't think you and I had a problem since what happened at the apartment building."

"It was to talk," he says.

"Then maybe don't send a messenger who tries to kill me."

"Ned is—was—a little overzealous. Look, I fucked up. I'm not so proud I can't admit that. I really just wanted to talk."

"Okay, sure. Let's talk," I say. I can feel him casting and I brace myself, but it's only a silence spell. The noise of the casino fades away.

"Why'd you break her out of prison?" he says. "She's fucking dangerous and you know it."

"Because what you did was fucked up. She's dangerous? She's not the psychopath building a Las Vegas empire. You're way more dangerous than she is. Should I shove this thing into your chest and dump you at the scene of a crime?"

"You don't know what she's capable of, man."

"I watched her burn down an entire fucking prison and a bunch of people inside. I think I have a pretty good idea."

"Fine. Whatever. That's not what I wanted to talk to you about. You've been here, what, two days? Three? Your name keeps popping up and I'm not sure what to make of it. It's like people are scared of you."

"Might have something to do with me marching some guy's head around a fighting pit covered in gore. Try it some time. It's very invigorating."

"We don't trust each other," he says. "We don't like each other. But really, I do just want to talk. I've got a question."

"Shoot," I say. "Poor choice of words, I know, but it's kind of a dare."

"Why are you here?"

"Because I thought it'd be rude not to come down after your goons tried to put bullet holes in me by way of invitation."

"You know what I mean. You know what? Scratch that. Maybe you're here because of me. Maybe it's a complete coincidence. I don't care. What I really want to know is what it will take to get you to leave."

Oh, now this is interesting. Not what I was expecting. I'm curious what he'll do. Fuck it. The truth will set you free and all that.

"Jimmy Freeburg," I say.

"Isn't that a Lynyrd Skynyrd song?"

"Now who's being obtuse?"

"What about it?" he says.

"You have him. I need to talk to him. Simple as that."

"Talk to it? You know that's not how the Oracle thing works, right?"

"So everyone keeps telling me," I say. "I'm not looking for a prophecy, I'm looking for an answer. And don't ask to what. It's none of your goddamn business."

"Okay. Yeah, I have it. If it gives you this answer, you're gone?"

"In a flash," I say.

"Then if you want an answer, let's go get you one." He stands up. I have a momentary panic that he's going to take me down to the vault and this whole thing'll go tits up. But this is David we're talking about here.

"You're a funny guy," I say. "You think I'm going to let you lead me into some hotel corridor where you and your buddies can jump me in the dark? No, I think I'll stay here with the crowd."

He sits back down. "I'm telling the truth, but suit yourself. If you won't come with me to talk to it, how are you going to get your answer?"

"Steal him," I say. "Obviously."

Chapter 21

David isn't quite sure what to do with that one. It looks like he's about to laugh it off and then stops.

"You're serious. Holy shit, you are serious. That's why you sprung Bridget out of prison."

"Well, duh. What the hell else was I gonna do? She can burn through anything, a safe, a bunker, whatever. Or did you not notice that?"

Now he starts laughing. "Oh, man. You're gonna need a lot more than one psycho pyro to get to it. You're welcome to try. You won't get ten feet, but go for it."

"Pretty secure, huh?"

"Believe me, you can't get anywhere near it. Alarms, traps, wards, and a big fucking safe. It's right downstairs. Take a crack at it. I'd love to see you explode."

"Sounds like I'll need a wardcracker," I say. "I wonder if I can track down Lucas."

"Fuck Lucas."

"What is it with the hostility?" I say. "Is the rumor about you and him true?"

"Don't say it."

"He bilked you out of fifty million bucks. You'd have to be really fucking stupid to fall for one of his cons. And we both know you're not really fucking stupid."

"Is that sarcasm?"

"Now when have I ever been sarcastic?"

"Fuck you," he says. "And it was twenty. There was no reason not to trust him. We'd been friends for years."

"We were all thieves, David. Do the math."

"Enough," he says. "Just fucking stop. Look, I want you gone. It'd be easier for all of us if I didn't have to have you killed. So how do we get you out of my hair without having to murder you in front of all these fine people?"

"Give me unrestricted access to Jimmy with no bull-shit."

"I just—"

"With the added guarantee of me having a razor blade to your throat."

"That's a big ask," he says. "Especially seeing as you don't have one."

"I'll make do."

David looks around at the casino. "How about this? We're in Vegas. Let's gamble, play some cards. If I win, you leave. If you win, I take you to the Oracle—yes, with a razor blade to my throat—and you ask your question."

Hadn't expected that, but it could work in my favor. I don't have to win, I just have to keep the game going until I get the all-clear from Rachel.

"I'm listening. What's the game?"

"Seven card stud."

"What, no hold 'em? I thought that was the big trend these days?"

"I fucking hate that game," he says.

"Seven card stud, then. To what?"

"Until you run out of money." David waves over a dealer. "Seven card stud. Straight? Nothing wild?"

"Works for me." I pull out the money clip and hand the five thousand I have in there to the dealer, who slides over a stack of chips. The man looks a little nervous. If I had to deal with David every day, I'd look that way, too.

"Gentlemen," he says. "Hundred minimum bet, no max. Fifty dollar ante."

We both toss fifty into the pot. The dealer gives us two cards down and one up. David has a seven of hearts showing. I have an eight of clubs.

"Check," I say.

"Pussy." David tosses a hundred into the pot.

"I get plenty, thanks," I say and match it. David gets an ace of hearts, I get a nine of clubs. Another bet. David goes in for five hundred, I match him.

"It's customary to look at your hole cards, you know," he says. I haven't so much as glanced at them.

"I will eventually," I say. David's king of hearts. My ace of spades. "I'm seeing a possible straight flush over there. You know never to go for an inside straight, right? Of course, you do. Losing teaches you a lot, doesn't it?"

"And I see a lot of crap in your hand there," David says. "You gonna tell me why you want to see Jimmy?"

"It's for a friend," I say. "Really hard to shop for. Thought he could give me some tips."

"Didn't think you had friends."

"Well, friends, acquaintances, people I have blackmail on. Really, what's the difference? Oh, hey. Look at that."

"Pair of eights, bets," the dealer says.

"Oh, let's make this one exciting," I say, I make a show of looking at both of our up cards. He's gotten a queen of hearts compared to my eight of spades. I give my most steely gaze, lean in, and whisper, "Check."

"Oh, for fuck sake." He slides five hundred in and I match him.

"Last card down," the dealer says. "Bet's to the pair of eights."

"So help me, if you check, I will fucking shoot you," David says.

"You or one of your people? Ned, maybe? Oh wait, no. He's dead. Dead Ned. Hey, that rhymes."

"Place a fucking bet."

"Cards don't really relax you, do they?" I say. "I hear yoga's really good for that."

"Look at your cards and fucking bet."

"And ruin the surprise? I don't know about you, but I hate spoilers." I slide a thousand into the pot.

"You're really fucking stupid, you know that?"

"Oh god, yes," I say. "Plenty of people tell me. You gonna match that pot? Or you gonna fold?"

He slides in a thousand. And then another thousand.

"Now we're talkin'." I match the bet. "Call."

David flips over his cards. His final hole card is an ace of diamonds, giving him a pair of aces. Everything else is crap.

"Nice," I say. "That beats my pair of eights. But let's see what Santa brought me this year, shall we?" I flip over my first two hole cards. A ten of hearts and jack of hearts.

"Sonofabitch," David says.

"Guess I messed up that inside straight you were hoping for," I say.

"I still beat your fuckin' two eights." I flip over my last hole card.

"Well, whattaya know," I say. "An ace of clubs. That gives me aces and eights. Dead Man's Hand. Kind of on the nose, though, don't you think?"

"Fuck." David gets up from the table and paces a bit, muttering to himself.

"Does he do this a lot?"

"I'd rather not answer that, if you don't mind," the dealer says.

David comes back to the table and sits. "Okay," he says. "Sacrificial pancake."

"Sounds like a pop-punk band from the nineties."

"When you cook pancakes, the first one's always fucked up. Maybe the heat's too high, you're not using enough butter. Something like that. How it's fucked up tells you what you need to change so that the rest of them don't turn out that way."

"And that's the sacrificial pancake. Was this your sacrificial hand?"

"Something like that. Let's play cards."

"Yes, let's."

"With a different deck."

"Oooh. Special cards? Why, David, I'm flattered."

"You ever play with sorcerer cards?"

"You mean a deck supposedly immune to magic so it won't let you cheat?"

"Exactly."

David nods to the dealer who pulls out a new deck, unwraps it and begins to shuffle. Sorcerer cards are our way of cutting down on magical cheating. They don't work as well as everyone likes to pretend. They're good with illusions, pretty bulletproof for them, in fact. And teleportation. They won't do anything to a diviner, though. If they can see your cards with magic, they're not gonna stop that.

Easier to just have mages hang around and watch out for anyone using magic. I didn't actually do anything and I'm just as likely to get a Dead Man's Hand as anybody. It's either a coincidence or the universe playing a joke on me.

"I'm hurt," I say. "I don't need special cards to cheat, but if you want I'll be happy to cheat with them anyway."

"Deal the fucking cards," David says.

I win some, I lose some. Sometimes I fold on good hands, sometimes I bluff with shitty ones. I don't care about winning. I just need to keep the game going.

"The fuck are you doing?" he says half an hour in.

"Playing cards."

"No, you're not. You're just dickin' around."

"What, because I'm not losing more?"

"Because you're not winning more."

"Maybe I'm just really bad at cards."

"I don't know what the hell you're doing, but cut it out. Let's play."

I had a roommate for a few months in Albuquerque a while back. Nice guy. I was a night owl and he had a nine-to-five, so we didn't see each other much.

This guy loved chess. He bought fucking magazines about the game. I had no idea chess magazines even existed. He kept a chess board set up near the door for I don't know what reason.

One time as I'm about to go out I see that he's moved a pawn. What the hell. I move a pawn. I get back the next morning and he's made another move. So I make another move.

Back and forth and back and forth. This goes for about a month and a half, maybe two. I get up one night, find him crouching next to the board looking at it with the intensity of a surgeon pulling burs out of somebody's dickhole. Multiple angles, from above, below, across the room.

"I can't figure it out," he tells me. "I thought I knew what strategy you were using, but then I thought it was something else. I can't tell if you're a genius or an idiot."

"That's easy," I say. "You're the only one who's playing. I'm just moving pieces." Yeah, he wasn't happy.

David is getting more and more frantic. I think at first he thought it would be easy. He's the casino owner, right? I'm some asshole from Los Angeles just begging to get my ass handed to me. Except I'm just moving pieces.

"I want a new deck," he tells the dealer. The man nods, pulls out a fresh deck, and unwraps it, then shakes out the cards and starts to shuffle.

"We can do that?" I say. "I didn't know we can do that. Can we get one with ponies on it? I like ponies."

"You're not taking this seriously at all," he says.

The dealer slides out our first three cards, two down, one up. An ace of clubs to David's nine of hearts. I slide in three stacks of chips into the center of the table.

"I have no idea how much that is," I say.

"I fucking hate you."

My next three cards are a ten, a jack, and a queen. All clubs. The pot's about half of our funds now. Two cards down. My phone buzzes. I pull it out and look the display. 1111. That went faster than expected. That's my cue. Then another text right on its heels. 'BRIDGET IN ELEVATOR NOW. COMING TO YOU.'

The game has finally gotten interesting.

Chapter 22

"Bet's to you," David says. From my seat I can see a bank of three elevators, one coming up from B3, which I assume is the basement.

"All in," I say. I push all of my chips into the center of the table.

"You're bluffing," he says.

"That's, what, eight thousand in the pot now?" I say.

"All right," he says. He pushes the rest of his chips into the center of the table. "I call." He lays down a straight flush of hearts, ace to five.

"Damn. That's a good hand." I flip over my hole cards. I needed a king. No such luck. "Beats my almost-but-not-quite-a-royal-flush. I guess you win. I'll leave town. Have a good life, David." I stand up from the table.

"Stop," he says. "The fuck are you doing?"

"Leaving," I say. "Just like we bet. I lost, you won. I'm outta here."

David nods at one of the two bodyguards, who pulls a small, silenced pistol from beneath his jacket. "You're going to fucking answer me. What are you doing?"

"Thought it was obvious," I say. "You were playing cards. I wasn't. Come on, David. You're not stupid. Put it together."

Confusion goes to realization goes to rage and he bolts up, kicking his chair out from beneath him. "You mother-fucker. What the hell is going on?"

"Two things," I say. A man in a suit bursts out of a side door in a panic and runs to the table. He whispers something to David, who turns a shade of red I thought you only got with lobster.

"That's one."

"I'm going to fucking kill you." David starts pulling in a lot of magic.

"Aaaand—" The elevator dings. "That's two."

The doors open and out steps Bridget. David glances over his shoulder. Takes him a second to recognize her, and when he does all the blood drains from his face.

The bodyguard steps in closer to me with the gun raised. "Oh, I am so not the person you want to be shooting at right now." I incline my head toward Bridget, who has just burst into flames.

There's screaming, the fire alarm going off, sprinklers kicking in. I already have a shield spell around me to keep the water off. The bodyguard must know enough about magic to see the spray pattering off the shield and understand he'd just be wasting bullets.

He turns around and starts shooting at Bridget. The bullets vaporize before they get to her. I do the bodyguard a favor and save him from the horrible fate of burning to death by manifesting the straight razor and slitting his throat through the back of his neck.

"Mind if I borrow this?" I say, picking up his gun. "Thanks, you're a peach."

The amount of energy Bridget's expending and pulling in is so much more than at the prison. She was always very efficient with her magic, but now?

It's not like drinking from a firehose so much as ramming a car into the hydrant and sticking your face in the hole.

And that's my cue. She is not going to be paying attention to anyone or anything that isn't David, guaranteeing

I'll be caught in the carnage. I haven't come this far to get killed again.

"Where the fuck do you think you're going?" A group of elderly men and women step in front of me with murder in their eyes. They all spoke in unison and they're moving the same way.

"David, you really should be focusing on Bridget," I say. "And not wasting your energy on me. You're gonna need it."

"I might go down, Carter," they say, "but I'm taking you down with me."

"Really? With a bunch of geriatric slot-machine addicts? I mean, I'm impressed. Splitting your energy between me and Bridget. And clearly holding your own, because you're not dead yet. But really, you don't stay focused, you're gonna burn."

"Maybe. Maybe not. Take a look." I glance over my shoulder, keeping this gang of oldsters in my peripheral vision. There's Bridget burning bright by the elevators. She's moving, but slowly. She has to repeatedly burn away these walls of ice that keep growing in front of her.

The reason for this is the group of three mages surrounding her, constantly replenishing the ice. They're not trying to hurt her, they're trying to exhaust her. If they can slow her down long enough, she'll run out of power and be a sitting duck. She'll never reach David, and it'll all be over for her.

I take a quick scan of my surroundings. There are a couple of Haunts nearby, and a Wanderer. It could be a problem if I don't move fast enough.

"Clever," I say. "But we can't have that." I slide over to the dead side and run to the glowing form of one of the mages. I slide back to the living side and take a quick swipe at the man's neck with the straight razor.

His head comes away like cutting through paper. From

the fountain of blood, it's clear he was dealing with hypertension. Probably have a heart attack in the next year or so if he didn't burn to death here. Really, I'm doing him a favor.

His ice wall disappears like throwing a light switch. The next mage over notices. I can feel him pulling more power to bolster his spell and compensate. In the chaos he hasn't seen exactly what's happened.

Dropping that one mage makes all the difference. I back away with an encouraging thumbs-up to Bridget. She sees me, waves a flaming hand, and pushes forward, darting to the side to take advantage of the new opening.

"You're gonna pay for that," say a weird harmony of old and young voices. I spin around and see that David has taken the minds of about fifty or so of his soaking-wet customers, all steadily marching toward me. He's going to try to smother me, which won't work since I can pop away any time I want. But what I really need to do is even these odds a bit.

"If he hasn't scooped out your minds like a melon-baller, know that I'm really sorry about this." I slash at the group of five directly in front of me, willing the razor to kill without cutting anything important off the bodies.

They go down like tenpins, a bunch of retirees who just wanted to play a little slots, maybe some blackjack, ogle the waitstaff. I feel each of their deaths, lightning flashes amid a storm of the dead and dying.

I really fucking hate myself, sometimes.

I do the same to a few others. Soon I have a pile of corpses that the other brain zombies are stepping over to get to me. They seem to be on auto-pilot. David's probably figured out that I'm the lesser threat and so given them a simple command, just to kill me.

I start pulling in power. It's actually not easy. Bridget

and David are both sucking a lot from the pool. There's no danger of draining it, but getting a connection takes a couple seconds.

One of the things a mage learns pretty quickly when people are trying to kill them is to draw in power and cast at the same time. All three of us are doing it. Drawing in and throwing out, like industrial snowblowers.

Technically we don't *need* to do that, but it's a force of habit we all seem to pick up. This way we're not tapping our own power. Some mages don't have a lot of their own. They depend on the pool of magic. I mean, if it's there, grab it.

David and Bridget's magic is a steady flow of power. They're both pretty much doing the same thing, trying to kill the other. I just have my shield up to keep everybody at arm's length.

But it's time to crank things up a bit. I think about Mictlantecuhtli's magic, form the spell in my mind. It still feels like speaking a foreign language, but it's getting easier.

It happens a lot faster than I expect and I snap out the spell with a single, massive burst of power that stops Bridget and David dead in their tracks for a second. I have the attention of every mage here. And possibly of every mage in all of Las Vegas.

"Hey, Davey-boy," I yell. "Want to make a bet my zombies kick the shit out of yours?" He might not be able to hear me, but when the corpses at my feet stand up and start attacking the mob, he takes notice. Biting, clawing, punching, kicking. I'm not telling them how to take these people down, just that I want them to do it. From the confusion on his face, I think David isn't sure which threat he needs to be paying attention to.

I watch for new dead as David's puppets go down. As

soon as each one falls, I make it stand back up again. The problem is that each one takes a lot of power, and with this much magic being thrown around it's getting harder to tap into the pool.

Like it or not, I have to tap into my own reserves. I've got a lot but it's not infinite, and every time I raise a corpse it's a big drain. I keep this up for too long, I'm gonna drop.

I think about keeping some power in reserve so I can slide over to the other side if things get too hairy and then realize that won't work.

I haven't been keeping track of how many people I've killed so far, or who've died in the stampede to escape, or been taken out by Bridget. But given the number of new ghosts I'm seeing here, it's a lot. If I slide over now, I'll be like a cow in a piranha pool.

Fortunately, I still have the portal ring. Though I've never tried it around this much magic. If it pulls any power from the local pool that could be a problem.

There's a gunshot and one of David's mind-controlled zombie's head explodes. Then another and one of mine goes down, its head shattering like a watermelon dropped from a ten-story building. Alive, dead, a zombie's a zombie, I guess.

"Shoot them in the head," someone yells and whoever they're talking to starts firing into the crowd. Bodies drop. They're completely indiscriminate. There's no point in raising any more dead if they're just going to pop their heads with hollow-points, so I pump more power into my shield.

Some of the bodies going down are mine, most of them are David's. Even more are innocent bystanders who just wanted to play some craps. On the plus side, they're being spared decades of therapy.

As a patch clears, I see that the shooters are the five survivors of the Venetian. They're mowing down everyone who gets in their way. They have no idea who's dangerous and who isn't. Might as well just kill them all.

Then they see me. It takes a beat for them to pick me out of the crowd. If David ever clued them into who I am and what I can do they've probably connected enough dots to know that I'm a big source of the current problem.

Of course they shoot at me. I mean, I would, too. Just on general principle.

None of their bullets connect. Mostly it's just noise. Gunfire, screaming, bullets stopping dead or ricocheting off my shield.

I can only imagine what this all feels like to the other mages in town. If they're smart they're packing up and getting the fuck out. We're slinging around more power than I've felt in a long time.

I've got a crowd of undead and mind-controlled zombies between me and a group of heavily armed murderers. Behind me are two hardcore mages who are trying to turn each other into greasy stains on the floor and a group of casino security guards who are all shooting at Bridget and occasionally dying when they catch the business end of a fireball.

Alarms are blaring. The sprinklers are soaking everything. The air is filled with smoke, steam, bullets, shredded poker chips, mulched furniture, and the certainty that it can't possibly get worse.

Which is when it gets worse.

One of the security guards has just run onto the casino floor with an LAW, which on the surface doesn't look that impressive. It's just a wide green tube open at both ends. Until you pull the trigger.

This is not the sort of thing you use indoors. I'm not

sure which surprises me more, that some idiot thinks a rocket launcher is a good idea in this situation or that David just happens to have one lying around in the back.

I see the guy with the rocket launcher. Some of the security guards see the guy with the rocket launcher. The goons trying to kill me see the guy with the rocket launcher. We all shoot the guy with the rocket launcher.

Unfortunately, we're a nanosecond too late. He pulls the trigger just before he's pumped full of a few hundred rounds of lead.

Everything feels like it's in slow motion. That helpless feeling of a train wreck, or when your car is already over the cliff but you pump the brakes anyway.

There's a roar of sound, a blast of light. I push everything I have left into my shield. Amazingly it holds, but bows inward with a crackling red glow when the blast wave hits. Then the wave picks me up and throws me like I'm a beach ball. I hit something hard and then it all goes black.

I don't know how long I'm out. Not too long, though, since the building hasn't collapsed on me yet. Everything hurts. I've been blown up enough times to know that's actually a good sign. If you hurt, you're not dead.

I'm covered in drywall dust, chunks of wall, unidentifiable bits of meat and metal. My shield held long enough to keep me from turning into either a pancake or a pincushion.

I push a chunk of drywall off me and stand up. The room is destroyed. The lights are gone along with most of the ceiling, sparks from exposed wires the only illumination. Water is pouring out of pipes somewhere. I can hear the occasional weak moan of a survivor, generally followed by feeling the unmistakable pinprick of their death a moment later.

That's likely part of what knocked me out. There are a

lot of dead here. Not just the ones caught up in the fight, but people all around the floor who hadn't gotten out in the panicked rush to escape and were caught in the blast. Good thing I was unconscious. Feeling all that death up close would be almost as bad as the shock wave. Like getting punched in the head by a gorilla.

The ghost population has swelled. Mostly Haunts, a few Wanderers. They don't seem to have caught on to the fact that they're dead yet. They walk in a daze, past Echoes standing at nonexistent slot machines going through the motions of feeding coins and pulling levers, hoping for a payoff that'll never come.

Between the mass die-off and the rocket explosion in an enclosed space it's a miracle I'm not a smear on what's left of the walls, with or without magic.

It's not like I don't have a scratch on me; I'm not sure how many places I'm bleeding from. One of my ribs is fucked up. But hey, I didn't puncture a lung. I really hate chest tubes.

I stagger over to where I think the elevators were. It's hard to tell with all the debris and smoke, but I can just make out what looks like three twisted doorframes that are all that's left of the wall they were set in. I don't see anyone else standing.

I come up to the remains of a circular bar off to the side. It's barely holding together. I feel a small flare of magic coming from it. A tiny blip that fizzles out a second later.

I don't have the gun anymore, but the straight razor is there in my hand when I think about it. I wonder where it goes when it disappears. Another physical location? A different space?

I slowly peek my head over the side of the bar and see Bridget awkwardly sitting on the floor and leaning against the other side, pouring a bottle of whisky with one hand into something I can't quite make out in her other.

Her body is covered in burns. Clothes either burned away or melted into her skin. She doesn't have any hair on one side of her head and not a lot of flesh there either. I can see the muscles of her jaw and exposed bone. Her right leg is bent out to her side in a way that legs shouldn't bend.

She notices me and smiles with one half of her face, the charred skin crackling as she does. Raises the bottle. "Hey, man. Want a drink?"

"Sure," I say. "Why the fuck not."

I limp my way through a blown-out chunk of the bar. The floor is covered in shattered glass and pools of alcohol. I don't really relish the idea of sitting and having half a jagged bottle of Jim Beam up my ass, so I kneel painfully down to her level.

"You look like shit," she says.

"That's nothing new," I say. She hands me the bottle and I take a swig. She raises the thing she was holding—

the top half of somebody's fire-blasted skull—and sips whisky out of the brain pan.

"David?"

"Yep. The rest of him's around here someplace. I burned out his eyeballs and then grabbed his head by the sockets. Tore it off like I was picking up a bowling ball. It was fucking awesome."

"Good for you. Fucker deserved it. You wanna get outta here?"

"Nah," she says. "No point. I really did burn myself out this time. Between the vault and all this I couldn't light a fart if I wanted to."

"Doesn't mean you have to die for it," I say.

"Dude, look at me. I'm already dead. I can't feel anything below my chest. I used the last of my magic to dull the pain everywhere else. And if I survive, what's gonna happen to me with no magic? They'll lock me up again, execute me, or just flat-out shoot my ass when they find me."

"You sure this is how you wanna go?" I say.

"Sipping whisky out of David's burnt-out skull? Fuck yeah."

"I can think of worse ways."

"Yeah," she says, raising David's skull. "Like him. Cheers."

I clink the bottle against David's skull and take a drink. "Before you go off into the great beyond," I say, "how'd it go?"

"Without a hitch," she says. "Kinda creepy, actually. It was like everything just sort of lined up. The guards let us right through, Lucas said half the wards had been deactivated, cameras were shut down because of maintenance. And then we find out somebody's left the electronic locks on the vault in a diagnostic mode. Cut our work in half."

"That's a lot of coincidences."

"Yeah. Kinda freaked Lucas out. He said for everything to line up a bunch of different schedules would have had to change like two weeks ago. But hey, gift horses and all that. We got your head for you. Or Nicole's head. Or, fuck, I dunno. Once it started talking, I was out of there."

Two weeks ago. Huh. I wonder if that's the reality quake I felt the other night. From what Shait was saying, two weeks sounds like it's Jimmy's current limit for fucking with the past.

"So, everybody else made it out?" I say.

She coughs, a ragged, wet sound. "I assume," she says. She wipes blood off of her chin. "I came right up here once they were packed and out the door." Another cough. "Oh, this doesn't feel good."

"Dying usually doesn't," I say.

"Rachel told me some shit about you being dead and coming back. Any of that true?"

"Yeah. I got gutted by a demon and bled out on a school yard. I don't recommend it."

"And what, Heaven? Hell?"

"Place called Mictlan. Took on the mantle of a death god. Hard to explain. Then a friend of mine yanked me back."

"Death god. That is so fucking metal," she says. "I'm tired. I've been so tired."

"Thirty years in stir is a long time."

She raises the remains of David's skull. "I wish I could piss in this thing. You think anybody'll remember me?" Her voice is slowing, drifting.

"I sure as fuck will," I say.

"Thanks, man," she says. "For everything. I mean it." Her face goes slack, then the rest of her. The top of David's skull rolls out of her hand and wobbles a bit on the floor.

I stand up, every muscle screaming at me. "You were a crazy motherfucker, Bridget," I say. "Glad I knew you. And I'm glad you're dead."

Now that pretty much everybody around here is a corpse, there isn't a whole lot of magic being used. I try the portal ring. I'm shooting for the Golden Nugget and it opens a hole onto a nearby alley. Range is probably the problem. I limp through the hole and close it behind me.

Chapter 23

I'm not sure where I am—I wasn't thinking of a particular place other than "away." I've never really tested this thing's range. The farthest I've gone has been about five or six stories when I went from the bottom of a building to the top.

I can hear sirens, screams. From the smell it seems like the Lilywhite's on fire. Between Bridget and the rocket launcher, how could it not be?

I can see the sign for the Gold Rush casino in the distance, where Nicole should be holed up with Jimmy. Lucas and Rachel are at Caesar's on the other side of town.

I can't walk onto the street looking like this. Hell, I'm not sure I can walk at all. I don't have any stickers or a Sharpie and casting any sort of invisibility is going to take focus. After getting slammed around by the blast, that would require more concentration than I muster.

Stealing a car is right out. The streets are at a standstill. Not sure I could drive right now anyway.

I start to open a new portal. I concentrate on the Gold Rush, but a wave of vertigo hits me as I trigger the ring. Suddenly I'm on the ground, trying really hard not to throw up. Concussions are fun.

Concentrating on anything right now seems to be a problem, but I had brain damage from multiple concussions before and it didn't kill me, so I'm not too worried. I should be able to take plenty more hits to this new noggin and keep going.

I try it again. The portal opens up, the edges of it ragged and shaking. The Gold Rush might be a bit too far away for it. I jump through before it can close on me or I pass out, barely making it onto the other side before it collapses behind me.

I'm only a couple of blocks away from the Gold Rush. The ring's got a much longer range than I realized, even if that puts a strain on it. Good to know. I do one more portal hop and I'm at the back entrance to the shut-down casino, inside the chain link fence surrounding it. Then I double over and puke my guts out.

I lean up against a stack of wooden pallets, the world spinning around me. A few deep breaths and the vertigo fades. Experience tells me I can expect to have this on and off for the next few hours at least. Once my head and stomach settle, at least temporarily, I'm able to get a good look around.

Nicole was right. This place hasn't seen anyone in years. Old construction equipment, rusted and faded from the elements, sits haphazardly around the site.

It's smaller than I remember. The penthouse, if you can even call it that, is only five or six stories up. The windows are covered with years of filth. The disintegrating signage out front and the Old West theme make it look like a ghost town.

I go around the building until I find a service door near the back. It's propped open. Nicole probably went in that way. If there were troublesome squatters, she would have run them off before I got here.

That doesn't mean there isn't still trouble. David might be dead, but this thing isn't over until I have my answers from Jimmy and get the hell out of here. Nicole might make that more of a challenge than I'm up for.

The straight razor appears in my hands as I think about it, and I nudge the door open with my foot. Inside, the casino might as well be a lightless cave. Where gaming tables and slot machines once stood, there's dust and mold. A handful of broken slots are scattered around the floor, cannibalized for parts.

Nicole said the safe room was on this floor. The question is where? If Sebastian put as much effort into it as she said he did, I don't think I'm going to find her.

This is where cell phones come in handy. "Where the fuck are you?" I say when she answers.

"Hang on." Thin lines of light appear in one wall, connecting into a rectangle that fades into a pair of steel security doors. Nicole opens one of them, steps out, sees me, and runs over to grab me before I faceplant on the floor.

"What the hell happened?" she says, helping me limp into the room.

"Bridget, David, and a rocket launcher," I say.

This is a nicer safe room than the one Nicole had in the house in Summerlin. It looks larger than it should be given its location. A mini pocket universe, kind of like the room I had at the ghost of the Ambassador Hotel.

Only that was a suite. This looks like it's a whole house. It's open plan, allowing me to see a sizable chunk of it. Living room, den, kitchen, stairs leading up to a second floor. Sebastian sunk some serious money into this thing.

"Hello, Eric." A voice I haven't heard in years. Sitting on the top of a secretary desk pushed against the wall is a suitcase-sized box of dark mahogany with a handle on the top and hinges and latches that allow it to be opened like a cabinet.

"Jimmy fucking Freeburg," I say. I can't see him too well because my eyes are starting to cross. "We need to talk."

"Yes, we do," he says.

"In a minute," I say, and pass out on the floor.

———

I regain consciousness halfway into a maroon club chair, my ass on the edge of the cushion and my arms precariously draped over the chair's arms. It takes me a second to remember that I'm not in the room in the Ambassador, passed out after getting shitfaced on the endless amounts of whisky the room kept stocked.

"Uh . . ."

"You're too goddamn heavy," Nicole says. "That's as far as I could get you into the chair. I don't know why I even bothered doing that much."

"Thanks," I say. "I think." I manage to pull myself all the way into the chair, which is surprising, because every part of my body should feel like I've been trampled by a bull. Instead it's more of a distant ache.

"What the hell did you give me?" I say. She tosses a pill bottle at me. I look inside at the bright red, slightly glowing pills.

"Take one when the pain starts to kick back in. Usually takes a couple hours."

"The hell are they?"

She shrugs. "Sebastian never told me."

"You gave me thirty-year-old glowing pills?"

"You gonna be an asshole about it, I'll take them back."

"No, I'm good," I say. "And thank you." And the fuck I'm gonna take any more of them. Not until I find out what sort of poison she's trying to kill me with.

I look around and see that Jimmy has been moved from the secretary desk to a dining table off of the kitchen. Something about him seems different. I mean, he looks the same: nerdy type; pasty skin, kinked-up hair that makes his head look lopsided.

"Lost the Buddy Holly glasses, I see," I say. I stand, walk over to the next room, and sit in one of the dining chairs, putting us eye to eye.

"Don't really need them," he says, "and they kept falling off whenever Nicole moved my case."

His voice is how I remember it, sort of. But it's calmer, more measured now. There's inflection, but not much. It's the kind of voice where you'd tell a joke and instead of laughing, it'd just say, "That's funny."

It's weird having a conversation with him again after all these years. When he was alive, Jimmy was a fuck-up with a meth habit who would panic at the drop of a hat. I bailed him out of jail six times before I killed him. Now he looks like an actual adult. As much of an adult as a severed talking head in a box can.

"Death suits you," I say.

"Thank you," he says. "You as well."

"Yeah," I say. "Some days I wish I could go back to what I was."

"I know the feeling."

But does he? And then it clicks. There's nothing left in there of the person I knew. Not sure why there would be. Everyone has been right. Jimmy's not a him. They're an it.

"What should I call you now?" I say.

"Jimmy's fine."

"I have questions," I say.

"And I have answers, though I suspect you've already figured a couple out on your own."

"The counterspell," I say. "How do I reverse the bull-shit that Liam pulled on Gabriela and Attila Werther?"

"Gabriela is easy," he says, "since she wasn't the one it was originally intended for. When Liam Werther hit her with the spell, her soul came to me. I've been holding onto it for you." "Holding onto it for me," my ass.

"We'll debate that phrasing later," I say. "How do I reverse it?"

"I simply let it go," he says.

"What's the catch?"

"No catch. Eric, I know you well enough that were I to use this as some sort of blackmail or hold on to it out of spite, you would make things very unpleasant for me. You are a god, after all."

I really wish people would stop saying that. "And Werther? How about him? Where'd you send his soul?"

"It's more a question of when," Jimmy says. "I used his past experiences to send it to an earlier time of Liam Werther's choosing. He thought it would be appropriate. Physically, it appears it's where Union Station is now."

"Bring him back," I say. "Now." I know Amanda wasn't sure if she wanted her dad back or not. But I am not letting Jimmy screw with me any more than he already has.

"I can't. It was *his* past. I could send him there, but I can't go after him. Not yet, at least. I don't even know when he landed. But if you happen to find it, you can retrieve it easily enough."

"I don't believe you," I say. "But I'm not fighting you on this one. Let Gabriela go."

"Eric," Nicole says, and tilts her head toward my hands, which are white-knuckling the table. I ease my grip. Mostly.

"Done," Jimmy says.

I pull out my phone and call Amanda. She picks up before the first ring is done. "Are you home?" I ask before she can say a word. I have no idea what I'll do to Jimmy if he screws me on this, but I'm sure I can come up with something imaginative.

"Yeah."

"Check on Gabriela. And cross your fingers."

I hear the phone fall to the floor, footsteps running away. A minute goes by, then two. My tension ratchets up with each passing second and I start weighing the relative merits of acid and fire, whether either one can actually destroy Jimmy. Probably not. Maybe throwing it into lava.

Another agonizing minute until I hear a click, and Amanda says, "You're on speaker."

"What the fuck happened?" Gabriela says. She sounds like she's just woken out of a nap. I can feel my entire body uncoil like a spring, and I start to breathe again.

"You've been cosplaying as Snow White," I say. "We hired a homeless guy to come in and give you true love's kiss."

"We were fighting Liam," she says. "I don't remember anything after that."

"Good," I say. "It was boring. Amanda'll give you the gist and I'll fill in the details when I get back."

Amanda comes back on the line. "My dad?"

"More complicated. We need to talk to your uncle. Liam's been holding out on us."

"Are you sure?" she says. "We put him through the wringer."

"He's good at surviving through loopholes," I say. "This time ask him *when* he sent his brother."

"When?"

"Special request from Liam to send his soul into the past. I don't know what that means yet, other than that we can't get him back as easily. You two okay?"

"Yeah," Amanda says. "Gabriela seems fine."

"Because I am fine," Gabriela says, irritation in her voice. When she sounds like she wants to kill something, that means she's fine. "You getting the hell out of there?"

"Not yet," I say. "I need to get some answers. I'll let you know."

"Don't go getting blown up or anything," Gabriela says.

"I think the odds of that happening are pretty low."

"You already did, didn't you?"

"Oh, you know me so well. I promise not to get myself blown up. Better?"

"Yes, thank you," she says.

"I'll talk to you soon." When she hangs up, I find myself listening to the silence, unwilling to put the phone down. There's a catch here. There has to be.

I slide the phone back into my pocket and look at Jimmy. Like really look at it. It's weird. This whole time I kept thinking about it as a person. Because I was responsible for its creation. Because it had a name.

It's a device, an artifact. Herb called it what you get when a monkey's paw fucks a hand grenade. It isn't a Magic 8-Ball, but that's a more accurate name for it than Jimmy Freeburg.

"How much of this did you orchestrate?" I say.

"Eric," Nicole says. "Just leave. You got what you wanted."

I ignore her. "Well?"

"Directly?" Jimmy says. "Not as much as you might think. Some words in the right ears at the right times, a few things that zigged instead of zagged. You make it difficult to plan ahead.

"Right now, I have no sense of you. I can hear your voice and see you, but that's not really how I perceive most things. You may as well not exist right now and Nicole is like—'static' wouldn't be inaccurate. You only become clearer the farther into the future I look. A week from now I can see Nicole clearly, but it takes years before you come into focus. And even that requires a lot of effort on my part."

"Your kidnapping?"

"I saw that happening," it says, "but I didn't know much

about it. But I knew that I was going to need to plan ahead as much as possible. When Liam Werther came to me, I was ready."

"I don't understand," I say. "If you knew about it, why didn't you prevent it?" And then the answer comes to me. "You didn't want to."

The device we saw the plans for is in a cardboard box on the table. Like the drawings, it looks like a birdcage sitting on top of a videogame console.

"This is the thing lets you make changes to the past, isn't it?" I say. I lift it out of the box, turn it in my hands. It's surprisingly light. I feel underneath and find the compartment you would normally put batteries. I feel around for the edges, angled so neither of them can see.

"How does it work?" I say.

"I doubt you have the math," Jimmy says.

"Jesus, you don't need to rub it in. So put it in layman's terms."

"It reverses the way I perceive time."

"Got it. And since you can view the future to make changes, this lets you view the past and affect it the same way."

"Yes," Jimmy says.

"See, was that so hard? Here's something I don't understand. If you knew about the device beforehand, why did you still want to get taken?" I say. I set the device back into its box. "Couldn't you just arrange things so the people around you make it for you?"

"I think you already know," Jimmy says.

"Sonofabitch," I say trying my damnedest to sound surprised. "You needed something only David had. One of the opals."

Nicole jerks like she's been hit with a live wire. "How do you know about that?"

I ignore her. "David got his hands on it at an auction a

few years ago and you needed its power for this contraption. You arranged for David to get hold of you so you could get access to it."

"Yes. Like you, the stones are resistant to my influence. I couldn't find a way to bring it to me."

"So you brought yourself to it. And the birdcage?"

"David built it."

"Bullshit. David was an idiot who couldn't change a tire. No way he could have made that thing."

"He could if I told him how to do it."

If it was able to get David to build it, why not direct Nicole to do it and save us all this hassle? I'm about to ask when the answer comes to me. He didn't just need the stone, he needed a way to get it out past David. If it was all together, Jimmy, the device, the stone, all he had to do was arrange somebody to get him out of there and then he's got everything. He didn't have to change the world around him much to make it happen, either. He just needed to make sure he got the right people in the right place at the right time.

"I fucking hate you, you know?"

"I do."

"Okay, what the hell did you need me for? Was it just camouflage? You couldn't see me, so you couldn't tell David I was coming?"

"Yes, and also so I couldn't give him any details on what was going to happen or when. He's not very good at asking the right questions. More importantly, I knew that your presence would throw him into turmoil."

"I was both camouflage and distraction."

"With you in the mix, he was bound to make more mistakes and make a rescue even easier. With you, I predicted that the odds of success were high. Without you, it would never have worked at all. Though I did my best to clear the path beforehand."

"The security cameras down for maintenance, the vault door half-unlocked. All that was you." Like I thought, that was the reality quake I felt, the one that changed the avatars of Las Vegas. But how would something so small do that?

Because it wasn't as small a change as it looked.

"That last change you did in the past fucked a few things up, didn't it? Or changed things enough that it affected the big avatars of Las Vegas."

"It was a side effect," Jimmy says.

"Yeah, I see that now. You get a lot of people coming to see you. They're not asking for anything extravagant. A lot just want big wins at the blackjack tables, become a star, find love.

"And you give it to them. You defy the odds and screw with their destinies. And because of that, you're just as much a spirit of Las Vegas as the two avatars I met. In fact, they wouldn't be what they were without you."

"When I arranged for the path to clear for you," Jimmy says, "I set some drastic actions in motion. And since it was done in the past, when it caught up with the present, the avatars were affected."

Drastic actions. What's such a drastic thing Jimmy could do that would affect them? Easy.

"You're leaving," I say. "In fact, as far as the avatars are concerned, you might as well have left two weeks ago."

"Bravo," Jimmy says. "Yes, to all of that."

"Tell me why I shouldn't just dump you in cement and drop you down a mineshaft," I say.

"Eric," Nicole says.

"I don't want to hear shit outta you," I say. "Why would I? You're just as complicit as this thing is. As I am. You've wanted to kill me for thirty years."

"Oh, fuck you," Nicole says. "You were passed out for

over an hour. I could have strung your intestines up like Christmas garland."

"Exactly. You could have." I turn to Jimmy. "So why didn't she?"

"I'm right here," Nicole says.

"Sweetie, do you mind? I'm having a conversation with our son. You still need me for something, don't you?"

"You won't believe anything that I tell you," Jimmy says. "So why should I say anything?"

"That is such a non-denial denial you should probably run for Congress," I say. "Nicole could have killed me. She *wants* to kill me. She's been trying to hide it and pretend we're all buddy-buddy but I don't buy it for a second. Now that she's got what she wanted, what's holding her back?"

"Because I'm tired, Eric," Nicole says. The defeat in her voice is solid as a brick. "I am so fucking tired. You think I like this life? If I want to keep breathing, I'm tethered to this goddamn thing. I'm stuck. Wherever he goes I have to go."

I look between the two of them. There's a game going on here and I haven't figured out the rules. Is Jimmy telling the truth? Weirdly, I think so. As far as I can tell it hasn't actually lied to me. But that's more by omission than anything else.

And what about Nicole? Maybe she is telling me the truth. The cancer's real. I know that much. Does it matter? I don't think so. I'm too tired of being manipulated for it to matter.

I had a choice last month that seemed to be between destroying Darius once and for all but probably dying in the process, or letting him run rampant through the world knowing that he might kill me and everything I cared about too. I told the people asking me to sacrifice myself for the greater good to go fuck themselves.

They were trying to twist me into their fucking puppet so I'd rescue them, and then me and Darius would disappear, like we were inconvenient warts they were freezing off.

I was ready to let the world burn just so I'd know that they'd burn along with the rest of us. I don't like being manipulated.

"I know a great cure for exhaustion," I say. I manifest the straight razor. Nicole sees it and her shoulders slump. She lets out a sigh like a deflating tire.

"Do it," she says. "I don't fucking care anymore. I got what I thought I wanted. Honestly, if I wasn't so freaked out about dying alone in a cancer ward or some run-down hotel in the desert, I'd leave. So do it. I won't fight you. Just make it quick."

Jesus fucking Christ. That might be the most honest thing I've ever heard her say. Sure, she might be lying, but if she is, it's to herself. There's nothing I can do here that's any worse than what she's dealing with right now. She's a slave to Jimmy and can't escape it on her own.

The kind thing would be to kill her. I fold the straight razor and slide it into my coat pocket.

I'm not happy about any of this, but what the fuck do I do about it?

The necromancy spellbook said an Oracle can't be destroyed. But what resources did a medieval necromancer have access to? Maybe there's something I can do to it they couldn't. Toss it in lava, maybe. Use a bandsaw? I wonder what a nuclear accelerator would do.

I don't know how to destroy Jimmy. I can't take it with me. If I kill Nicole, it'll just arrange for somebody new to stop by and find it and who knows what sort of fuckery will come out of that. Better the devil I know and all that.

I need time. There's only one way I'm going to get it. Leave it alone.

"You're right, Nicole," I say. "I got what I wanted. I'm outta here. Have fun, you two. Either one of you ever tries to screw with me or mine again, I will make goddamn sure neither one of you survives it."

I fight every instinct and desire I have to start chopping away at both of them with the straight razor and leave them behind.

I'll see them again soon enough.

Chapter 24

A wise man once said, "Buy the ticket, take the ride." Well, I bought that goddamn ticket and I took that fucking ride and it is time to get out.

Las Vegas leaves scars. Be there an hour, be there a year, when you walk out of there you'll be missing chunks of yourself you don't realize until the scabs peel.

I've stolen a Ferrari Portofino whose owner clearly didn't appreciate it, because they parked it on the street where I could drive off with it and speed out of town in style.

The traffic on the 15 is pretty light, all things considered, and I'm making decent time.

Now that I don't have anyone trying to kill me or manipulate me I can focus on important things; the hell am I going to say to Gabriela when I see her? Somehow offering to pick up where we left off sounds a little crass. I must be maturing, because crass has never stopped me before.

"Hey, baby, wanna date?" I say, trying on the sound of it. Yeah, no. How about, "Hey, sailor, wanna dance the hornpipe?" That's not an improvement.

What I should tell her is the truth. Unfortunately, that truth is, "I have no idea what the hell is going on, what I want, or even how to recognize it if it came up and bit me on the ass."

I have a few hours to figure it out. I suspect that's not going to be nearly enough time.

This car has more fancy shit in it than I can figure out. I've got brakes, gas, clutch, paddle shifters, and that's about it. There are buttons in this thing I don't recognize and gadgets and doohickeys that mean absolutely fuck all to me.

But it automatically connects my phone. So when it rings as I'm coming up on Buffalo Bill's Resort and Casino, about half an hour from the state line, I don't have to dig it out of my pocket to answer. I get a sinking feeling when I see THE TWINS pop up on the car's center console.

"What's wrong?" I say the second I pick up. Because I know something's wrong. I can feel it in my bones. I hear breathing on the other end, labored, wet. "Ken? Kendra? Come on, talk to me." Then the line goes dead.

I stomp on the gas, hitting the Primm off-ramp at a hundred and twenty. I skid around the turn, almost clipping a delivery truck. I'm back on the freeway heading back toward Vegas in about two seconds. I don't slow down. For all that speed, I'm afraid I might be too late.

———

It's clear there's a problem as soon as I pull into the Candyland parking lot. One of the double doors to the club is half open and there's nobody out front. They won't open for another six hours at least, but they always have security watching the door.

Doesn't take me long before I find the front door security. He's just inside, lying face down in a puddle of his own blood, his foot keeping the door from closing.

He didn't even get a chance to draw his weapon. I turn him over. It's the first bouncer I met, the one who was so freaked out I might not be on the list. His throat's been cut.

I take his pistol, check it, chamber a round, and get

down low. I can feel a couple new ghosts further inside, but they're just Echoes.

Echoes keep repeating a loop of their death. There might not be any consciousness there, but you can still learn a lot from them. I can see and hear what happened, though it's like listening to one half of a phone conversation. An Echo is the person who died, not the person who killed them. The only time I've seen someone's killer in an Echo, it was two guys who took each other down.

Some rockabilly song is blasting through the sound system. The song ends and then kicks back in again. With that much noise somebody could toss a grenade in here and I wouldn't bet on anybody hearing it.

At first I think the front room is empty, chairs stacked on tables, daytime lights revealing all the dark corners. Then I find the bodies of a man and a woman behind the bar, their throats slashed.

See enough murder scenes and you can figure out how somebody died with just a quick glance. They were stocking the bar. The man was taken from behind. Blood spatter tells me the woman was facing away from him when it happened.

If she heard anything, which is doubtful with this music, it would have been the smash of the bottle of Jägermeister lying shattered on the floor. No, she probably felt the blood spray on her back and turned right into the blade. A bloody handprint on the left side of her head tells me her killer grabbed her by the hair, pulled her in close, and slashed. Deep cut, clean edges. Right to left.

I walk further in toward the stages, staying low and near the edges of the room, working to keep the tables between me and who knows what. I doubt whoever did this is still here. Those bodies were already approaching room temperature.

I find the sound panel along with the body of the sound guy lying on the floor. Another cut throat. All of the levels have been cranked. I cut the sound. If whoever did this is still here, then they know I'm here now. But they probably did anyway. At least this way I'll hear them.

I run across the first Echo on a stage near the back of the club. One of the dancers was practicing a pole dance routine when someone came up to her, she said hi, and then took two shots right through the heart. She knew her killer, and this time they used a gun. With the music so high nobody would have heard the shots.

I watch the Echo loop a couple more times, trying to see if there's anything else to glean from it, but I don't notice anything new.

I can feel the next Echo upstairs, but there are plenty of bodies at the bottom of the staircase. Dancers, cleaning staff, security. Most of them are wearing the same expression of surprised confusion.

One dead at the top of the steps. I watch an Echo take out their gun and wave somebody behind them, as if trying to protect them from whoever's down below. And then he gets shot in the back of the head.

There aren't any bodies behind him. If the killer shot him in the back, why didn't they shoot whoever he was trying to protect?

Simple, that person was the one doing all the killing. Another big check mark in the Knew the Killer column.

I hear a quiet thump down the hall, a slow metronome of somebody weakly batting at the door to one of the rooms. I head over with a shield ready to go and open the door. It's one of the Twins. They don't look injured. At least I don't see anything.

Then I catch sight of the bright red arterial blood sprayed along the walls and up to the ceiling. I look behind a loveseat that's been pushed out of the way.

It's the other Twin. Shot in the legs, shot in the hands, and then finally shot in the head. But why leave the other one alive? And why drag out the pain with nonlethal wounding shots?

Both questions have the same answer. Cruelty. Both Twins probably felt the gunshots equally, and then when one of them died it would be like a normal person having half their brain carved out with a shotgun.

I get down on the floor with the survivor, if I can even use that word. Their breath comes in shallow, hitching gasps. They move their head weakly to look at me and their eyes are so filled with tragedy I almost can't bear it.

They put a hand over mine, tug it closer, angle the gun up. I know what they want me to do and there's really no other choice. They're already dead, they just haven't stopped breathing.

I pull them close, hold them tight. "I am so sorry," I say, and put a bullet through their heart.

When I find who did this I'm going to make them suffer for days, weeks, before I kill them. And when I finally do, it'll be slow and painful. The kind of death where I can pull up a chair, grab some popcorn, and watch the fun.

Who would do this? A lot of people know the Twins. Disgruntled employee? I wish it was but I know it's not. The timing is too much of a coincidence to not have something to do with Jimmy.

I grab my phone and call Rachel. No answer. Lucas. Nothing. I don't really care about Nicole, but I call her anyway. It goes straight to voicemail.

I haul one of the Twins over to the other, lay them side by side. Place their hands together. Wherever the two of you crazy fuckers have gone, I hope it's a non-stop party. You deserve nothing less.

"I will find who did this," I say. "I will kill them. I know you would tell me some horseshit about how vengeance is a bad idea and leads to male pattern baldness or some shit and you're dead anyway so why bother because you think it'll somehow diminish me, break me, turn me into some kind of monster."

I squeeze their hands and feel tears stinging my eyes. "You don't need to worry about me," I say. "I'm already a monster."

———

Getting the room number for Lucas and Rachel's suite at Caesars is simple enough. I don't even need a Sharpie to convince the guy at the front desk to give it to me. A spare couple hundreds did that for me.

It helped that I took a minute to find a clean shirt at Candyland. The Twins always have spares of everything. Sorry, *had*. It's a little big on me, but it has the benefit of not being covered in blood.

Their floor is quiet. Probably why they picked it. Middle of the week in the late afternoon. Not going to be as many neighbors as the weekend.

I draw the gun, stand to the side of the door, and knock. Nothing. I try again. Louder. Fuck this. I move in front of the door, try an unlocking spell and . . . nothing happens.

Of course. Lucas has set wards. Now that I know they're there, it's easy to see them. Aside from the one that blocked my spell, none of the others look to have been triggered.

I try it a second and a third time before the spell works and pushes the door open.

Rachel and Lucas are both here. Lying on the floor, blood everywhere. I step in, closing the door behind me, moving cautiously. I don't want to join them, after all. Doesn't take long to clear the room. I avoid looking at either of them until I'm reasonably sure it's safe.

Lucas has been shot in the chest with a shotgun. Rachel, though, took it in her face. There's not much left above her jaw but flaps of hair and skin. But she had her throat slit first.

This whole thing feels off. There was definitely magic involved. There's no other way to completely silence a gun. And a suppressor for a shotgun is over a foot long. Kinda hard to conceal without magic.

The door wasn't broken and the wards weren't triggered before I came in, so the killer either had a key or they were let inside. Neither of those sound very likely.

If this were me, how would I do it? First of all, I wouldn't switch up weapons between here and Candyland. I'd use a pistol. Maybe two. Easy to conceal, quick reload. Downside is accuracy. Me against everyone at Candyland, I'd have to make every shot count.

An assault rifle? No. Bring an AK to the club and the fight starts the second I step out of the car. Same with here at the hotel. Casino security doesn't like people wandering the halls carrying military hardware.

I definitely wouldn't use a shotgun. A short-stock sawed-off is easy enough to conceal and has the benefit of not needing to be accurate. But it's slow to reload, with a limited magazine and shorter range. Terrible choice for Candyland.

Would I use a shotgun here? Maybe. Not that it wouldn't work. It would work great and did. But if I want to do all of this fast between the two locations, switching up weapons is just extra work.

And then the really weird thing. Why would I slit Rachel's throat before shooting her? That seems personal. But it also means they subdued her. There's no way she would have stood there and let them go at her with a knife. Lucas, either.

None of this makes sense, but process of elimination points to only one person who could have done it. Nicole. She's the only one I haven't found dead yet.

But when? While I was unconscious? It would have to have been. But that doesn't work, either. I got the phone call from the club while I was there.

There's no way Ken/Kendra would have waited to call me. And I doubt they passed out and woke up. With what happened to them, if they'd gone out, they'd have stayed out.

I check the bodies again. Did I miss anything? Yes. Lucas's phone under the bed. He doesn't have it locked so when I touch the screen it springs to life.

He has a photo of his kid as the background. Happy, smiling. Probably just farted. Goddammit. I check the call history. He tried getting hold of me but the call never went through. The hell is that about?

I feel a Wanderer a few rooms over. There's so much blood you'd think it wouldn't be necessary to slice my arm open, but this is given freely. Or offered, at least.

The Wanderer is in the room in seconds, staring intently at me, waiting for the cue to eat like a dog at their food bowl. It's a pretty recent one. Strong, solid color. A man in his late twenties, I'd say. He has a hatchet stuck in his head. There's a story there, I'm sure, but I don't have the time to ask about it.

"The people who were in this room? Did you see them?" There's no guarantee he can even perceive the corpses on the floor, but if he was close enough, he would have noticed the bloodshed when it happened.

He looks around, then slowly nods. "You mean the ones the lady killed," he says.

"Lady," I say.

"Can I eat now?"

"Tell me about the lady."

He shrugs. "It was a lady. Can I eat now?"

"Details. What did she look like?"

"Like a lady," he says. "Can I eat now?"

Recent or not, this ghost is an idiot. Who knows, maybe because it's got a hatchet in its head and died with a brain hacked in two. I've dealt with his type enough times to know that I'm not getting anything else out of him.

"Sure," I say. "Knock yourself out." He descends on the dribble of blood already soaking into the carpet.

A lady, huh? I wonder who that might be.

Chapter 25

I pull up to the Gold Rush in a stolen sedan after ditching the Ferrari. Yeah, it was a nice car and all, but driving away from two murder scenes in a three-hundred-thousand-dollar sports car would probably get noticed.

I risk a spell and slide over to the dead side. From here, if Nicole or anybody else is in the building, they should light up like a bonfire. Nothing. Doesn't mean she isn't in there, though. I can think of lots of ways to hide.

The Gold Rush has always been conspicuously without ghosts. If it were any other place I'd be surprised, but nobody's been in here for years. Any Haunts or Wanderers probably faded a long time back.

The casino is as I left it. Little light, dust motes dancing in the occasional sunbeam punching through a hole in a piece of plywood covering the windows.

The door to the safe room is wide open. There's a dim light inside. I make my way over to the room, gun in one hand, razor in the other. When I get to the door I stop, not sure what to do with the sight in front of me.

A side table has been pulled into the center of the room a little inside the door. On it is a wide envelope on which is written ERIC in big, bold letters.

I look for trip wires, triggers, pressure plates, but don't find anything. I take the envelope and pull out a generic birthday card. I open it up and notice two things right off the bat.

The first is that it's one of those digital music cards

with a chip and a super-thin speaker playing "Pop Goes the Weasel." The second thing is the folded piece of paper inside. I pick it up and unfold it just as the music from the card ends.

It says *KABOOM*. The song ends. I don't have to think too hard to figure out what's about to happen next.

I slide myself over to the dead side. Even then I'm not quite fast enough. I feel a punch in my chest as I catch the barest edge of the blast, blowing the air out of my lungs and flinging me several feet away. I black out.

Fortunately, it's only for a second. Passing out over here is a really bad idea. There might not be any ghosts in here now, but there are Wanderers not too far away that are smelling blood in the water. In this case, literally. I can feel cuts on my face and hands, showing me just how quick on the uptake I wasn't.

I need to get out of here, but if I slide back here it'll be in the middle of falling timbers or straight into a fire. I limp out past the car and across the street before sliding back.

Across the street is barely far enough. Car alarms, blown-in windows, cracks in the walls of the buildings behind me. There's still-burning debris fluttering down and the air is filled with smoke.

Of the Gold Rush, there's nothing. It's rubble, blown-apart timber, twisted metal. The computer chip in the card must have been the trigger for the bomb. Once it finished, it probably sent a signal to a detonator. "Pop Goes the Weasel" was a nice touch.

People are coming out to see what the hell happened. Pretty soon I'm just one more face in the crowd. Even the cuts and blood aren't that conspicuous. It might not be rush hour but there are plenty of people on the road.

I get a couple blocks out from the casino, find a place

away from the people and the emergency crews, pull out my phone, and call Gabriela.

"Hey, remember how I said I wasn't gonna get myself blown up again?"

———

Amanda has a new lake. As the new head of her family she seems to be carrying on the tradition her dad had of periodically changing the landscape in the Werther pocket universe. I've seen it look like a severe black-and-white nightmare palace as well as a Willy-Wonka-inspired fairy-tale land complete with candy trees, chocolate rivers, and gingerbread houses you could really eat but that would kill you if you tried.

Before I left for Vegas it looked like an old English country manor. Now it's got more of a German Black Forest vibe to it, with a castle looming in the distance that could rival Neuschwanstein.

I like the lake. It's quiet. After everything that happened in Vegas, I could use quiet. I got back last night, passed out, and haven't seen anyone since. I spent the morning changing bandages.

All I could find on my way back from Vegas was a box of children's Band-Aids in a gas station outside Barstow on the edge of the desert, so I drove back with a bunch of green and purple dinosaurs on my face. Most of the cuts are gone, or nearly so. I stopped the bleeding with a spell and that seemed to help knit the tissue. I haven't tried it on a sucking chest wound, but for what are essentially a bunch of tiny papercuts it works a treat.

I pick up a flat stone and skip it across the water. Three before it goes down. I sit down on the grass, listen to the birds, feel the warmth of the sun on my face.

I know this environment is artificial, but when magic's

involved, what isn't? I never really knew much about the Werther family and even after what happened a few days ago I still don't know much about them. I like Amanda. She's very much her father's child. Better looking, nicer, but just as ruthless and bloodthirsty.

I pick up another wide, flat rock and throw it across the water. I get four skips this time before it plunks down into the water.

I hear a team of horses and a carriage approaching. Amanda has really embraced this particular uber-cosplay. She used to have cars that would drive you wherever on the grounds you wanted to go.

Now it's stallions made of light and stardust carriages. If I see glass slippers or anybody starts singing I am getting the fuck out of here.

There's a pop next to me that's still a little disconcerting. Bigsby. It's a construct intended to look like a Jeeves sort of butler. It's part of the house, and it's tried to kill me a couple of times, but Amanda assures me that it's safe now. As far as she can tell.

"Excuse me, sir. Miz Cortez was wondering if you were receiving visitors."

"Yeah," I say. "Send her over."

"Very good, sir." He disappears. A moment later Gabriela appears from the treeline separating the road from the lake. She's wearing jeans and a black t-shirt, her long, black and purple hair pulled back into a ponytail.

"Hey," she says, sitting on the grass next to me. She picks up a stone and throws it. It skips six times before sinking. Well, shit.

"Hey yourself."

"You want to tell me about getting blown up?"

"Not much to tell, really. Nicole murdered everybody, figured, correctly, that I'd come for her, and I walked into a trap."

"That's fair," she says. "You know where she and the magic head might have skedaddled to?"

"If I did, I'd be over there right now burying an axe in both their melons," I say. "But I know I'll see them eventually."

"They want something from you," she says.

"If they didn't, they do now." I fish the opal out of my pocket and flip it to her. Even under an artificial sun it catches the light in ways that don't seem possible.

"The fuck?" she says. She turns it in her hands. "Yeah, this is one of 'em, all right."

"Same as the one in your pal?"

"Shape's a little different, but there's no mistaking the feel."

"How do you mean?"

She hands it back to me. "You can't feel just how much power is in there?"

"Never been what you call a sensitive sort," I say. "I palmed it out of that weird birdcage device of Jimmy's when I picked it up. If we're lucky, they'll think it fell out at the casino and they'll have to dig through the rubble to find it."

"We'll have to see if we can spread some rumors around," Gabriela says. "But if they don't know you have it, eventually they'll put it together."

"That's what I'm hoping. I need time to figure out what the hell to do. I have no idea how to destroy Jimmy. Speaking of, I've got the spellbook being couriered over. Should be here in the next day or so. It was in a safe deposit box in New York. Hopefully that'll give us a clue."

"I've got a couple ideas that might help," Gabriela says. "Come on, I'll show you." She starts to stand but stops when I take her hand.

"How about we don't," I say. "For a few minutes, at least."

"You all right?"

"I think so. I was just thinking I haven't really stopped moving since I got back. To life, not Vegas. This is the quietest place I've been in a while. Let's just sit."

It's not long before we both start to fidget. So I figure now's as good a time as any.

"What are we doing?" I say.

Gabriela doesn't move. I can't tell if she's a deer hoping a wolf doesn't see her, or the other way around.

"What do you want to do?" she says. Caution in her voice.

"I went to Vegas because you're my friend," I say.

"Ah," she says. "Friend. Not exactly the—"

I lean over and kiss her. I think we're both surprised but that doesn't last long. We both lean into it.

"I came back because I'd like a try at something more," I say once we break apart. "Not that I know what that looks like. I suck at relationships."

"Not as bad as I do," she says. "Killed my first boyfriend and stuffed his head into his family's mailbox in Mexico."

"That's so very you," I say.

"I like to think I established my brand early. How about you?"

"You mean besides the car crash that was me and Vivian?" Vivian and I were together from high school until the day I bailed from L.A. There were a couple gaps but for the most part we were inseparable.

Then I disappeared and came back fifteen years later and found she'd hooked up with my best friend growing up. Who, of course, I ended up having to kill.

She doesn't like me much.

"Yeah, that was pretty bad," Gabriela says. "I got ya beat."

"Do tell."

"Last year of grad school. She was a normal."

"Oh, no."

"Yep," she says. "I thought being totally honest with her would be a good idea. It wasn't. We should have alcohol for this conversation. Why don't we have alcohol?" I pull a flask out of my coat and hand it to her. She unscrews the cap and takes a sniff.

"Oh, my," she says. She takes a swig. "What is this?"

"Pappy Van Winkle 15-year bourbon."

"Nothing this good should be named Pappy Van Winkle." She takes another swig. Her eyes are a little unfocused and it's not from the alcohol.

"The grad school girlfriend," I say. "It ended badly?"

"So, you and Vivian," she says, ignoring the question. "Who else?"

"Miranda," I say, taking a drink from the flask. "She was a lamia. We were fine for a while and then one night she decided I'd be a better late-night snack than a boyfriend. I was on a plane to Belize the next day."

"Belize?"

"Long story."

She takes the flask and has another drink. "We're both really fucked up, aren't we?" she says.

"Was there any doubt?"

"It's nice to be around somebody who understands my sort of crazy," she says.

"Likewise."

"So whattaya say?" She hands me the flask. "After all that, you wanna give it a shot?"

"I have a question first," I say. It's sort of the elephant in the room. Or the elephant in the ceiling, I guess.

"Amanda? She knows how I feel. About both of you. I'm not going to stop being who I am and I'm not going to apologize for it. You get me, you get the whole package. You have a problem with that?"

"I can work with that," I say.

"You realize we're going to end up killing each other, right?" she says.

"I can't think of anyone I'd rather be in a bloody triangle of murder, passion and rage with than you."

"I can work with that, too," she says, and kisses me.